OWLIGHTERS ALIGNMENT

NOCTIS VENARI #0: THE WANDERER

ARU

authorHOUSE®

AuthorHouse™ UK
1663 Liberty Drive
Bloomington, IN 47403 USA
www.authorhouse.co.uk
Phone: UK TFN: 0800 0148641 (Toll Free inside the UK)
          UK Local: 02036 956322 (+44 20 3695 6322 from outside the UK)

Published by AuthorHouse 07/27/2020

ISBN: 978-1-7283-5494-1 (sc)
ISBN: 978-1-7283-5495-8 (hc)
ISBN: 978-1-7283-5493-4 (e)

Print information available on the last page.

To my Mother Tracey, and the cast of much-loved Aunties:
I have grown up with all of you and you have supported and
shaped me as I matured. Thank you for being there for me
and making me the ever so slight nut job I am today.

To my Partners Quinn and Ashe and my Closest friends Adam and Bobby:
I can only apologise to for having to listen to my semi-insane
ramblings. I'll give you a few weeks break after this.

To Meek: The other half of my singing voice and
heart, my sister in all but blood.

To Elijah:

All I can say to you is that I am terribly sorry for what's coming.

And to everyone else who was there for me. I thank you from the bottom
of my heart. There will be other books and further dedications to come.

Benjamin and BeBe

May the road rise up to meet me,
May the wind forever be at my back,
May the Owlight guard and guide me,
And may my compass always point true, to home.
<u>The prayer of the Owlighters.</u>

TERMS

Ameliora- Ah-may-lay-oar-ah – Healing Rune.

Akashi- Ah-cash-eye - Information gathering and recording Lense.

Archir – Arc-ear – Architect of the world.

Auran - Oar-An - The Auran is believed to be the Guardian born with every person. An extension of the Soul which protects the integrity of said Soul.

Cumhacdor - Coom-Hack-do-ar - The sword the felled Arthur. Known colloquially as Excaliburs Bane. It translates as Dark Power. Wielded by Mordred at the battle of Camlann. The Duskphizer Clan crafted it centuries earlier.

Draiohba - Dry-Ock-Bah – Markings that are a natural feature of the Leanai species.

Drucapaturam – Drew-cap-at-oor-am – Portal Rune.

Ennaorban - Aen-yah-or-bah-n - Enchanters Orb.

Faemiliar - Fay-mill-ee-ar - Summoned creature.

Frostaur – Froz-tor- Minotaur-like creature, part of the Chimera family.

Fuinnestra – Foo-ness-trah – Window or viewing device.

Gieldr – Gee -el -dar – A Magick sung continually to keep the effect.

Iudex - Eye-You-Dex - Lead Inquisitor surname.

Leanai – Lay-An-Eye – Second of three species of Human.

Nagual - Nay-Goo-aal - Pillar of Magick – Missing.

Ontogenic Field - One level of one's Aura.

Phasmastis - Fas-mast-ees - Rune of Phantoms.

Raot - Rah-Oat - Rune/Spell of ending.

Rikuvan – Ree-coo-van - Tree/Oil and an energy.

Rikuvani – Ree - coo - van - ee - Pillar of Magick/Council of elders – Active.

Seidhr – See-der – The old ones/powerful entities and precursor to humans.

Seid – Seed – Branch of Magick.

Seight - See-eye-ht - The ability all Seidhunters have which allows them to see the world "as it truly is."

Studis - Stew-Dis - Rune of Study and knowledge.

Wyrd – Weird – Type of energy.

Wyryd - Wih-Rid - Pillar of Magick – Active.

Wyrydryth – Wih-Rid-Rith - A council of elders.
Vulacdrek – Voo-lack-dreck – Summoned elemental spirits related to the mythical salamander.

True Magick is spelt with a K at the end. Everything else, for example, stage magic – is spelt Magic.

HELLO READER,

My name is Wytch, one of this universes Archir. I'd like a few moments of your time, to explain things. Namely the mechanics of how this works. Now I'm willing to bet that you think the book, currently held in your hands is just that, a common household book that which can be found at any bookshop or library. In a sense, that may be true. The object you hold is known in our world as a Fuinnestra or viewing pane. Though unfortunately for you, the Techno-Magickal capabilities of the world in which you sit seems to have limited your viewing pleasure to words only for now. How sad. Then again, it means you can make up your mind about how everything looks etcetera. The Fuinnestra will translate as much detail where possible but, well... *sigh* There've been some issues here in the last century or so.

I suppose I should explain the basics of the events which have been artfully named, not by myself mind you the Cosmic Fuckaroo. I hope that you're old enough to be reading this. Or at the very least, your Parent or Guardian has read this beforehand to approve it. I mean, if they haven't pass it to then and ask them to read it and maybe even take it to their next book club, won't you? *Chuckles* Apologies for the shameless self-promotion but you can't blame a guy for trying, can you? Now, back to the topic at hand.

A brilliant young experimental Physician and Mage named Lewis Bertram perpetuated The Cosmic Fuckaroo. Bertram lived in London during the Victorian era. Somehow, he got it into his head to make Magick accessible to everyone in the form of all things, a Game. By obtaining all Thirteen Grand Codices which contained every single Rune and Seal which we used to stitch and weave this universe together. They allowed people to live again. Made it possible for Magick flow and even for dreams and nightmares to come true. Infuriatingly, we still have no clue just how he did it!

Regardless, he did it.... Gathering them in one place, in what we now know as the British Museum Reading Room. That grand circular room is not only *perfectly* shaped so that even a whisper can be heard anywhere within, it still is today one of the few, man-made places on earth where Magick can be invoked, focussed and controlled masterfully. You didn't think the oculus in the ceiling was just for decoration, did you? Once all thirteen books were present, he had created a focus out of stone, an intricately carved board game based on runic tiles. Well, as I'm sure you can imagine that much power, didn't favour being confined into one place, I mean we separated it into Thirteen volumes for a reason! The power exploded outward from the focus and tore apart the very fabric of this universe. Magick had all but disappeared. Now, this world works similarly to a computer program, one building toward a cascade failure, all those lives and all of our work would unravel. We did the only thing we could think of, we patched it. We created the system of Lensing and many other systems of Magick. Each with an identical goal, to slow the Cascade. It somewhat worked. It's still going on nigh imperceptibly. There are glitches and bits of corrupt code, but we can handle those things. Sadly, rather than binding to the patched systems, a large majority of the Runes and Seals hid themselves in universe. We now have people looking far and wide for them, the more we find, the more stable the program becomes.

During your time interfacing with the Fuinnestra please bear with us, my compatriots and I as we try to compensate for this. You may see Glitches, Mistakes or even places where the story stops as we edit the Worldlines. we will identify this with: -***- and the text will display in **bold**. Once the edits are complete, the symbol sequence will repeat and the Worldlines will resume. We the Archir can only apologise for this necessity and will try to keep the interruptions to your vicarious living in our universe to an absolute minimum.

One final note: though the headers for some chapters may seem odd, there is a rhyme and reason to them - pertinent to the subject. I believe I have taken up far too much of your time already and should let you get on with your travels via this wondrous device.

I have no doubt we will commune again.

Wytch

CHAPTER 1

OWL-LIGHT – NOUN – 1. THE DIM LIGHT OF TWILIGHT, 2. AN IMPERFECT LIGHT.

⁂

*Veroah deknichan ter.... *sigh* perhaps the old tongue would be better, it's easier to document things directly instead of concepts and ideas I suppose. My name is Thedas North, and I am now officially the last person in this universe. Since the incident that released Entropy aeons ago, life has been systematically eradicated as Worldlines became severed one by one. I stand here in a room that vaguely resembles a set from a fantasy film. Then again, the entire Owlight Library looks like a hodgepodge of fantasy, science fiction, medieval, classical and even alien architecture. Each aspect, though disparate, melds naturally into the next, metal to stone, glass to some alien material and so on. It is a wonder to behold. The library is vast. Surrounded by an energy field that shows hundreds of cracks as the roiling darkness outside tries savagely to breach it and destroy this last vestige of life. Nothing else remains - even the sea of stars known as the Triangle Sea. I haven't seen a star in decades - I need to fix this, I don't know how but I know I'll have to, use the last of the Owlight Energy to light my way through history to where it all began...*

CRACK... CRACK...

Thedas stood from where he had been leaning over the desk dictating to a leather-bound book which until he removed his hand had been recording everything. He looked around the circular stone room searching for the source of the almost deafening cracking sounds, that were still reverberating around him. He listened for the next one and, upon realising that it sounded like ice cracking, sprinted across the room, through open stained-glass doors and onto a wide terrace. An ornate metal orrery, which depicted a ten-planet system,

1

dominated the terrace. Two planets were shown holding a mirrored orbit to each other. One planet at one side of the star and the other one hundred and eighty degrees around the other side.

He looked up and blanched as he recognised that the cracking sound, which was increasing in intensity and frequency was being caused by cracks appearing in the energy field. Upon closer inspection darkness was beginning to seep through. Thedas remained rooted to the spot for a moment before springing into action. Turning, he ran back into the tower, held out his hand and barked "Kahlir". A ripple of greyish power around the room which multiple items including the book from the desk to fly toward him whilst packing themselves into a battered-looking patched leather satchel. By the time it reached his hand the satchel had packed full, its bronze clasp locked shut. With practised ease, he caught the bag and hooked it over his torso before turning back towards the door.

"Leonard!" He called over his shoulder. "We need to leave. Now."

Behind him from the balcony above came a chittering reply and the scratching of claws on metal before there was a thunk as a heavy-looking rucksack fell from above. Miscellaneous artefacts and trinkets falling out of the flimsy toggles. On the balcony above a small creature around a foot high stood, pride showed in his features. The creature appeared to be a hybrid of many small creatures, the body of a pudgy squirrel, a chipmunk's face, long cats' ears with furry ends and a racoon's tail. A soft coppery, down-like fur covered all of his mismatched features, making them look natural. The strangest thing about it was the colourful hawk-like wings that spread from its back. These were five times his height, in width. Leonard chittered excitedly, gesturing at the bag, metallic whiskers catching the light as he did.

"Hey bud, way too much. The extra Seid rating might destabilise the Lightway." Thedas says in an exasperated manner. His only reply was a series of rapid chittering sounds from Leonard who gestured insistently at the rucksack again.

"Come on boy, we can replace it all. I doubt we will need any of it when we are going."

Leonard pulled an obstinate face and planted his small fists on his hips. Leonard wouldn't go anywhere without his bag of trinkets; he was sure of that. Thedas was about to argue when the cracking sound intensified and stopped the words on his lips. He sighed explosively. A quick gesture at the bag and it began re-packing itself. A second gesture which involved the closing of his right hand, caused the bag to shrink to almost a quarter of its size. It now looked like one a child might carry. Leonard made excited sounds and glided to the floor after donning the backpack, another proud look on his face as he ran on all fours toward Thedas.

Thedas looked down to check his appearance. Crisp black trousers, well-polished shoes, a grey shirt ironed to almost military precision, adorned by a blue tie with golden clips. his hair covered by a grey turban, below which, a blue sliver of fabric peeked. The sharp line of the most prominent fold of the turban had thirteen tiny symbols embroidered, by hand at the peak in silver thread. His ensemble was completed by a swallow-tailed ghostly grey leather, mid-length jacket. Thedas pulled back his left sleeve and began expertly twisting a set of gold, silver and bronze dials strapped to his wrist, muttering under his breath as he did. The metallic hues of the device complimented his tawny complexion.

While Thedas set about doing this Leonard padded to the door and grabbed two miniature lanterns on ornate chains. Both were crafted from a rainbow metal. The first was a ship's lantern and the second a miner's lantern - each was stamped with an ornate owl symbol. Leonard put on the Ships lantern and handed the other to Thedas with a small insistent squeak.

"Thanks, buddy. We better go." Thedas appraised the room wistfully. "Sure, will miss this place." From his pocket, he produced a small, acid-green hard candy wrapped in a piece of plastic. The crackling of the wrapper caught Leonards attention, and he looked up hopefully. Thedas chuckled and pulled another out and passed it to his furry companion who unwrapped it and popped it in his mouth at the same time Thedas did. Both enjoyed the fresh lime taste for a briefly before turning to the door, crossing the terrace and mounting the stone railing. As he gazed upwards, Thedas noticed that the once perfect shield now had enormous holes in it and nebulous darkness was pouring in. Everything it touched aged and crumbled before his eyes.

Thedas looked downwards carefully as all sound seemed to stop, below him saw the silver-grey ribbon of energy. All that remained of the flow of Owl-Light, winding its way around the outside the castle.

"Well bud, let's hope this works, or it's going to be quite a short story." He chuckled and immediately swan dived off the terrace directly into the stream of grey energy.

Thedas breathed a sigh of relief as he was swept through the air by the energy flow and soared around the perimeter of the Library, taking in its features one last time. He could vaguely remember, aeons ago arriving here as a child. A small, scared traveller lost in the darkness and swept by the tides of time to the end of everything. A single island on an otherwise barren world, in a desolate universe. He had made friends and enemies during his time as an Owlighter in the Great library of Terradox. He had even found love. Though they, like everyone else he had ever known, was now gone, lost to Entropy. The very same nebulous entity that was currently devouring his home. As he zipped past the turrets and parapets, he was convinced that the spectral figures of those who had gone before looked out at him, almost encouragingly, from the windows and atop the roofs. That wasn't possible, they were gone, spirit and all, weren't they?

His mind worked this over as his speed began to drop. The grey energy that was carrying him was being absorbed by his lantern and he knew the same thing was happening for Leonard. They were taking the last remnants of his home with them to power a jump that might in the end fail, his last-ditch attempt to make things right. Almost no energy remained in the stream as he approached the ground and righted himself so that he did not land on his face. The moment his feet touched down he glanced behind him and sure enough, the spectres still stood, their collective ethereal presence seemed to slow the billowing cloud of nothingness. Unbidden tears began to fall from his vibrant purple eyes. He had to reign in his emotions and turn away to focus on his goal, the Lightway Portal.

"Kahlir..." The collective voices of those beautiful phantasms thundered over the deafening silence of eternal nothingness. He gasped as he experienced a rush of power, the last fading memory of the ribbon of Owl-Light washed over him. From the dark waterless sea, a beautiful, intricate stone archway rose silently. The Runic symbols that covered it, began to glow in a softly multiplexing light. Thedas looked through the aperture saw nothingness beyond. It had been so long since he had walked this once-familiar path into history.

"May the road rise up to meet me..." He commanded, his voice though wavering carried the heavy tones of power. Indeed, the road rose to meet him inside the now gently glowing aperture. The road itself was made from spectral images of a cobblestone pathway which were made of pure Owl-Light.

"May the wind be ever at my back..." He intoned again and once more he was answered. A wind of no natural means whipped his clothing from behind, blowing directly into the shadow-filled gateway before him. He was about to speak when the phantasmic voices commanded in chorus.

"May the Owlight Guard and Guide you..." Immediately the lanterns around his and Leonards neck roared into life. A silver-grey flame lit, and both were encompassed in an aura of that very light. Leonard flew into the aperture and Thedas stepped in and immediately whipped around as they once again spoke. Shock evident in his features. They spoke the one line that sparked hope in his heart, a line that he had not expected to recite. The line that would allow his return.

"And may your compass always point true, to home."

Thedas barked out a laugh as the aperture snapped closed, though it did not close before an image of his love smiled at him. "Maybe there's hope. Perhaps I can pull this off." He thought quietly. He turned once more and began to run down the pathway, his aura and flame shifted through the spectrum until it shone the brightest of ruby reds. Thedas relished in the familiar sense of running through rapidly melting gelatine.

On the other side of the Aperture, the spectres smiled at the familiar scent of Lime Jelly before they and their home were engulfed in darkness. Now surely, they had become nothing but memories?

CHAPTER ONE

VOCEM PERDIDIT

The expansive Attic was dim, damp and dusty at the best of times. Though tonight lit by over a dozen guttering candles which cast sinister-looking shadows which danced around. It was downright creepy. Carefully piled and catalogued stacks of collected ephemera dominated the space. Over it's time The Forge, on the outskirts of the small northern town of Crosstown, had been home to the Duskphizer family. Even by Leanai standards were hoarders. Items ranging from Uncle Harry's well used Heavy-Metal Vinyl collection to Aunt Ophelia's' Platinum Tiara. Even an old steamer trunk that bore a sticker for the Titanic. It contained thirteen beautiful, if slightly yellowed wedding dresses which had belonged to Great-Grandmother Emerald and her string of ill-fated marriages. In reality the attic had become a family museum. Everything in there was truly irreplaceable.

Crash! A large pile of boxes was knocked over by an unseen force. The noise barely drowned out the expletives, uttered by the culprit. The small creature had a high-pitched nasal voice. It clambered out from under fallen family documents and other paraphernalia. It stood around about foot high it was dressed in a red and black hoodie with a pair of jeans. With an almost feline grace it extracted itself from the pile and over to a sphere of light emanating from a small group of candles. It surveyed itself in a beautiful antique mirror which sported a deep, crack right down the speckled glass due to of the creatures' fall.

"Seven years bad luck." It muttered quietly. "Bah." In the light figure was revealed to be a small brown teddy bear with black beady eyes. Its eyes were partially covered by its fur so that it was hard to tell if it was annoyed or just simply squinting. In its reflection, it noticed that several of its badges were askew but, with a sharp prod and a small grunt of a word in no humanly recognisable language, they moved back into place. Snuffling slightly in satisfaction, it turned its gaze to the floor noticing that the dust was moving of its own accord, another word in its language which sounded like a swear word and it followed the path of the dust. The bear padded silently through the dusty maze of heirlooms in the huge attic it stopped every so often at intersections, to study the direction of the dust, and changed its course to follow. Steadily the dust led the bear to the middle of the room.

It took several long minutes of walking for the bear to reach his destination, he stepped into a large circular clearing in the very centre of the Attic and gasped. At the epicentre of the space was a Pentagram chalked onto the floor, its lines hummed and glowed as though alive with power. As the bear watched the dust around the edges crackled and sparked as it touched a seemingly impenetrable wall of power whilst moving in a clockwise direction. Inside the Pentagram stood a huge ornate mirror of black glass with a frame of polished lead which was inscribed with strange symbols. The surface of the mirror moved with an ethereal mist yet did not reflect anything in the room nor the heavy cold iron gates which were chained closed over its surface.

In front of the mirror knelt a young boy of ten years old wearing a soft fluffy green dressing gown and bright pink slippers that were one size too small. His shoulder-length copper coloured hair fluttering in an unnatural breeze and his amber eyes glowing from within as he chants in an almost practised manner. He was reading from a large ancient-looking book. Bound in cracked blood-red leather. The book rested on a large wooden lectern, that seemed to be growing out of the floor, and was covered with symbols and diagrams of an Arcane nature. At the head of the page from which he read, were the words "Vocem Perdidit" written in a looping script and green ink. He continued to chant the litany of Latin words; the boy stammered over a few words as the temperature rapidly dropped. He shivered as his breath condensed when he spoke, sending small white clouds into the air. Slowly the symbols on the gate and mirrors frame began to glow and languidly move over the surface of the metal like oil on water. These symbols spoke of Guarding and Warding, Binding and Holding. They held a warning to potential thieves. Apparently, in response to this, the gate began to radiate a bone-chilling aura of power which caused the boy to shiver violently as his lips rapidly turned blue.

"Elijah..." The bear said quietly, worry evident in his voice. He is interrupted before he can say anything else.

"Benjamin quiet..." Another bear stepped out of the shadows speaking softly in a deep voice, he was dressed in a long bobbled grey woollen hooded jumper with a zip. It was way too big for him yet seemed to suit him. He had brown eyes and very fluffy fur which was slightly darker than that of Benjamin. "You know what would happen if he stopped now, without a reversal."

"He shouldn't be able to open the Grammerie. Let alone read and Lense from it at his age Be-Be." Benjamin implored, emotion filling his voice.

"Obviously, he..." Said Be-Be sarcastically, jabbing a Paw in the direction of Elijah "... didn't get the memo."

"Quiet! Something's happening,"

Indeed, something was happening - Elijah's chanting had reached a quiet crescendo as he threw his arms toward the mirror. This caused the gates to rattle violently and then become still again. The bears both breathed a sigh of relief while Elijah looked shocked, pleased even, he repeated the last few lines and threw his arms out anew this time holding them steadily in front of him, his face a mask of concentration and a sheen of sweat formed and froze, on his brow. This time the gates rattled more violently; it did not subside instead the noise became almost deafening. Then with an unearthly screech, they flew open, inwards through the glass, opening into the writhing darkness beyond.

Elijah sighed in triumph before, his eyes rolled back and he fainted dead away, collapsing in a boneless heap. Immediately both bears sprang into action, hurling themselves over the still pulsating boundary line of the pentagram and landed at Elijah's side in an instant. Be-Be stood sentinel at the boy's head, a paw stroking his still sweating brow and murmuring reassuringly. Benjamin meanwhile began pacing back and forth at Elijah's feet, staring intently into the darkness. In the impossible distance, there were multiple flashes of light and Benjamin began growling and snarling in a manner that did not match his cuddly exterior. A few seconds passed and a figure could be seen sprinting towards the opening in the mirror, ducking flashes of red and purple light, retaliating with blasts of pure white light.

Benjamin snarled a word in a language that no human could ever speak, a shining silver sword appeared in his paw. A similar sound came from the other bear who now held a silver staff, immediately he ran around Elijah dragging the tip in the wood on the attic floor. Another word when the circle was complete, and a silver dome sprang up around him and Elijah. Be-Be could be seen stood bravely over the boy still murmuring comforting words. Benjamin snuffled and nodded before charging through the Mirror into the darkness brandishing his sword overhead, a roar emanating from him. The roar was feral and animalistic. He sprinted headlong into the void toward the oncoming figure and leapt into the air, only to be swept up into a grip that resembled an embrace. Benjamin struggled against his captor snarling and biting at him.

"Stay still you infuriating creature or we're both done for. I'm being chased and need to cross the threshold and close the aperture before it can follow me into life." The figure says in a reverberating voice which caused Benjamin to still immediately.

"Lord Richard?" The Small bear says in disbelief. "How?"

"When Elijah sent out the Vocem Perdidit to me, I felt it resonate and began to come home but when he stumbled over those syllables, let's just say he caught others' attention..."

With that Richard sprang forward and dived through the gate and into the attic, landing on the floor with a thud. A hurried gesture with his free hand and a word caused the gates to clang shut. Now in the light, Benjamin could see that it was indeed Richard, almost exactly like he was before he passed, dusty brown hair and matching beard, his brown eyes showed so many emotions - irritation and anger chief among them. He wore a sleek fitted green suit with tiny golden symbols that shifted and moved embroidered on his collar and cuffs. His black shoes still shone, and he wore a blood-red, single shoulder, hooded mantle. Exactly what he had been laid to rest in. He looked at the bear in his arms, anger radiating in every fibre of him.

"Benjamin Bear." He almost growled. "What did you think you were doing allowing a thirteen-year-old boy to attempt a calling of that magnitude? He could have been killed. Even I used to struggle with that one. It's not even a Lense it's Old Magick." Behind them, the barrier came down and Be-Be Stepped forward, behind him Elijah was stirring.

"He's only ten Richard." Be-Be says quietly

"How could both of you le..." he pauses, shock evident on his face. "Ten you say? Impossible,"

"He waited until I was asleep and snuck out. I saw him last week looking through the Grammerie and he stopped at that calling. I warned him against trying it. I even hid the Grammerie from him, well thought I had."

"You could have told his mother or..." Richard started but was interrupted by Elijah who had made his way quietly over to them unnoticed.

"Don't be mad at Ben Bear Grandpa," He said softly, grabbing Benjamin into a tight hug. "I made sure he stayed 'sleep long enough for me to get started. He's a good bear. I called you to get you to come and see mummy and stop her crying" Elijah softly pleaded. Richard sighed and stood up, made his way from the circle and sat heavily in a nearby rocking chair, patting his knee as he did so. Elijah picked up Be-Be too and made his way over allowing both bears to clamber from his arms to the sides of the chair before he scrambled into his Grandpa's lap. For several moments they were all quiet, Richard surveyed the young boy in his lap smiling slightly it never quite reached his eyes though. They held concern. He cleared his throat softly to gain Elijah's full attention.

"Yes, about that..." he started in a measured tone. "I am very proud of what you have accomplished on this night young one for it's astounding but..." Elijah stiffened. "I need you to listen carefully Eli, whilst I applaud your ability to call power nearly three years before your awakening, I must ask you to make me a promise. Please not try any more callings until after your thirteenth birthday."

"I promise Grandad." Eli said.

"Delightful boy." Replied Richard "Also no-one outside the manor is to know what has happened here tonight, they may not think kindly of you for your power. I will speak to your mother and Sarah. You are right that your mother and I need to settle this ridiculous feud. For your sake, if not our own. We didn't part on the best of terms." He finished in a wistful tone.

"I know, but she still loves you," Asserted Elijah.

"Yes Eli, and I her. I must tell you something. Time is short. On the eve of your thirteenth birthday under the light of the full moon stand in front of the Dark-Gate and watch as the power awakes in you. Pay attention to the size, shape, colour and position of your primer marks. Those will tell you what form of Lenser you will become. I have but seen snippets of your future and I could not be prouder. Do this every year until your ascension on your twenty-first birthday where you will change to become your true self and find out your True Name, just like the rest of us."

"I will, I promise Grandpa." Eli smiled in response causing Richards stern gaze to soften slightly.

"Now do not worry if you don't notice much of a change in your markings over the coming years, until your ascension, this is no real reflection of your power - no matter what people would have you believe. My own marks lay dormant for the full eight years until they grew overnight and look at me, I am or rather, I was, quite powerful" Richard grinned cheekily. Eli smiled yawning slightly. "Come now, off to bed with you. You must be exhausted. I must see your mother; I love you dearly" Richard smiled and this time it reached his eyes.

"I love you to Gwandpa" Eli Slurred a little. "I'll see you again." He smiled tiredly, eyes already drooping.

"That you will son, that you will, goodbye for now." With that he faded from view, leaving Eli to float for a moment before he plopped down into the chair with a soft thud. He chuckled at the sensation.

"Come Eli, that's enough for tonight." Benjamin said firmly as he hopped down from the chair and over to his sword which had lain forgotten. With a whispered word the blade melted into a pool of light before it faded completely without a trace. "Off to bed now. We'll drop Be-Be off with Hollie." The bears both grabbed Eli's hand and they all left the attic. Carefully avoiding the threshold of the Dark Gate.

Once the attic was empty with no-one there to witness, Leonard flew out of the Gates aperture followed by Thedas. Thedas surveyed the attic, smiling thoughtfully at this familiar place, for the first time. After a moment, his form shimmered, then vanished. In his place was a stunning grey owl which hooted and then flew off, through the roof.

CHAPTER TWO

FAMILY REUNION

At the far side of the Manor, unaware of everything that had transpired, a tall lithe woman with long curly blond hair and deep blue eyes which had star-shaped pupils. Her face and any skin left exposed by her long elegant evening dress, was covered in light blue star-shaped markings of varying styles and sizes. She sat at an antique dressing table, typing rapidly on a sleek red laptop, only pausing every so often to take a sip of strong steaming black coffee.

Richard faded silently into the room, unnoticed by the woman. He stood observing her, regret plain on his face. He sighed quietly as she took another drink from the cup, draining the last of the contents before setting it down, empty, on the side with a dull clunk.

"You won't sleep you know..." Richard said out loud, still quietly in his reverberating voice, making his presence known. Humour lacing his tone. "Coffee this close to midnight, you'll be up past dawn."

The woman released an animalistic, almost feral snarl and jumped up, turning in the air. By the time she was facing Richard, her right hand had extended like a claw and a ball of intensely burning blue flame crackled into existence suspended between her clawed fingertips. She saw Richard at the same moment she was rearing her arm back to throw the ball of flame. Her eyes widened and immediately the flame guttered out and she fell back onto the desk, winded.

"F... Father but how? You're... You're" She stuttered, totally at a loss for words. The colour seemed to drain from her face almost matching her Father's deathly pallor. This made the marks on her skin look sharper, more pronounced and her dress seemed even more vibrant.

"Dead? Yes, well that has been known to hinder one's ability to visit loved

12

ones." He chuckled dryly. "How long has it been? I had assumed Elijah would be thirteen but to find out he's only ten..."

"Just under fourteen months," Emily replied sadly. "I never got the chance to..."

"Yes, to that end," He cut her off. "It seems fortunate for both of us stubborn mules that you have a resourceful and frankly powerful son Emily."

Emily reared back as though slapped staring at her father incredulously. "Eli? Impossible, he's only ten years old. He simply couldn't access power that great at his age. I doubt I could, especially not to allow you to roam free of the Circle..." She trailed off, confusion and worry lacing her voice.

"I am technically still within the circle. The physical circle is still in the attic surrounding the Dark-Gate, preventing any further egress. The Mirror thankfully does not display his image as yet. But he evidently desires us to reconcile and as he has no real preconceptions of the Wyrd, and it enabled him to create a metaphysical barrier circling the house. On my way here I examined the boundaries, and it seems as long as I do not try to go outside then I am free to roam the confines of the manor until dawn. This certainly demonstrates his power." Richard replied matter-of-factly.

"Wow..." Is all Emily can say slipping heavily into the comfortable chair.

"I must say from what I have been able to glean of his future and he'll do great things, though he will be bound closely to another as equals. Though I cannot see their face or even detect what type of person they are, as though it's not set yet. I'm thankful that it's still distant."

"This's rather alot Father. Elijah seems to have a rather interesting path ahead of him. He said that he wants us to reconcile?" Asked Emily softly.

"I think his exact words were 'To stop Mommy crying...'" Richard replied. "He is right of course. I had no right to meddle in your love life and I realised shortly after, but my own stubbornness prevented me from coming back to you, then I died." He says thoughtfully.

"Father, I accept your apology, but as it transpires Walter was nothing but a money-grabbing Low-Life Bigamist, he had three other fiancées' dotted around the country. He was after the Paper Father. There's a distinct probability I would have either become ill or simply disappeared. He's being held at the Bailey for trial and probable execution. He was apparently under investigation in connection with at least three other disappearances in which he inherited either an estate or a business. Anyway, I digress. Will you be visiting often?" She finished. Her voice laced with something like hope.

Richard smiled a smile that was a mix between happiness that he had reconciled with his daughter and a pang of sadness that he was at the end of the day, dead.

"The rules apply as normal, dusk until dawn and no more than twice in twelve months, from today. The gate will open for me until Eli unfocuses or unravels the Lense." Richard said quietly.

"Shall we say, midsummer and midwinter? A Shorter visit in the summer and a nice long one near Christmas?" Emily replied in a Business-like manner smiling slightly.

"That sounds perfect." Richard replied smiling, happiness shining in his eyes. His smile turns into a mischievous grin. "Do you have any of that Brandy we used to share?" He asked, almost as an afterthought.

"Yes." She smiled, remembering the better times. "I'll ask Sarah to bring us some."

Emily turned to the desk and passed her hand over a Quartz orb, around the size of her fist, which rested on a delicate, silver and gold filigree stand. The orb immediately glowed with a soft blue light which emanated from within and pulsed softly.

"Sarah..." A pause before the glow became a steady light and a soft female voice sounds from within the orb which rang with a crystal-like resonance.

"Yes, Mistress Emily? How can I help?"

"Please could you bring the decanter containing the MacDonald Eighteen Seventy-Three, along with Three glasses to my study?" Asked Emily politely.

"Yes of course Mistress." Sarah replied, her voice wavering with uncertainty and barely concealed curiosity at such an odd request so late. Without another word, the light within the orb winked out, and it became inert once more.

"You should promote her, or better yet pay her off with enough money so she doesn't have to work anymore. She's Eighty-Four though she does look good for her age and she's been working for us since she was Nineteen." Replies Richard thoughtfully smiling.

"I've been considering that very thing for a few months now, today is her birthday. I think I'll do just that." Emily replied happily, already rummaging through the desk drawers.

"Good Girl, she was a good maid." Richard said proudly.

"She still is..." Emily muttered distractedly.

14

A soft knock at the door interrupted them, alerting them to Sarah's arrival. Richard immediately sat in one of the wing back chairs facing the crackling hearth with his back to the door. A quick flick of his hand, an almost lazy gesture toward the space between the two chairs behind the table that rested there. The air rippled with an unseen force causing the two chairs to shift slightly aside and the table moved forward and widened noticeably while a third armchair identical to the others faded into reality. In a moment, the arrangement changed. Emily thought that she might leave it like that. She smiled happily, pleased that she had the chance to share a drink with her Father again and heal old rifts. Facing the door, she spoke.

"Come in Sarah."

The door opened smoothly and silently and in walked a woman of average build, her long black and grey hair was tied in a tight bun on top of her head. She wore a fitted pair of black pants and a deep forest green blouse which offset the pale green vines and leaves which adorned her skin. On her feet a dainty pair of green slippers matched perfectly in shade to her blouse. Sarah stepped across the threshold carrying a silver tray on top of which the requested Decanter filled with amber liquid and the three glasses sat neatly accompanied by a small selection of small bowls with snack food therein. She looked confused and slightly nervous as she had allowed no guests entry and had felt no-one cross the Ward boundary. The way she looked and moved would have you believe that she was barely half her Eighty-Four Years.

"Where shall I put this Mistress?" she asked quietly.

"Emily, call me Emily. For the hundredth time of asking. You've known me all my life." Emily chuckles. "On the table will be fine. Take a seat, Sarah."

"Oh no, ma'am. I wouldn't want to disturb you or your guests, when shall I expect them?" Sarah replied earnestly, shaking her head lightly.

"Sarah sit down, we need to talk to you about some recent developments. You are one of my guests and the other is right there." Emily indicated the seat containing her Father behind Sarah where he sat patiently. Sarah's head whipped around, and she gaped as she registered who was sat in the chair.

"L... Lord Duskphizer?"

Richard held up his hand in a slight wave smiling jovially before he spoke kindly.

"Please sit and do call me Richard, again after many years of telling." He chuckled. Sarah flushed nervously and sat hesitantly in the proffered chair.

"L... Richard, how is it you come to be here?" She caught herself from calling him Lord again. He offered her a drink which she accepted hesitantly but took a large sip. Richard gestured to the third glass on the tray which he had filled while Sarah spoke to Emily and it floated up from the tray and made its way across the intervening space toward Emily. The glass rocked slightly, the amber liquid sloshed over the edge onto the cream carpet much to the chagrin of both Emily and Sarah. He had overfilled the glass slightly. Emily reached forward and took the glass from the air before it could spill anymore smiling in thanks to Richard. Immediately Emily turned back to her desk and began writing a cheque as well as and noting the information in a ledger.

Richard began explaining the events which had transpired in the manor that evening. The explanation was interspersed at appropriate junctures with gasps and muttered exclamations. Near the end of the story after Sarah had nearly fainted from shock Emily turned in the chair, cheque hidden in her lap, she sipped her drink lightly while listening to the last of the story. Once Richard had finished explaining Sarah spoke impassionedly before anyone else could.

"He won't be attending any of the schools then. He'd be held back and made fun of; they wouldn't understand him. No," She paused before continuing decidedly. "That won't do, not at all. He needs someone who knows him and understands him." She speaks mostly to herself, but her tone dares anyone to disagree.

"I wholeheartedly agree, Emily?" Richard said smiling.

"One hundred percent agreed but we will revisit that issue in a moment. Sarah, I am aware that it is your birthday today." Smiled Emily.

"Oh, missus Emily you know it is, I got your lovely Card, Gift and Flowers a few minutes before you called me. Tulips have always been my favourite." Sarah gushes happily.

"Yes Well, after discussing the situation with Father and we both agree and realise that you have you have worked here in your capacity as Housekeeper for too long." Emily said kindly.

Sarah gasped and released a mournful wail before promptly bursting into tears, sobbing violently.

"Ooh..." She wailed. "I'm too old, a'n't I? Did I speak out of turn? Sometimes it's hard to forget they aren't my own. I know I ain't half as fast as I was when I was a gel but I'm still capable. I... I'll do better, I'll keep my nose out, I promise. Please give me another chance. Please..." The last word is drawn-out and descended into a wail accompanied by a fresh round of sobs. Emily looked up at Richard imploringly, but he looks back at her bemused and mouths the word "Smooth" rolling his eyes at his daughter's apparent lack of tact. Emily rushed over to Sarah's side dropping into the vacant chair still clutching the cheque in its envelope. She pulled Sarah into a tight hug.

"Sarah... Sarah calm down a moment and look at me." After a few seconds, Sarah calmed down and looked at Emily, mixed emotions flitting over her tear-stained face. "We're not firing you..."

"R... Really?" She asked haltingly.

"No, Quite the opposite. Here." Replied Emily reassuringly while slipping the envelope into Sarah's Hand.

Carefully Sarah opened the envelope and withdrew the crisp cheque and gaped at the figure written on the paper in Emily's razor sharp script before her eyes promptly rolled into the back of her head and she passed out, slumping in the chair. Richard launched into action, rapidly refilling Sarah's glass and running it under her nose, the strong sweet-smelling, amber liquid did the trick and Sarah slowly began to rouse from her stupor. She groaned groggily, reaching for the proffered glass and downing half its contents. When she looked up at Emily she gaped openly, clearly still in shock.

"Two hundred and Fifty Thousand Pounds?" She spoke the number in an almost reverent tone. "Two Hundred and Fifty Thousand Pounds? I don't know what to say, Thank You. Thank You. But I can't accept this, it's too much."

"Sarah, this money is for you to do with as you please, and you certainly can and will accept this." Richard smiled kindly.

"I fear we, as a family have been remiss and have never truly shown you how much you mean to this Family." Emily held up a hand forestalling any argument. "You have served this family unerringly for sixty-five years. You were a mother to me after mine vanished. You became mother to Eli and Hollie when I couldn't be there. We took you for granted, whether you felt that way or not."

"I'd rather stay here even without all this money. The Manor's the only home I've ever known." Sarah replied in an almost desperate, pleading tone.

"You are barely middle-aged in our world as you know and deserve to have the means to live the life you would like. If you wish to remain in residence at the Manor, then that is certainly possible, but I would also like you to think about picking a plot of land on the Manor Grounds and we will build you a Home there if you have any preference. The money however is non-negotiable." Emily said smiling properly now.

"I've always dreamt of owning a small cottage by the river."

"Then in the morning, we will retain the service of Fred and the other local contractors from the town to design and build your dream home." Richard smiled happily.

Sarah looked tearful again as she took another drink from her glass. "How could I ever repay you?" She asked a little nervously.

"The money and the house are gifts and are yours. Of course, it will take some time. Your room is always open to you. In the meantime, we would like to have you put through the courses and exams that the government requires you to become a registered instructor which would allow you to teach Eli what you think is best and Hollie when the time comes. Would that be acceptable? That way you would also be named Guardian if anything happens to me." Emily rambled excitedly, smiling happily.

"Oh my... Thank You both for your faith and the wonderful gifts, I will not let you down." Sarah gushed.

"We know you won't." Smiled Richard. "You have carte blanche where education is concerned. This'll give you more free time for a life." This caused Sarah to smile tremulously.

"Thank you again. I Accept." Repeated Sarah.

"Think nothing of it, Sarah. You are Family." Emily states smiling still. She raised a glass which has again been refilled. "A toast, to Family and the Future."

"Family and the Future." Richard and Sarah Echoed clinking their glasses with Emily. They Spoke and Planned into the small hours, all three growing closer, their relationship changed for the better. Finally, just before dawn, the three proceeded to the attic and after a round of hugs, Richard happily stepped over the threshold of the Dark Gate and returned to rest.

The next three years passed in a mostly uneventful manner and a blur. Sarah's dream home was built in the woods at the back of the house, almost exactly where she had always dreamed. A few hundred meters away in another clearing a second building was built, a training/school room which contained all the modern conveniences not generally available to the public. This was prompted by a major tantrum thrown by Hollie when she found out that her brother would be taught by "Aunty Sarah." As she had always called her. This tantrum lasted over an hour before Emily could calm her down and finally agreed to let her be taught at home as well. This turned out to be a good thing as shortly after her eleventh birthday she began to show abilities early. Namely the ability to port herself from one place to the other without physically moving through the intervening space.

As agreed Richard visited twice a year and helped make a few bigger decisions that Emily held off on until she could consult with her Father who still had a vast network of contacts none of whom, ever seemed surprised to hear from him despite them having attended his memorial service.

By his next visit, Sarah had been certified as an instructor as she already had most of the pre-requisite qualifications after many years of doing free and discounted correspondence courses in her spare time. As it transpired, the rest of the staff were happy to help with the new endeavour and asked that their children, current or future be taught on the estate. Sarah and Emily Agreed almost immediately, happy that Eli and Hollie would have some classmates. The Manor's inhabitants fell into their new routine with ease. Time passed uneventfully.

CHAPTER THREE

SARAH

The Manor and its Grounds were a hive of activity as there were only a few short days until Elijah turned thirteen. In Leanai culture the Thirteenth birthday was a coming of age, on the eve of the Thirteenth Birthday the Wyrd calls to the child and awakes their powers in the form of their Primer Marks. These marks represent one or more of the Thirteen Affinities, the marks or Draiohba change, grow and evolve along with the Leanai Child. The Draiohba show what the Leanai find easier, their speciality they do not in any way restrict their ability to use other Affinities. After their Awakening, Children see the world how it truly is. Sights and creatures that were hidden from them and the things that humans are incapable of perceiving. Awakenings were always a grand occasion. There was always a miniscule chance that the child may be lost.

Emily and Sarah sat in Emily's Study in the same positions that they had taken almost nightly since that night. The room had remained relatively unchanged since the night that Richard had changed the layout as Emily had decided to keep it that way instead of changing it back twice a year. They sat chatting amiably, taking a break from the rapid preparations eating sandwiches and drinking tea. Sarah often still marvelled at how she had been made welcome, like a member of the family by everyone including the staff who seemed genuinely pleased for her as they gave her the same reverence and respect as they gave Emily and the Children.

"So, Sarah, how are Elijah's studies progressing? Is he ready to Awaken?" Emily asked lightly, her voice was tinged by worry.

"His studies are progressing brilliantly; I assume that he shouldn't have any issues in future. He's certainly taken to the meditation techniques and is scoring well on the psychometric tests. It all depends on who comes through to guide him. Any thoughts on who it might be?" Replies Sarah Curiously.

"I don't think it will be Father, considering his unique circumstances it would be a wasted opportunity as he will be arriving in a few weeks for his regular visit, anyway. My guess would be Aunt Ophelia, she died a few months before he was born but made him a lot of things, like clothes and toys. Ever since he was a baby Elijah has been obsessed with Ophelia's Tiara, it's one of the few heirlooms he's ever connected with." Emily replies.

"I remember Ophelia, she was very kind but wilful, her main affinity was Spirit if I remember rightly." Sarah said thoughtfully. "I wonder what his first officially recorded Lense will be?" Asks Sarah smirking.

"It's always interesting someone's inherited Lense, I got mine from my Great Uncle twice removed Augustus. It was a Live Light." Emily smiles fondly. She opens her hand and a luminous butterfly flutters above her palm for a moment before fizzling out.

"I got the Light Lense from my Aunt Helena; she died a few days before my calling." Sarah said with a hint of sadness evident in her tone.

The women sat silently for several moments sipping their tea and working their way through the selection of delicate cakes and sandwiches, lost within their thoughts. Finally, after she had finished a particularly tasty and delicate chocolate cake glazed in a shining chocolate ganache. Sarah straightened her back and smoothed a few errant wrinkles from her crisp, conservative blue dress before she spoke in a business-like manner.

"The preparations are almost complete; space has been cleared in the attic for the observers and the ballroom has been decorated as we planned, and I've ordered the gifts from the relevant stores in London and they should be delivered later."

"That's good, there are four others over the next few days." Replies Emily happily. "Has the Barrow Gate been opened yet?"

"No, not yet, I can't open it and make it stay accessible until noon, that's what I put down on the Application. It will stay open for free Ingress and Egress for five days as long as the traveller has an invitation. Allowing everyone free access to the Warren during that time. That reminds me, I need to go into the Warren and travel to Aetherius for some supplies. Do you need anything?" Sarah asked.

"I don't need anything, really. Although…" Emily paused and grinned. "… could you grab me some Chocolate Marshmallows from Sweetbriars on Yewdale Road please?"

"Of course, I'm heading that way, anyway." Sarah smiles, glad to indulge her friend and glances down at a delicate silver full hunter pocket watch, its cover adorned with a stylised image of a classical Fairy and was hung from a fine silver chain. The time read Eleven Forty-Three. "Actually, I'd better be off soon. I think I'll have lunch and return later this evening if that's ok?"

Emily smiled warmly but inwardly rolls her eyes. Even after three years Sarah still thought she needed permission. Sarah seemed to sense her friend's thoughts and blushed mildly.

"Sarah, you don't have to ask permissions." She chides playfully. "Go, have fun and I'll see you for a drink when you get back."

"I keep forgetting..." She grins awkwardly. "See you later then."

Emily smiled warmly and nodded as Sarah rose and tidied her things away. With a final few parting words Sarah left the room and headed down the corridor, past the library and games room, down the marble staircase into the busy foyer leaving Emily alone with her work.

Once she reached the cloakroom Sarah picked up her Messenger Bag and slung it over her shoulder, retrieving her deep blue cloak and gloves she donned her gloves and draped her cloak over the bag. Finally, she retrieved her hat and set that upon her head securing it with a hatpin and left the room, crossed the foyer and out through the black stone archway. Sarah strode past the heavy oak doors barely noticing the silver and gold symbols inlaid into the wood which shone in the summer sunlight. She walked down the marble steps and was just about to step out onto the baking tarmac drive, when a white two-door low riding sports car came screeching out of nowhere. It would have hit her if she hadn't jumped back and grabbed the handrail to stop herself falling on her backside.

After a short pause, the driver's door opened and out stepped a tall young man with cropped, dyed grey hair. He was dressed in a crisp dark blue suit which was accompanied by mustard accessories and polished brown brogues. A smile graced his face which quickly vanished as he saw the thunderous expression on Sarah's face as she pulled herself upright clutching her chest with her free hand. The man rushed forward and helped her upright only to be struck repeatedly by Sarah's surprisingly heavy messenger bag. He cried out in shock.

"Jason, ye stupid bugger, you could have killed me. Me in the prime of life." She shouts at the top of her voice, smiling as she continues to beat him. The scene causes many of the workers and guests to stop and laugh.

"Oh, I'm sorry Aunty S, I didn't realise it was you. I thought it was a beautiful Gel to impress." He says wringing his hands earnestly.

Sarah stops beating him and snorts, pulling him into a bear hug which he falls into easily. "The day you go chasing after a pretty Gel is the day, I take the Leanai throne, Jason Duskphizer." She mutters into his ear causing him to snort in turn. They stood for a few moments before she pulled back and stared into storm-grey feline eyes. She could see the faint pretty grey spiral patterns of his Draiohba which adorned his skin and glancing down she could see the jagged red tribal design faint but present on his hands and knew the pattern and colour changed toward his legs to a natural brown pattern. His affinities were Air, Fire and Earth and he used them well.

A persons Draiohba could shift, blend and change many times on a person's body depending on the number and combination of affinities a person had. In Leanai culture it was considered vulgar to question a person on their Draiohba, you take the visible ones as they are, the rest were for lover's eyes only.

"I'll forgive you this time charmer." She smiled rolling her eyes "but I want that car parked in the garage, not here. Other guests will be arriving soon." She finished in a mock stern manner.

"Oh, ok." Jason says backing away slowly his arms held up in surrender grinning cheekily. "Keep your wig on." He said the last as he turned and ran to the car as Sarah screamed in mock rage her bag swinging ineffectually. He jumps into the car starting the engine quickly before pulling away spinning the wheels.

Sarah shook her head in exasperation before she stepped onto the drive, looking both ways, and resuming her walk across the grounds. She follows the road over the baking black surface until the drive began to curve. A red brick path joins the edge of the drive and heads off into the distance to a wooded area at the east of the Manor. She stepped onto the well-maintained path which looked as though it had just been laid but Sarah knew it had been laid twenty years before to replace a similar path which had become damaged. She crossed the interlocked bricks, across a sprawling wildflower meadow towards the treeline. After meandering over the field for a minute or so she crossed the tree line and into the cool damp shade of the woodland which was a welcome relief from the summer heat.

Around fifty feet in the ground rose and immediately fell, the path turning into equally pristine steps down the side of the embankment into a wide concave depression. In the centre of the depression, the ground rose once again into a large mound. The path cut into the hillside. As she crossed the edge of the depression, she felt a static tingle wash over her skin, the wards. Sarah had always pictured a ripple in the earth when she imagined Blackstone Barrow. As she hurried down the steps, she carefully followed the path and made sure to stay on it, glancing at her watch she saw that it was Five to Twelve. The clearing

23

filled with sunlight as the sun passed overhead. The path ended in a thin passage of matching red brick, at the end of which stood a solid black marble door. There was no visible keyhole, but the surface of the stone seemed alive with symbols in Ogham and the Sidhe runic language.

Observing the moving symbols on the door Sarah waited and watched for repetition in the pattern, after a moment she saw the symbol for unlocking and revealing repeated many times. She held each symbol in her mind as she saw them until there were no individual repetitions left. She kept an iron grip of the symbols in her mind as they kept trying to slip away and placed her hand on the door. Immediately the movement of the symbols ceased, they were frozen in place. She let go of the symbols she was concentrating on and the seemed to flow out of her and onto the door, their counterparts glowed with a soft deep green light as the door lurched under her hand sliding backwards an inch or so and with a low grinding the entire slab sank into the ground. She coughed lightly as a cloud of dirt and dust was released. Once the sound subsided, she stepped into the long dark corridor ahead.

It was noticeably colder in here and she reached down and took the light cloak pulling it over her shoulders, adjusting her bag as she did so. She stopped at the threshold and cupped her hands blowing lightly on them. A flickering liquid-like ball of bright white flame, which held a slight green tint, sparked into life. When she opened her hands, the ball of light floated upwards until it hovered just above her head, illuminating several feet in each direction. The sides of the long corridor were lined with silver urns in recesses in the wall, the nameplates beneath each urn held names as well as life and service dates. The Blackstone Guard, serving in death as in life.

She walked briskly down the corridor which quickly opened out into a large, wide circular chamber, the floor was a single sheet of polished marble and the walls were the same stone as the house. The chamber-like the corridor was lined with recesses, floor to ceiling, some held urns, others coffins and the odd white skeleton. They stood sentinel holding weapons at the twelve points of the clock were twelve black boned skeletons clad in rags and remnants of armour. Empty eyes seemed focussed on her. Sarah shuddered and tried her best to ignore them, striding across the glassy floor toward the centre of the room her Wyrd light bobbing above her.

At the centre of the room, a large circle of white marble about ten meters across was inlaid seamlessly into the floor. On the floor she saw a square tile of white marble around the size of a paving slab is at her feet, in the centre of which is a large cold iron keyhole set in. Sarah knelt and withdrew a large ornate key from her bag and slipped it into the keyhole with a whisper of Iron on Iron. She turned the key clockwise. The resulting hollow thunk reverberates through the chamber and she swore she could hear the rattle of bones hidden in there. She shook it off and removed the key before putting her full weight on the white slab which sunk into the floor slightly before sliding back up. The outer edge of the white circle seemed to fall into the floor and formed a spiral staircase which fell into the darkness.

She walked down the spiral staircase for a short time before she came to the bottom. There stood the thirteenth Obsidian Skeleton, she had anticipated. It stood in a geode-like alcove opposite the stairs, with an empty alcove to its left. In its clasped hand it held a thin full-length Staff of Gleaming silver which was razor-sharp on one side and serrated the length of the other. Nothing alive could wield that weapon. She stopped far enough back that she would be out of reach of the staff, at least on the first swing and focussed her mind using the meditation techniques every Leanai knew, calling her Wyrd to the surface causing her Draiohba to glow in a deep forest green light.

"Guardian, I am Leanai and seek passage into the Warren. I request that per the terms of the Permit I carry, that you remain on guard with the Barrow-Gate open for five days hence. By the Throne above and below." She stated confidently, ending with the standard pronouncement acknowledging the Leanai Throne and the British Throne.

The skeletons head moved an inch to stare fully at her for a moment, its empty eyes appraising her as though considering her request. As it did so it began to glow with a red light from within heat palpable like a smouldering log. With a rattling of bone, it tightened its grip on the blade, Sarah remained impassive, it nodded to her and immediately moved aside into the empty alcove. It stood there still glowing. The geode-like structure seemed to melt away revealing a well-lit exceptionally clean tunnel where a clearly impatient group of three people waited.

"You're four minutes late Sarah Dear, not like you." Commented one of the group, a short stout man dressed in traditional robes that human children always drew their Wizards dressed in, though these robes were more tailored and well fitted than that depiction.

"Sorry, Sorry I got held up. In you come Gerald." Behind Gerald two Girls, twins Katherine and Katerina Hawkins. Though they were twins their Draiohba and affinities would be different as it was common for twins to have opposite affinities but the Draiohba would always be unique to the person and shaped by their personality and experiences. Sarah knew that the Girls had opposing Affinities, Katherine was Water and Katerina was Fire and they had a shared affinity for the Wyrd which allowed them to share power, as was common for twins.

Sarah stepped back and allowed them to enter, they stepped through the gate and entered the Barrow, past hr and the Guardian, she could feel the heat emanating from the Skeleton. Gerald and the girls walked up the spiral staircase and out of sight Gerald muttering about tardiness all the while. Sarah rolled her eyes Sarah moved to exit the Barrow and enter the Warren. With a smile and a nod at the Guardian who returned the nod and Sarah often liked to think, the smile. She held her breath and stepped through the gate, a wave of nausea passed over her but passed as she landed in the corridor, the warm breeze tickling her face.

The corridor of the Warren was wide and branched off often into the distance. Though knew she was underground, the beautifully detailed paintings on the wall made it feel as though she could just walk off into the distance. The scent of fresh baking and the smell of cut grass wafted on the breeze made it feel even less claustrophobic. A wooden signpost pointed in a multitude of directions. As she approached the sign and scanned the names of the places, Bowrigg Dell, Low Cliffe, High Cliffe, Aetherius and multiple others. Sarah stopped at the sign for Aetherius and read it.

"Aetherius Sidhe, 36km, Corridor Red Thirteen."

Nodding to herself she glances around until she saw a painted red sign on the wall pointing to a tunnel about a hundred meters away which had the numbers "10 to 20" written on it. Briskly she walked to the red section, passing several people she knew and nodding to them companionably. Upon reaching the correct platform she stood primly at the edge behind the red line and looked at the Solari Tab board opposite, which showed the time and was counting down to the next Tram. The board displayed Fifty-five and was counting down. She looked into the distance down the hill she could see the lamp on the front of the train approaching at breakneck speed.

"The next tram to Aetherius Central now approaching Platform Thirteen, Red Section and will depart at Twelve Fifteen sharp." She hears the soft female voice announcing the Tram.

The Tram screeched to a halt, hitting the Buffers with a resounding crash the force of which jarred every passenger aboard. Once the doors were open, the passengers streamed out of the Tram Car at the rear as Sarah and the handful of other passengers boarded at the front. She saw the seats resetting themselves to face forward and picked the seat behind the driver's seat and sat down strapping herself into the harness, her bag on her lap. The driver moved to the front of the car and sat in the tractor type seat immediately clicking switches and turning dials with learned ease.

Abbie, the Clippie, Sarah deduced from the worn name tag worn against her breast on the pristine red uniform which matched her skirt and hat perched on a tight set of chemical curls. On her left wrist was a ticket dispenser with the days' tickets mounted within; yellow in the slot marked single and purple in the return slot. A cigarette clutched precariously in the corner of her mouth which has a heavy coat of pink lipstick which was also covering her sharp front teeth.

"Single or Return?" Her voice ragged from years of smoking.

"Return Please." Sarah replied, smiling.

"Seven Eighty please." Abbie replied, pulling a purple ticket out of the Return slot, the ticket had the date, journey and the word return in gold writing. She clipped the Outbox with a star punch and handed the ticket to Sarah who gave her a Ten-pound note. Abbie clipped out the correct change from the metal coin dispenser on her belt handing the change to Sarah. "Have an enjoyable Journey." She said before moving onto the other passengers at lightning speed she had just finished when a loud bell rang on the platform and the doors clanged shut. Abbie stood by the window frantically puffing at her cigarette before throwing the butt out of the window and strapping herself into a harness, standing at the back of the cab. She reached up and pulled on a cord that ran the length of the cabin which caused a dull bell to ring. "Ding" Pause. "Ding, Ding"

The engine roared, and the car lurched forward to the edge of the hill, picking up speed even after the engine fell silent. Sarah was pressed back into her seat as the speed kept increasing, all she could hear was the rattle of the wheels on the rails and the roar of the rushing air through the open windows. The car sped through the darkness of the tunnel for what could have been hours for all she knew, in reality, it had only been around five minutes before the car hit the bottom of the decline and moved up the hill toward the station. The onboard engine revved into life and began pushing the car up the hill at a similar speed to that of its descent. The remaining journey was as uncomfortable as its beginning. She was glad that she was almost at the Station of the Subterranean Sidhe of Aetherius and that the journey was not as long or as deep as say the trip to London, she blacked out on the Grav-Tram descent last time she rode. The bell dinged again, and Sarah braced herself as the Tram slammed into the buffers, knocking the wind out of her a little. Grav-Tram journeys always made her sick, but they were faster than the surface trains and Metros the humans used. She exited the car at the rear and headed straight off the platform, into the tunnels following the crowds until she emerged from the red section in the cavern which housed the Sidhe of Aetherius.

Sarah fought the urge to look up which would have triggered a bout of Vertigo. The city itself was housed in a vast cavern under the west coast of the United Kingdom and stretched around five kilometres in diameter. The walls of the domed cavern had lights and balconies dotted around looking over the city proper. Everything seemed washed out and Ghostly by the glaring white electric streetlights. This overcompensated for by the bright and oftentimes gaudy colour schemes of the Buildings and plants which were kept alive by local UV lights. She stuck out her thumb at a Taxi Stand. A Black Clockwork Carriage whirred to a stop next to her. She glanced at the driver who inclined his head to her and grinned a toothy grin to her motioning for her to enter through the door below him. She nodded back and said, "Sweetbriars, Yewdale Road" loud enough for him to hear over the loud whirring. As the door closed, the carriage whirred to life, lurching into the busy street.

The gaudy colours looked washed out in the stark white light as the storefronts and homes rolled by. Sarah could hear the driver, perched atop the carriage talking on what she assumed to be his telephone. He was talking animatedly. It seemed that his daughter was having her awakening in a few weeks and he was having to plan it while working to pay it off. They pulled into Yewdale Road which was lit with thousands of LED lights. Yewdale Road had always been a popular trading centre and was remarkably busy that day, an enormous crowd of people moving in and out of shops and perusing the wares at one of the many wooden Chalets that lined the pavement. The carriage ground to a halt outside the green double storefront the signage on which read "Sweetbriars Confectionery – Est 1813" emblazoned in thick golden script. Though the shop was wider than any other store, the shop was still dangerously overcrowded.

She climbed out of the carriage and looked up at the driver who smiled politely and said: "Four Seventy please ma'am."

Foraging around in her purse she pulled a crisp Five Pound Note out and handed it to the driver who thanked her and opened a cash drawer below the Solari Board meter. With a single he pulled out two coins and handed her them while slipping the note inside before closing the drawer, causing the tabs to flip and reset.

"Have a nice day now." He said while pumping his feet up and down on two peddles which made a ratcheting sound. Several repetitions later and they lock into place flat. The driver tipped his hat to her with a wink, she blushed, before he pulls several levers, flips a switch and deftly steers the whirring carriage back into the busy traffic.

Turning, Sarah moved into the thronging mass of people who were walking toward the storefront. She deliberately looks toward the window displays and takes in the intricately modelled chocolate forest-scape which included animated woodland creatures and fairies which were modelled out of spun sugar and other confections. As the thronging mass of people slowly funnelled her into the store, she took in the details, though she had seen the interior of the store many times before they still amazed her. The ceilings were vaulted, and shelves and drawers filled with confections of every kind were fitted floor to ceiling, even following the curve of the building meaning that items and drawers were facing the floor at odd angles and yet the items remained in place. The oak and black marble counter was polished to a shine, and it stretched from one end of the store to the other and behind it the staff who were immaculately dressed scaled the railed ladders with a natural grace as they served customers. Sarah made her way to the counter and caught the eye of a young boy of around seventeen who she knew was Simon. He was the youngest of Penelope Sweetbriars eleven children, most of whom staffed the store today. Simon glided over toward her on a ladder and hopped down onto the black marble floor in front of her.

"Good Morning Miss Sarah, come to collect your order?" he smiled and asked in an accent that said he had been born and bred in the world below.

"Yes, thanks Simon, can I also get a crate of Chocolate Marshmallows and the same of Rhubarb Custards, Fondant Fancies and Those filled chocolate animals please?" She asks quickly.

"Crates!?" He exclaimed taken aback.

"Yes Crates," She smiles back. "We won't be back in the area for a while and Eli is being home-schooled after his awakening tomorrow."

"Ah I see, couple of things. What colour Fancy? What flavour in the marshmallows and which batch of animals?" he says recovering from his shock at such a large order.

"Can I have an even mix of the four Fancies, a random selection of the animals and Emily prefers Strawberry so can I have half a crate of strawberry and the rest mixed, please? Oh, and two bars of Chocolate Raisin." she says confidently.

"No problem. All on the one bill?"

"Please." She smiled.

Simon looked down at a ledger and his eyes widen again as he added the figures up double and triple-checking the figure several times. Sarah watched on in amusement before clearing her throat gaining his attention.

"The figures will be correct Simon." She says softly, almost inaudible above the noise of the crowd.

"Well..." he clears his throat. "the bill comes to £574.98,"

"I'll sign the bill so that the money can be transferred directly to you before I leave."

"Okie Dokie." he says sliding an Authorisation slip across to her. "We'll deliver it to the access hut at Southwaite as usual?"

"Thanks, but I'll keep the two bars of chocolate raisin." she smiles.

"Now that that's done, mother wants to see you before you go if that's ok?"

"Sure, I haven't seen her in a while."

"Come on through" Simon smiled whilst tapping the counter causing a section of it to fade from existence allowing Sarah to step through and follow Simon into the back room.

The workroom at the back of the store was a hive of activity, people were stirring vats of chocolate adding various flavourings and liqueurs to the vats. Others were working at stations crafting delicious looking treats to be displayed in the store. Simon led her to one of the many small rooms around the main work area. When she entered, she came upon an interesting scene, Penelope Sweetbriar looked as though she were holding court. Penelope was a portly woman who looked no more than fifty, her long hair was lightly greying and she wore an unfortunately fitted blue dress that hugged her a little too tightly, by Leanai standards she was a large woman as the Leanai metabolism is much faster than that of a human, but 200 years of sampling your own confections will inevitably catch up to you. That's not saying she wasn't a pretty woman, as she was. After all she had numerous children to many different men.

"Penny." Sarah smiled warmly striding over to embrace her friend.

"Sarah, how are you?" replied Penny in a warm melodious voice. "Come sit."

Penny turns to a slim woman who looks nervously at her and smiles in an almost encouraging manner.

"Lyla be a dear and bring that bottle of good scotch from the safe and two glasses. I mean the good stuff dear not the bottle at the front." She chuckles.

"Y... Yes, missus S" Lyla replies stammering lightly before rushing off into the back room. Penny turns to Sarah smiling warmly.

"My youngest Simons fiancé, talented lass but I can't show favourites." She giggles girlishly.

"Ah I see, always keeping em on their toes I see." Smiles Sarah.

Lyla returns quickly with two glasses containing ice and a warm looking amber liquid and hands each lady a glass before heading off into the main room. Penny and Sarah sit and drink the scotch in silence for a moment watching the organised chaos unfold in the room before Penny turns to Sarah and begins to speak.

"That cake of yours was an absolute pain to create, the fourth tier with the clock kept running backwards and the other layers wouldn't sit, the prophetic icing kept activating as soon as I laid it and showed some weird things, must have been a bad batch. Showing the young lad with a snake's tail and wings fighting in a war that couldn't possibly happen. Among other disturbing things. I destroyed the entire batch and started over, four times. But it's working now, look."

Penny gestured to an empty table behind her in a complicated hand movement. The air fizzed and shifted as a beautiful four-tiered cake materialised. The base tier was covered in a silvery icing and it was decorated with intricate leaves. The second tier showed a motif of woodland in black icing over the silver icing. Tier three had an animated train circling it the rest was plain silver and the final tier had roman numerals one to thirteen and a hand that slowly circled the time down to the end. On the top, a model of a winged wolf sat howling at an invisible moon.

"Oh, Penny it's truly stunning, I can't wait to see the icing change later." Sarah said in Awe.

"I'll box it up and have it sent with everything else to the drop-off. I can't hang around long though love as I have four more to finish by tomorrow. Though we can catch up at young Eli's awakening party." She grinned. "Extended family gets to pick where they attend,"

"True, I have a load of shopping to do then I'll have lunch and head back. Jason's picking me up at 6."

"I'll have it all there by then for you dear." Smiles Penny already standing.

Sarah took her cue and stood, quickly embracing Penny before heading out of the bustling store onto Yewdale road. She made a beeline for the expensive robe store and bought the expensive elegant red robe she had had her eye on in for a while. She coyly gave her measurements, signed the bill and asked for it to be sent to the service station for 6 pm. For the next few hours, she continued like this, going from shop to shop over multiple streets. She paid for the gifts for the children and a few for Emily too early on before continuing her own shopping spree. Why not? She hadn't spent much of the money she'd been gifted. Maybe the odd trinket here and there. Emily often encouraged her to spend money on herself, so she would finally follow her friends' advice. Friend, she smiled to herself, still strange. As she walked towards some other shops, checking her watch, she had two hours left, she felt as though she was being watched. Usually, she was not wrong about these things, so she ducked into a quiet secluded Pub and walked briskly over to the Bar.

CHAPTER FOUR

THE MEETING

The barman, a short balding man with smoke-stained false teeth smiled, causing his teeth to slip slightly making him curse as he righted them. A human then, she thought to herself. The barman greeted her in a gruff but kind voice.

"Welcome to the Tavern under the hill, where our beer is cold, but our welcome is warm. I'm John what can I get you?"

"Large red wine please." She asked softly before replying to his unasked question. "House"

John nods and turns to the shelf behind him, picking up a bottle and pouring out a generous measure of crimson liquid into the delicately decorated wine glass. While he does this she looked around the bar taking it in. Behind him, through an office door which had been left ajar, she could see a larger woman counting coins while smoking and listening to the radio, chuckling every so often. Everything in the bar was clean and well kept, the tables were arranged irregularly with varying numbers of seats, a common tactic to break up the flow of energy around a room, making Lensing harder in the room. Three large fireplaces on the far walls with several seats around each, blazed with a glittering light purple flame, Wyrd fire which was by virtue smokeless, in keeping with the laws of the warren to limit carbon output. The silvery glitter showed it was a government Lense. Other than those details it was a fairly unremarkable bar. The barman cleared his throat.

"Four Seventy please Lass."

Sarah smiled and grabbed her purse pulling out the correct change, handing it over before picking up the glass and moving off into the far corner of the bar with a good view of the door. The shadows in the booth slightly occluded her from view. For a few minutes she watched the door before it opened and a tall lithe man walked in, he had short brown hair which was feathered into soft peaks each tipped with silver. A delicate beard adorned his face and his eyes scanned the room intensely. His Draiohba, a stylised eye in the centre of his forehead which had intricate lines flowing outward down his face and neck vanishing into his clothes. The eye radiated speckles of pink light as it glowed softly, he was Lensing thought Sarah. As she thought this his eyes flicked to her and he smiled a little before turning his attention back to the barman.

She watched as he approached the bar, John's eyes narrowed at him, which was interesting that he could sense something off, maybe he was psychic in some way. A moment later his expression cleared, and he served the man a drink and took the money. The stranger turned and walked directly over to her booth. What Sarah observed that the stranger did not was John immediately turned to a solid black orb on the counter by the register. The orb was mounted in a black and gold claw, the symbol of the Inquisition. John didn't even speak just waved his hand over the orb which immediately glowed, blinking rapidly with a blue and red light meaning they would arrive soon.

"Sarah Aubrey, Long time no see." He said as he approached, his voice like honey.

"Ethan Forrester, Subtle as ever." She smiled, somewhat warmly. "You realise he's summoned the Inquisition? It's illegal to use a mind Lense on a human you know."

"I was using a generalised glamour and if he's pure human, I'll eat me 'at. He overacted his Part." Gesturing over his shoulder in a swift motion directly at the orb he muttered under his breath, the orb flashed in a complicated sequence and before going dormant once more. John watched and sighed, muttering under his breath before entering the office where his wife worked. Sarah rolled her eyes at Ethan as he said. "They won't come now."

"People will still talk you know?" she said exasperatedly.

"Let them." Ethan shrugged taking a sip of his drink, a sweet-smelling blue mead. "how have you been since we last spoke?"

"Fine, busy but fine. How is everyone?" She asks him in a guarded tone.

"They're fine really, always on the move travelling from Sidhe to Sidhe over the world. They're in Aetherius and would very much like to see you." He replies quietly causing Sarah to frown.

"Is that a formal request?" she asks, worry lacing her voice."

"No, a simple wishful expression from certain family members." He smiles lightly.

"Then as I have said each year. I am unavailable at this time." She replies calmly.

"I will pass along your regrets." He replies in a resigned tone which was tinged with sadness. With that, he drained his glass and began to stand. Sarah leans forward quickly grabbing his hand. Immediately Ethan stands upright hissing in pain, cradling his now blistering hand.

"Stay..." she pleads.

"It is forbidden." He says sadly. "You know this" he turns on his heel and strides out of the bar rapidly.

A tear streaked down her cheek and she wiped it away impatiently. She sat staring off into the distance absently finishing her wine, she didn't notice the Barman's wife approach carrying a slice of chocolate cake and a fresh glass of wine. As she placed it down in front of her, she heard the woman whisper kindly "No Charge". Sarah murmured "Thank You" Emotionally, tears still flowing as she ate the cake, which was delicious while sipping the wine. She had been there for the best part of an hour before she pulled herself together and finished up. Even though they'd been gifts, she felt bad for breaking down like that.

As she stood, she withdrew a twenty-pound note and a piece of card, quickly scrawling "Thank You. X" on the card and slipped both under the glass, surreptitiously adding a tiny Lense so that only a staff member could take it. She walked out of the bar, her mind light for once as she nodded at the old couple behind the bar who both beamed back. Checking her watch, she realised it was five twenty, so she made her way to the taxi stop and hailed a carriage.

The whirring cab pulled up and the same driver from before smiled at her and motioned her to enter the carriage. "Surface lifts, please" as soon as the door closed the driver ratcheted the pedals, and they set off to the other side of the Sidhe, it took nearly twenty minutes for them to arrive due to the holiday traffic. She paid the driver ten pounds and told him to keep the change before walking over to a silver filigree gate and waited as the lift stopped. She boarded carriage thirteen and instructed the operator to take her to the surface entrance. After a further five minutes in the lift, she stepped out of it into the warm evening air at the rear of the motorway service station.

Sarah exited the lift and walked quickly across the carpark to a small wooden shack and smiled at the attendant, a young man with speckled bland and brown hair. "Hello, I'm here to collect my purchases. Sarah Aubrey."

"There was a change of plans and Ms Sweetbriar had all of your purchases taken directly to your home an hour ago as the Magic Mirror Glaze would not allow compaction disc usage." He said kindly.

"Oh right, convey my thanks to Penny." With she dropped a tip into the slot and walked off around the kiosk. She walked into the woods. For several minutes she walked deeper into the woodland until the only light came from above through the dappled canopy. She stepped into a clearing and stopped in the centre, slowly turning in a circle until something caught her eye on the trunk of a tree. As she approached slowly the thing that had caught her eye, a symbol which consisted of two circles intertwined and bisected by a line, began to glow in a strange Greenish-Purple light. The closer she walked the brighter the light became until Sarah vanished from sight.

Immediately a pulse of the Greenish-Purple light left the tree and began travelling underground, rapidly seeming to cause the grass to become greener and flowers to bloom as it passed.

CHAPTER FIVE

THE GLITCH

The moment Sarah rooted into the grounds of the Forge and emerged from the Greenish-Purple Light; she knew something was wrong. Around her, the air sparked and crackled with raw power, all of her senses were being assaulted by it, sharp static on her skin, the heavy scent of ozone, bright intermittent flashes of raw power that left afterimages on her retinas, a deep droning hum of power that seemed to be climbing to some deafening crescendo and finally the taste of acidic copper in her mouth. She was panicking and beginning to breathe hard as she felt her innate hidden self, responding to such a powerful call.

Sarah began to glow softly and lift off the ground slightly, her arms and legs became long and willowy, her face sharpened and shifted to a somewhat terrifying level of ethereal beauty. Rapidly her skin seemed to dry out and change becoming thin and brittle until it stopped and looked as though she were made from dried leaves. Her neatly bunned hair now cascaded to the middle of her back, each strand like a thin blade of dull red grass, on each side of her head triple pointed leaf-like ears showed through her hair moving seemingly of their own accord similar to that of a cat. Her clothing now seemed like it was woven from the gossamer threads of a spider's web. As her eyes opened, they glowed a deep golden colour fuelled by the power within. She radiated an aura of vibrant golden power.

The moment her transformation had ceased there was a loud sound like the tolling of an ancient bell, the Barrow door flew open and out marched the thirteen guardians from within. Immediately they focussed on her and encircled her, their impossibly sharp weapons charged and trained on her. Around her the air rang with barely controlled power, Sarah reached out with her passive senses and found that the guardians did not recognise her power signature. She forcibly reigned in her power and began slowly forcing the transformation upon herself. Her features began to melt back into her usual Leanai visage. Seconds later she stood looking almost like her old self if a little younger though power was still rolling off her though now it was her usual deep green.

"Peace Guardians, I am keyed to the Wards of your domain." She said with an air of authority that was usually hidden. She reached into her bag and held out the key which pulsed with raw power.

Nothing could be heard over the roaring power as the Guardians heads moved as one. It was as though they were considering her words. Without warning their posture relaxed, they filed away into the Barrow and the surrounding air quieted, the normal sounds of the day returned. Immediately Sarah's expression became panicked as she whipped her head to the path just as there was the sound of static electricity from just beyond the wards. She watched in fascinated horror as Emily appeared in a flurry of electric blue sparks, her expression a mix between fury and fear. She looked directly at Sarah, trying to reconcile what she had seen with the woman who had helped raise her.

Undeniably Emily was standing looking at Sarah, she knew this in her heart and yet she could not reconcile the sweet nervous woman she knew with the beautifully terrifying entity that she was now aware slumbered within her. The stories she had heard as a child of the Fae were of bloodthirsty, beautiful tricksters who dealt in half-truths and shady deals. If this were true could she ever trust her friend again? Therein lay the rub. Sarah was her friend, her confidant and if she couldn't trust her, then who could she trust? Immediately her posture relaxed as she made up her mind, it was still Sarah no matter her species. Sarah noticed the change in posture and relaxed slightly, a single tear escaped the corner of her eye.

"Mistress Emily, I... I can explain."

"I'll bet," Emily replies smiling slightly. "But I'm sure my father is well aware of your identity?"

"Yes, he hid me here over seventy years ago from my mother."

"Whom I'm sure will be listening on the winds. For any hint of a conversation like this... On fathers next visit we will all converse in the security of the ritual chamber. I'm not angry, just confused. It doesn't surprise me that my father has a hand in this. The old fool could restart the war." She snorted causing Sarah to chuckle too.

"Richard is aware of my nature; he hid me here over ninety-three years ago. I wanted to tell you but..." Tears began to form. Sarah moved forward past the ward boundary and everything went to hell in a handbasket.

Black lightening exploded forth and vaporised Emily instantly. With a scream Sarah vanished in a further flash of blinding black lightning which arced from the clearing and obliterated a sizable chunk of the Mansion on the hill behind... The world froze, bricks and mortar ejected by the explosion hung in mid-air...

-***-

"Crap, it's a doozy this time. Hello reader, please don't worry your viewing will resume as soon as possible. Remember when I spoke to you at the start of the book? About the issues that the Cosmic Fuckaroo caused? Well, welcome to your front-row seat. We've just lost the Dark-Gate, Emily, Eli and a dozen other people. Sarah is floating in the space between spaces giving us all a headache but at least she's safe. So, excuse me while my compatriots and I fix this minor glitch."

While you wait you watch as the frozen world begins to fix itself, the building putting itself together brick by brick, though not exactly as before, one tower has moved a few feet and gained a floor. This is perfectly normal I assure you. The Dark Gate appears and repairs itself in the clearing, atop the barrow hill itself and the warding strengthens tenfold, now a faint golden dome even in full sun. Throughout the woodland, the redbrick path seems to dig itself up and relay itself in black and green aged looking bricks as though it has always been there. New flower borders are laid, and trees shift and repair themselves. It looks like a vastly different place, yet the feelings remained the same. As though it had always looked this way. Which after this, it always will have. Sarah and Emily reappear, sitting on the grand patio on a new/old table with two comfortable looking seats, finishing the scene is a worn well-used parasol under which a lush cream tea and steaming (well steam is there but not yet moving) tea service. On a table nearby, all of Sarah's purchases, and more can be seen.

On the sprawling lawn nearby, Jason is entertaining Eli and Hollie who are sat cross-legged, Ben Bear and BeBe in their laps. He is showing them something similar to fireworks which he is creating from between his hands. Everything now seems almost back in order.

"Phew, that took us days, I hope it doesn't translate like that to you? What seriously like three paragraphs? It doesn't do us justice. The others are re-writing memories as we speak, Emily still remembers the events earlier before the explosion. As far as they are concerned, they walked peacefully to the house. There were a few complications, like having to move the Dark-Gate, the thing weighs hundreds of tons in Magickal energy alone, but it's a lodestone, it has to exist. Also, the others couldn't resist a few cosmetic changes as you can see, easier to do it after a glitch when we're repairing, anyway. At least I didn't have to rewind time this time, I sleep for days after. So, once they've tinkered with everything, time will shift forward to dusk, several hours later, some plans have changed like the location and time of the awakening, but it'll all come out in t' wash I suppose. See Ya."

The time of day shifts, the suns position changing and clocks righting themselves, it is now around Nine in the evening. And as though someone had pressed play on the video.

-***-

Sound returned as the world restarted. Sarah and Emily partook in the tea service, continuing a conversation that they had been having. Emily chuckled mid-sentence.

"... and they said that Amanda had just so happened to pick it up?"

"Yup, as if picking up a leather bag out of somebodies car and trying to walk off with it was normal. She was stopped by an officer who had witnessed it. He asked her, in front of a crowd of people what the bag contained." Sarah replied smirking, in a slightly malicious way.

"What did she say?"

"Well, the Officer was a Guy. Frank something. So, she thought to put him off by saying feminine products. This didn't put him off in the slightest, so he made her open the bag, in front of everyone."

"He didn't, Amanda is the Mayor's daughter..."

"So, she opens the bag and well, feminine products indeed, one of those products was as big as my arm, I think even our Jason would have baulked at its size..." She broke off suddenly roaring in laughter. Emily joining a moment later. It took several moments for the women to calm down and resume speaking after gulping down tea.

"Oh my, Amanda must have been mortified. Who did she rob to pick up a bag with that in?"

"A rep's car... That wasn't the only one, just the biggest apparently it was a replica of an ogres..."

"Hem... Hem... Aunties perhaps that conversation is best left until after the sprogs are in bed?" came Jason's amused voice from the steps nearby. They looked up and sure enough, both children and their picnickers were listening with rapt attention which they only usually focussed on adult conversations where sweets were involved.

"Replica of an Ogres what mummy?" asked Hollie innocently.

"Arm, it was a replica of an Ogres' arm dear." Replied Emily smoothly, showing easily why she owned one of the most popular newspapers of the day.

"Huh, Huh, huh yeah arm…" Chuckled BeBe and Ben Bear together.

"Both of you shut it or I'll send you to my mother's for a few weeks." Emily glared at them both, grinning as both bears' eyes widened, and they silenced themselves. "Now all of you get some sweet treats from the kitchens and head upstairs to your rooms, tomorrow is a big day. I'll be up shortly to see you both as will Aunt Sarah."

With good-natured grumbling, the foursome wandered quickly into the house and out of view of the adults. Jason smoothly summoned an identical chair and sat down, cheekily pulling out a small silver hip flask and topped up his teacup with amber liquid. With a glance at both ladies. He did the same to their cups. They all drank in silence for a moment, enjoying the summer Breeze and the company. Each aware that tomorrow would be long.

"Is everything set up? I saw a lot of people arriving." Asked Jason, coughing slightly at the teas burn.

"Everyone's here and settled into their rooms. There'll be a buffet breakfast, then people are free to enjoy the town." Emily replied primly, the alcohol colouring her cheeks. "The Quecks point has been enabled at the main gate and is linked to the town and city."

"Just a quick note for those of you who don't know a Quecks or QEX points are Quick Exchange Points. They are folded pieces of space where two places are linked. Activating one with the correct key will allow near-instantaneous travel between the two locations. Some people report mild effects but other than that it is perfectly safe. They are also known as Quick Exit points for people at functions if there is an emergency. Well, this was cheaper than a footnote… Oh sorry, they're still talking."

"… so that's it then, awakening all set up? Nervous Emily?" Sarah asked kindly.

"Of course, I am, over the last century the mortality rate during Awakenings has risen by Twenty Percent. I just want my little Eli to survive."

"He will Auntie Em, after all, he called Grandfather at ten years old…" Jason stopped at Emily and Sarah's' sharp looks. "He came to me the first night Eli

41

called him, he's asked me to train and guide him after his awakening, something is coming he says."

"He had similar messages for us that night, apparently he can see things in the darkness about Eli's future but not how it will all turn out. The fact that he sees things does reassure me, mostly."

"Come now, let's not be maudlin. We should have another drink and talk of more pleasant things." Jason said quietly with a soft smile.

Both ladies readily agreed, they sat for another few hours as the last of the daylight faded and the moon rose. Eventually, they entered the house after sending the dishes to the kitchens with a quick Lense. On the grand staircase, both ladies parted with Jason after a quick hug and kiss on the cheek. After checking on the children as promised, who were both asleep soundly, almost strangling their picnickers. Sarah stayed in the guest room near Elijah's room and Emily returned to her room. All three fell into an uneasy sleep, their preternatural senses quietly but insistently telling them something was coming. None of them saw Leonard skitter out of a bush and take off into the air where he was joined by an eerily glowing Silver/Grey Owl. They circled the estate before flying through a set of patio doors into the attic.

CHAPTER SIX

SHE SPEAKS

Emily was rudely awoken by hammering on her bedroom door, she glanced at the old-fashioned clock next to her bed which read "08:15". Fine, she'd slept in but for someone to be banging on her bedroom door like a mad person at this hour there had better be a fire. Better yet, she thought grumpily, someone had better be on fire. She threw off the light summery cover and stepped onto the blessedly cold floor as the room itself was rather warm even at this hour; it was probably going to be a decently hot day. Emily threw on a silk housecoat and walked barefoot to the door and opened it, to be hit quite hard in the shoulder by Jason.

"JASON DAMIAN DUSKPHIZER! You better have a bloody good reason for hammering on my door like you are being hunted in the night by Gwyn's Hounds..." She roared, making the small crowd of onlookers scatter, the Lady of the House was in no mood for an audience this morning. Jason pales even more and stutters an apology.

"I... I... I'm sorry Auntie but I came to get you as soon as I heard."

"Heard what?" Asked Emily quietly, concerned now.

"She Spoke...." Whispered Jason, voice still tripping over words.

"Who spoke and how does that explain you hammering on my door like a maniac." Asked Emily, starting to get angry now. This was probably something inane that could wait until she dressed. How wrong she was, Jason's next words made her almost faint.

"Great Aunt Belladonna, she set up in the ballroom and asked, in front of about twenty people for Eli to be brought to her."

"In... " She dragged him into her room slamming the door in the faces of

43

the nosy people nearby. As soon as they were inside, she became a whirlwind of action, she tapped on the communication orb on her desk in a specific pattern. "Find Sarah and tell her to come to my room as soon as possible please." The orb flashed green twice and winked out with a crystalline ring. Once that was done, she stood in the middle of the floor, whipped her hand upwards and an Oriental style privacy screen materialised. She began getting dressed as Sarah knocked and entered the room. Jason took a seat on the beds edge which had made itself.

"Em? What's going on?" She asked causing both Emily and Jason to snort. "What?"

"It just amazes us both how your naming conventions for Aunt Emily changes breath to breath. One minute you're like sisters, then you're matron, then you're something out of a bad novel." Jason supplied helpfully causing Sarah to bluster and blush.

"Err... well." She stuttered.

"Jason, leave her be she can refer to me how she wants to. Now my boy, explain what the hell is going on." Came Emily's irritated voice from behind the screen, it was accompanied by the rustling of fabric.

"Well, Great Aunt Belladonna set up in the ballroom with that weird butler of hers, what's his name?"

"Wathelbury." Supplied Sarah quietly, she didn't like where this was going, something was setting her teeth on edge.

"That's him, the guy that makes a room seem colder and you can't tell how old he is. One minute he looks in his twenties and the next he looks like he's ancient. Well, they set up the alcove at the back of the ballroom. Then she got produced the cards."

"She's using the cards? She hasn't used them in years. That deck is rumoured to be the Noctis Venari, the deck of death himself. Whenever she's used that deck something big has happened."

"Probably a rumour like you said, but her using the cards in the first place sends up questions. Well anyway her Raven, Harfan began cawing orders for tea and breakfast to be supplied. By this point, the room had filled with guests for breakfast. Lovely fare by the way. Quiet conversation bubbled over the room when all of a sudden, her voice rang out. Terrifying, quiet with power like it had come from the grave. "Fetch me the boy, Bring me Eli the one who will find my husband."

"WHAT!" roared Emily and Sarah together.

"That's what has set everyone gabbling, not one family member plans on leaving the property, there will be no privacy for this visitation." Replied Jason, still holding his calm.

"I mean, we all suspected he wasn't dead, or fully dead as she aged rapidly and didn't die. But Eli, he's thirteen how is he to find her husband? I think she has finally lost it." Emily stated.

"Well, in the family structure she still outranks you, Emily, we have to get Eli properly presented and the as soon as possible."

"Fine but keep Hollie far away from her. I don't want her scared more than she will be today." Replied Emily stiffly. "Well let's get this done with."

Emily stepped out into the room dressed in a constricting emerald green dress that had flared sleeves, looking every bit the lady of the house. On her feet, she had a pair of shimmering ruby red high heels. She was adorned in beautiful jewellery to the naked eye but to any Leanai it was a statement of power. Each item of Jewellery hung sang with her power, she was a woman prepared to defend her child. This may seem an overreaction but to Leanai, children were everything, and any perceived threat would be met with the promise of a painful death.

"Sarah get Eli ready please, in the nicest clothes you can find. Fetch him to the top of the stairs and I'll meet you there so we can walk down together. Jason, go down to the ballroom and tell everyone to bugger off into town, I want that ballroom as empty as possible. Yes, they're here for the Awakening and they can stare at him then. Not before. If they aren't immediate family, to the third generation then they can f..."

"Emily!" Barked Sarah. "Language. If you start that now, then you'll slip all day." Snapped Sarah, Emily's jaw snapped shut with an audible click.

"You're right. Sorry. Come on then, I've calmed down. Off we go." She replied calmly. "I will meet you in fifteen minutes." The other two left with a small smile to her, leaving her alone in the spacious bedroom. For a moment she stood stock-still staring blankly at the door before a tear rolled its way down her cheek. Immediately she wiped it away with an impatient huff and turned to her dresser. Her laptop was closed neatly, she lifted it by both sides with a whispered word. as she lifted the laptop the section of desk rose with it, revealing with a soft silvery glow three shelves that couldn't have fit in the thin vanity unit without Magick. Each of the shelves let off a rolling cloud of cold, keeping all of the bottles chilled and the small ice bucket cold enough that the ice was still frosted. Quickly, with a small glance at the door, she picked up a silver coaster and put it nearby on the desk then picked up a black bottle of her second favourite sweet sherry. Immediately and with a strange sound, that can only be written in its onomatopoeic form as "bwoop", a small crystal sherry glass materialised on the silver disc.

With a grim glance at the glass, she poured a measure, barely controlling her tremoring hand. Replacing the bottle, she quickly pulled out a small brown glass bottle of pills. The bottle was labelled by the local pharmacy and was covered in a rime of frost. She poured two pills into her hand and tossed them into the back of her mouth, grabbing the glass and washing them down with the bitingly sweet sherry. A small shudder of pleasure washed through her body as the ice-cold alcohol warmed part of her she had not realised was chilled. She replaced the bottle and placed down the glass on the coaster where it instantly vanished with another "bwoop". A light knock at the door startled her.

"One second." She said quickly, waving her hand which caused the coaster to fly into the shelving unit which immediately sank back into the desk. Once she was satisfied that everything looked normal, she strode to the door and opened it.

Outside Sarah stood now dressed similarly to Emily though her dress was a deep sapphire blue. She glanced down slightly to see Elijah stood smartly dressed, in his finest grey suit. He looked tired but happy, his copper hair neatly tied in a small ponytail and shimmering in the light. Emily smiled happily to see her son looking so smart and happy. Eli had always been a happy child but also threw himself into his studies and didn't socialise with others his age. The moment she smiled; Sarah raised an eyebrow at the distinctive waft of alcohol that lingered on her breath.

"Em dear, your breath is smelling rather sweet, perhaps a mint wouldn't go amiss." She smiled warmly, though there was a warning in her tone.

Emily let out a small sigh as she reached behind her and mentally called for the tube of off-brand mints she kept by her bed, they slammed into her hand quite noisily which caused Sarah to snort. Quickly she opened the tube and popped two into her mouth, pocketing the rest of the container. She opened the door fully and stepped into the hallway. Eli even at Thirteen grasped hers and Sarah's hands. He stopped and said in a good affectation of a Gentleman's voice.

"May I escort you lovely ladies to breakfast?" He bowed slightly and offered both an arm.

Both women looked at each other over his head and giggled girlishly as they both had raised one eyebrow at his actions. They both hooked an arm each and began to walk in companionable silence. They walked down the elegant main staircase and into the large marble main hall which was watched over by shimmering marble statues. The early morning sunlight streamed through the stained-glass windows and painted pictures on the floor in shining pools of light. They allowed themselves to be led by Elijah along the familiar route to the ballroom. Soon they stopped and Emily looked down to Eli.

"Now Eli, Great Aunt Belladonna may look scary but she's not, she's just lonely. Her husband was a Seidhunter who vanished in the '80s. Now stand up straight and it'll be over before you know it."

"Okay mum, we'll go. Then can I open a present?" He grinned cheekily.

"Of course, sweetie, I'm sure there are one or two hidden around here." Smiled Emily.

Sarah snorted knowing that there were more than one or two presents from the family hidden in the manor. She straightened the front of her dress as Emily stood and gestured for the doors to open. The ballroom itself was truly magnificent, arched windows on all sides and a stained-glass dome designed by some famous company or other. The entire thing was a mass of Iron and Glass, perfectly balanced. But it was the floor that took your breath away, a giant marble mural of the Duskphizer crest. The setting sun and day and night represented equally on both sides. In the centre of the half-circle of the sun was a flaming egg of black and white. Legend had it that the family held the secret to the last remaining Phoenix Egg. Sarah thought, probably just a legend. Not all the legends could be true, right? Finally, the marble pillars had been wrapped in enchanted ivy that changed colours and chimed when touched. It was a very understated way to decorate the room.

The three strode across the room. Toward the back where an alcove and everything within had been covered in deep blue cloth. It looked like a fortune tellers' tent at a carnival. They were followed by the whispers of family members who were milling about at the long buffet table. Everyone trying not to obviously watch but all eyes still glued to them. By the time they stood in front of the opening, Eli looked nervous. He received a squeeze on each shoulder from the women. From the "tent" a tall man walked out, he was very tall, though the slight curve of his spine belied, his long shaggy dark brown hair obscured his eyes. The man was dressed in a crisp black suit with a blood-red tie. He looked as though he was in his mid-twenties.

"This 'im?" Asked the man in a British accent that sounded remotely southern and a little upper class.

"Yes Wathelbury, this is Eli." Replied Emily stiffly.

"Come in lad, she don't bite. Not with these dentures anyway." Wathelbury chuckled at his own joke. As the other two moved to follow he held up his hand. "Mistress Bella only asked for him."

"Well… Fine." Emily started, but she repented under Wathelbury's withering look from under his flyaway fringe.

Eli gulped but walked forward at the gentle push from the Butler, as he entered the tent there was a shimmer of violet light behind him as a Privacy Lense was activated. As his eyes adjusted to the light, he got his first good look at his Great Aunt. He gasped. She was old, dusty-looking and decrepit. Her clothes hung at odd angles on her frame as she was so thin. her face was gaunt and sunken and her hair that was probably once long and silky had lost its lustre. Each breath she took was ragged and looked like it took a lot of effort. On the chair behind her, a majestic Raven sat staring at him intently.

"Well," She spoke, not unkindly, in a gravelly voice that sounded straight from the grave. Eli Shivered. "come closer boy and sit down. None of us here will harm you."

He did as he was bidden and sat at one side of the circular table clutching the velvet tablecloth in his lap almost like a security blanket. This small space really could not have been more cliché, the heavy scent of sandalwood overpowered the air, charms and talismans guarded the space and three long dripping candles were the only real light. In the sinister light cast from the small collection of candles Belladonna Hawthorne looked utterly terrifying, her sallow shin hung loosely off her, even her dress was dusty, her hair hung in tangled knots on her head and her face looked like it was carved out of aged stone. She tapped on the table with a long bony finger which had a sharp claw-like blue painted nail.

"Elijah or do you prefer Eli?" She asked carefully.

"I prefer Eli, Great Aunt." He replied nervously.

"Now, now less of the great, I may look ready for the grave but I assure you I'm not. You may call me Aunt or Auntie. Do you know why I have called you here?"

"No Aunt, apart from it being my awakening."

"That it is. Has your mother ever told you about me?" She asked grinning in what she hoped was a reassuring manner. It was not.

"Not really, just that your husband was a Seidhunter, one of the best and he vanished a long time ago."

"Well that about covers it, but I've been looking at the cards and you will be the one who allows us to find him."

"Me, how?" Eli asked, clearly confused.

"That I don't know. I called you here to give you a gift and a warning."

"A... A warning?"

"Yes, a warning. Time stutters around you boy, you are an anomaly. Any seer that looks at you can see it; you are the proverbial rock in the stream. The flow moves around you but do not be too rigid for it may well submerge you. Now for the gift..." As she spoke, she reached behind her neck and unclasped a delicate silver chain and pulled the pendant free handing it to Eli. Carefully Eli took the chain and held the charm in his hand and looked at it. The charm was a small Owl that seemed to be made of five different coloured crystals perfectly fused, the colours seamlessly melding into each other. The owl had its wings closed. Purple, Pink, Green, Blue and Red instantly Eli recognised the colours of the five Pillars of Magick. Even to his young eyes, he knew this was a powerful gift.

"That charm is a Seid Stone, as you know it represents the five types of Magick that permeate our world. A Seid Stone can glow with any of the six types of power including Seidhr Magick which is Grey/Silver. Now when in use the owl will spread its wings and provide light only to you and those you choose to share it with. Listen well Elijah, when you reach the River take the less travelled path the night train will open your path. To get the owl to respond thick of it and say Nocht which is Irish for reveal. I'm sure it does more than light, but I've never bothered to try. It should allow you to find hidden things depending on which light you use. I know it responds to thought and intent, but I leave that to you to experiment with. You were taught, Irish?"

"Yes Aunt, I rather like learning it. If it's a Seid artefact will it only respond to Irish?"

"No, but Irish will be the easiest to figure out as a lot of our Magick has a Celtic and Gaelic base."

"Thank You for the wonderful gift Aunt." Eli beamed happily; all hints of fear gone.

"You're very welcome young man. Now, send in your mother and Aunt in all but blood. I want a word with them."

"Yes Aunt, I'll send them in now." With that, he reached over the table and gave her hand a soft kiss before standing and bowing slightly to her. The privacy screen fell, and he stepped out of the tent into the ballroom proper. Quickly he clasped on the necklace and turned to his Mother and Sarah.

"Your turn, Aunt Belladonna wants a word she says." He tells them smiling brightly before happily pottering off toward the breakfast buffet. The women looked at each other nervously before they sighed and entered Belladonna's domain.

They crossed the boundary and the privacy Lense once again silently activated behind them. Both women stood nervously in the overly warm tent waiting to be told why they had been requested. They were shocked when a Lense matrix unravelled on the table and a tea service appeared cakes and all.

"Come on then sit down. I haven't got all day. Obviously, I'm not getting any younger." She cackled softly.

They sat down in nervous yet companionable silence as Wathelbury skilfully poured the steaming tea, knowing each of their preferences by heart. For a moment they all enjoyed the taste and smell of their respective teas before Belladonna spoke again.

"I'll not beat 'bout the bush. The boy has a destiny." She stopped as Sarah snorted.

"My father said the same." Said Emily before Belladonna could respond.

"I'm well aware of that. I'll get to your fool of a Father shortly. Elijah has been given a gift by me that will help him along. The Wyrd is not all he'll know, not all he will be. But he is in danger from she who listens to the whispers in the shadows. Send him away tonight. Pack him all the artefacts and relevant clothing food and money you can. Use my brothers Kleiner camping bag. While not infinite it can hold a heck of a lot. Should keep him going for a while. If you do send him anyway, send him to the riverbank, he knows what to do after that."

"What? Send him away? Why?" Exclaimed Emily.

"Listens to whispers on the shadows... Em, that's her below." Sarah said quietly causing Emily to stop still.

"She comes near my son and..."

"You'll what Emily Ann Duskphizer, take on the Storm Queen, risk our family place in this world. No matter how you hate my sister at this moment you wouldn't risk her life?" Belladonna said heatedly, her aged voice cracking.

"No, I suppose not. If it becomes safer to send him away I will. Is that all about Eli you will share Aunt?" Emily asked in a defeated tone.

"One more thing, be careful of your sister. She is wavering between sides at the moment. Also, on that subject tell your idiot father to come today."

"The conditions of the ritual..." Emily said unsure as to what her Aunt was saying.

"That ritual only applies to the dead. Not the Wanderlost. Amelia your sister has his body somewhere under spell and key. He didn't die, he was projecting at the time and has just forgotten. Idiot."

"I'll call him right away."

"Off you go then. We will speak again one day. When I look quite different from now."

"Sarah, stay a moment will you."

Before Emily could argue she was ushered out by the tall butler, she noticed that his hands were ice cold. Once she was through the privacy Lense, she noticed that even the overpowering smell of sandalwood was even blocked. How paranoid could you get, she thought. She walked over to Eli and hugged him tightly.

"Mum look what Aunt Belladonna gave me."

Emily looked down at the small owl pendant and blanched with a primal fear. Belladonna had given him a Seid Stone. Those were rare, expensive, powerful and many other things besides. It would paint a target on Eli, but her Aunt did nothing without reason and for her to break her silence. Emily decided that she could not interfere, or she could cause a lot of issues. Besides from what she knew about Seid Artefacts no-one could separate them from their owners without wilful passing of the Artefact. Even death could not break the bond, apparently.

"That's pretty Eli, what does it do?" Asked Emily, with genuine curiosity.

"Auntie said that it would allow me to find hidden things and that it can shine with the light of each Pillar of Magick and the Seid. Shall I show you?"

"Yes, please Eli. See if you can find your presents from us." She smiled.

"Okay." He beamed. Eli lifted the small crystalline owl to eye line in his palm and focussed on the Wyrd and finding his presents. "Nocht" He spoke, his Irish almost perfect.

With a crystalline tinkling sound, the small bird opened its beautiful wings and emitted a soft amethyst coloured light. At first, only Eli could see it and the effect of the light, but Eli focused on sharing it with Emily and she gasped.

"What am I missing, not off adventuring without me are you?" Came Sarah's voice as she appeared over Emily's shoulder, wiping a stray tear from her cheek.

"Are you ok Sarah?" Asked Emily concerned.

"We'll talk later, near that wonderful cabinet of yours." She smiled.

"No problem, it is great at times." She replied and grinned as Sarah snorted.

"Eli was just showing me the present that Aunt Belladonna gave him. She gave him a Seid Stone." Sarah choked. "Show her Eli."

Eli did as she asked and showed Sarah the Owl and added her to the view, like Emily she gasped. The small owl glowed still glowed with light which washed over everything in the room. On the floor rippling footprints, the same colour as the bright light rippled, leading them from where they stood out of the room. With significant interest, the three of them followed the footsteps a short way. Before Jason intercepted them, who like Sarah was added into the group and joined the hunt. For several minutes they followed Eli through the vast house until they came to Emily's room. With a glance to his mother who nodded in return they entered and followed the footsteps until they led to the foot of the bed where the impression of an old chest could be seen, made from the same light. Emily had concealed the chest so Eli couldn't get to it. She was about to unveil it when Eli shocked them all.

"Nocht" He ordered gesturing at the chest which exploded into view in a wash of power. The power of the command had unveiled several other hidden things which made Emily's cheeks burn as she concealed them again with a hasty Lense before Eli could see them.

"Oscail." he said again. With the popping of several locks, the trunk sprang open again along with several usually locked things in the room. Emily relocked everything including the trunk which caused Eli to glance at her confused.

"Irish in Magick requires delicacy. Let's not forget you shouldn't have any access to power until tonight but let's try opening it again with less force behind it, visualise only the trunk opening and keep a rein on your power." Said Emily kindly.

"Ok Mother." He replied. Everyone watched with interest as he turned to the trunk again focussed on it. "Oscail." he said again. This time the power was like a lance and struck the chest which popped open with the clunk of its locks. Nothing else shifted.

"Well done Eli. Now, go open your presents while we nip outside for a moment?

"Ok mother. Thank you." With that, he hugged the three adults and set about opening his gifts. The three adults left and stood in the hallway.

"I'd like to spend some time with Eli if you both don't mind, Jason could you help Sarah pack the bag please?"

"Bag?" Asked Jason confused as he hadn't been in the tent with them.

"Come on my lad, I'll explain on the way to the attic. See you later Em." Sarah said as she led a still confused Jason down the hall. Emily turned and entered her bedroom to spend time with her son before she possibly, lost him.

CHAPTER SEVEN

GIFTS FROM BEYOND

The day passed painstakingly slow for the inhabitants of The Forge, Sarah and Jason packed everything they could think of and more into the Kleiner Bag and then joined Emily and Eli in her room and enjoyed watching Eli playing with his gifts. They ate tea as a group in Emily's room and as Eli dozed off for a while they drank and leant on each other for support. After the sun went down Emily called upon Richard and told him what Belladonna had told her, leaving nothing out. He lost his composure and vanished; the wave of power produced on his exit did not bode well for anyone. But she had done as she had been instructed and now, she had but a few scant hours left before her sons awakening and she wanted to spend it in the company of her family.

Hours later as the full moon hung high in the night sky a stream of people following the woodland path by lantern light towards the clearing where the barrow lay. No artificial light came from the Victorian lamppost or The Forge itself. Night shrouded the manor and its grounds in a veil of darkness but not silence. Those that walked toward the Barrow talked in hushed tones. They talked about nothing of import just what they thought would happen a few even speculating if Eli would survive.

In the clearing, Eli stood inside the ward barrier of the Barrow which shone gold in the moonlight. He stood in front of the Dark Gate which looked foreboding in the half-light. Emily Sarah and Jason were nearby with Hollie, all being immediate Family. They counted Sarah as such because of the Families feelings toward her. A few minutes later and the Barrow depression filled with family members watching and waiting. Emily stepped forward at five minutes to midnight, as an owl hooted in the background and called for silence.

"Family we are gathered here on the auspicious night in the presence of our ancestors to bear witness to the Awakening of Elijah William Duskphizer. I call the Barrow Guardians to Guard from threats within..." As she said this the Barrow Door opened and the Onyx skeletons, each glowing with fire marched out and took positions at the outer edge of the circle facing inwards, weapons at the ready. "and I call the Gaergohl to protect from threats without." In response thirteen points behind each of the Barrow Guardians, the ground boiled and bubble. Out of the boiling ground rose Thirteen fearsome looking beasts, each different and around the size of a bear. The creatures stood, fangs bared surveying the woodland and the sky outside the wards.

"The moon reaches its peak and the power will now call to my son. Let us bear witness."

"We bear witness." Replied the gathered crowd.

As they spoke this Eli now topless wearing only a pair of shorts stood and faced the Dark-Gate. A beam of pure moonlight lanced down from the moon and struck Eli and the gate. The Gate opened as Eli gasped. Power spiralled in all directions around the boy. He rose into the air eliciting gasps from the gathered attendees. Eli shone with a deep silver light. Someone in the crowd screamed. Two figures pushed their way toward the mound where Eli and his family stood. One a man dressed in an inky purple almost black suit and a green tie, the other looked like a shaggy dog on walking on its hind legs. Before they could reach the mound, a storm the likes of which no-one had seen before whipped up out of nowhere. Lightning rained down and struck trees, setting them ablaze and sending showers of dirt into the air where it struck the ground. Over the noise of the wind, thunder, lightning and rain there was a pair of deep groaning wails. Everyone presents knew that sound from storybook and nightmare. From the sky, a pair of nightmarish Wraiths made of black smoke and green flame swooped down. These were the Vanguard of the Storm Queen, the Shada. The pair circled and screech as a bolt of lightning gathered in the sky and lanced down leaving behind a figure that was made from storm clouds and lightning. The Gaergohl let out a roar as one that seemed to ripple space itself. But that was not the loudest scream, Eli let out an inhuman wail as power slammed into him. A screech of an owl which swooped down and shifted into Thedas.

"Stop it all you pair of fools." Thedas roared at the two figures behind Emily.

"Owlighter..." Growled the Wolfen figure.

"Not now. Do it before he explodes." Thedas shouts at the suited figure whose eyes widen. A snapped word, a flourish of hands, the world froze. Eli did not. Power kept pouring into him and the three unfrozen people watched at the golden threads of time seemed to wind and unwind around him.

"What have you done Owlighter?" Roared one figure (That's me Wytch)

"I have done nothing except rectify your mistake. You cannot send a Thirteen-year-old boy off into the world. He needs aged before the power pops him like a water balloon." Thedas replied.

"That re-write would have more holes than the titanic."

"Like everything about this world, write now patch later." Thedas grinned. "She won't wait; she will hunt him down." He motioned to the frozen Storm Queen.

"Granted. Now, what do we do? He must be sent away." The Wolfen one said.

"That has already been seen to, they have a Kleiner Bag behind the gate. Belladonna warned them this morning. Eight years should do it."

"Well that's a lot easier in a way. We can turn this into his Ascension."

There came another pain-filled wail from Eli and the three beings turned as one to watch what is happening to him. Before their eyes, Eli's body twisted and contorted as the power still relentlessly sank into him. His hair lengthened and became a brighter red, his body stretched and grew and elicited another scream. The poor boy was living through puberty all at once. Acne appeared and cleared in a heartbeat leaving some scarring on his face and body which faded a little. His muscles filled out as though he had worked out during his non-existent teenage years. Freckles became more pronounced on his face. The next rush of power caused another scream, deeper this time as his larynx grew.

Over Elijah's heart, his Draiohba formed a five-pointed flower, each petal an identical labyrinth. Each of the petals was coloured differently; Purple, Pink, Green, Blue and Red. In the centre a knot of Grey, White and Black made a smaller rose binding the five petals. Lines of woven Grey, White and Black branched out forming thorny looking vines from which labyrinthine leaves sprouted. These vines spread and wrapped around the now lithe muscular body. Tiny flowers blossomed along his hairline, around his eyes and near his mouth. Elijah's eyes sprang open the once amber eyes now held a braided gold and silver ring and they shone with power. His skin began to become scaly momentarily and his legs shifted and were replaced with a long beautiful serpentine tail. His tail split with a gush of blood as it shed off allowing his legs to reform. The final shock was one final scream and a spray of blood as two pairs of wings one huge with a span of at least fifteen feet and the other slightly smaller with a span of around ten feet. The wings were had black feathers with tiny flecks of silver and gold intermittently.

The Seid Stone that Belladonna had given Eli rose from his neck and began to grow until it was the size of a large fist, the silver chain seemed to melt and change. Along with wood which had flown from the surrounding woodland, oak to be exact, the boys birth wood, it melded to become a large staff of around six feet high. The staff was perfectly straight and had a silver double helix chain with large links down the length. Finally, the owl stone clasped its claws to a large link at the top becoming part of the staff. Overall, the staff now stood a few inches above the boys' height.

Rapidly the power winding around Eli began to sink into him and fade away. As it did so he slowly fell to the floor and his wings sank into his back, the Draiohba forming delicate wing designs on his back and torso. Luckily for the boys' modesty, the shorts had been charmed to expand but the sheer power of his combined Awakening and Ascension had started to unravel the charms and fabric.

Wytch closed his eyes for a moment and gestured to Eli. A pair of Grey trousers and shoes materialised on him, a loose shirt and a long black fitted jacket which he had charmed to allow the wings free. Eli was panting heavily but grunted out his thanks.

"No trouble lad grab the staff it's yours now. Seid artefacts become what they need to be. Use it to hold yourself up while we sort out the rest of this mess. How Old Are You?"

"Thirteen." Eli replied.

"Crap we're going to have to rectify that. Haru go back to the house and edit his bio. Leave me the master copy."

"Catch." The lupine figure grunted throwing a book. "Back soon." With that, he vanished between breaths.

"Owlighter I assume you have a copy too?"

"Not with me." Thedas replied.

"Fine, I'll do it myself. When it hits the fan, take the boy to the riverside but don't linger. You'll be too easy to track until he gets into Glight." Wytch spoke authoritatively but not harshly.

"No problem. You're not banning me contact?" Asked Thedas quietly.

"No, we'll need you to train him. His powers are close to yours. Wherever this new plot takes him, you'll be there."

"Thank You."

"It's no problem, I may not like you, but you don't do anything without cause and if our plotline last run failed then thanks for rectifying it. Now shush, the boys frozen meaning Haru is editing him personally, he'll add knowledge and training as well as memories for the last eight years, so it seems real. It's for me to edit the rest." Wytch replied opening the book and taking out a pen.

The rest of the world froze...

-***-

Hi there friend. Yes, it's me Wytch. You've just been watching me through the Fuinnestra but now I've frozen and am speaking to you. Confusing yes? Well, let me explain before I edit this mess. Hopefully, this will be the last edit for a while. So, when you're reading the Fuinnestra you are seeing the events as they happened a few minutes ago. Whereas during edits, it's live. Make sense? Think of it as a TV broadcast, they send it out a few minutes after it starts in case there's an accident or swearing. Don't want another Tommy Cooper, do we? Anyway, that's as simple as I can make it. Now I'd better get editing.

While you watch, you see things begin to change as time changes around the frozen people. A mist covers everything leaving a light frosty rime for a moment before it fades. That's the memories taking hold. The clearing changes, new plants and trees appear while others fall and die. The grass and meadowland change slightly as other small changes are made. New lanterns. New patterns in the grass where things were planted or buried. Other changes that take place are minor. Things that would have been updated and changed in eight years.

The guests clothing is changed and updated to suit a fictional new trend that has been added. Each person shows some tiny hint of the passage of time, a few wrinkles, a grey hair or two but luckily for us the Leanai age slowly, much slower than humans after their Ascension. Hollie is now nineteen and looks hugely different. She is tall and though slim she is not skinny; her red hair is streaked with blue she wears a fitted robe-like jacket in line with the new fashion. Before your eyes, a few new younger children appear in their parents' arms or standing near their parents. Some children have gone through awakening or ascension as they now have Draiohba as well as having aged.

Only the Shada and Storm queen are unchanged. They are as they always will be. While you wait and watch for the world resuming, she seems to shrink and change as the Archir force her into her humanoid form. Even in her humanoid form, she is intimidating. Her hair is black and grey and topped with a crown that looks as though it is made from solidified lightning bolts. She wears a long blue-grey dress and is decked out in finery befitting her station.

Well, we've done as much as we can to make it believable. The date was June 23rd 2020, but it is now June 23rd 2028. We've fabricated memories, mementoes and news articles. We just have to hope that there aren't any glaring holes or places where people can add things in to take advantage. Oh well, as Thedas said write now and patch later. Haru and I are knackered after over a month of editing for us, so we'll resume now, I'll come and watch the events and then go and join Haru for a long, long nap.

The world restarts again as time catches up, the storm clears.

-***-

Everyone gasps as they see Eli, power rolling off him and seeing the staff in his hand which they remembered seeing form. Eli spread both sets of his wings with some difficulty but smiled when he succeeded, and they passed through the shirt and jacket with ease. He would have to thank that weird man properly later. When he glanced at the man he saw he was reading a book and as he glanced up, he gave Eli a strange look before he burst into silent laughter. Eli looked to the Storm Queen who was still frozen as a figure walked out of the Dark-Gate and into his view. The figure was a young-looking woman who was rather short and let's say curvy. She wore a long billowing dress and seemed rather solid for a spirit.

"Eli, do you know who I am?" the figure asked, her voice echoing.

"You are Aunt Ophelia, I pay respect by counting you as near kin." Replied Eli bowing low to her. "Aunt you are as beautiful in death as you were in life. I may not have met you personally but the memories of my family allow me to know you."

"Oh, you are a charmer young one. You'll go far. Now due to the strange circumstances of this visit and how certain beings are playing with things I'm bending the rules. I've brought you five gifts, four given to me by other family members who are resting to help you along." She gestured with her arms and five orbs of light appeared. "The first is a simple gift from my own Uncle Captain Arturo Duskphizer a naval captain. It is his compass tuned to the Forge, so you will always find home." The compass materialised and floated to Eli. He examined it before stowing it in his pocket. "The next gift is from your grandfather. He's looking for something at the moment. He gifts you access to the Flow, as is proper for him to do so. He also snuck in a capture and release Lense." The second orb hit Eli, and it was as though he was submerged in water for a moment. Eventually the sensation passed, and he began to feel normal again. Right hand burned for a moment and a Lense matrix appeared in his palm "The Third gift is from your Aunt Bessie. She's sleeping at this moment; the strangeness has messed her up a little. She gifts you her ability to sense the truth." Again, an orb hit Eli and he knew everything yet nothing at once. "The fourth gift is from Great Grand Uncle Elijah for whom you are named. he gifts you the simplest of things, a message. Your family will always love you no matter what. Know this and be happy." The fourth orb hit Eli, and a tear escaped him as unconditional love washed over him and warmed him like a fire inside. "Finally, my gift, as is tradition I give you a Magick as I am allowed. I gift you the ability to call your Faemiliar." She snorted as did Eli. "I like a good portmanteau as much as the next ghost but that one just seems like lazy writing. Like we're in a cheap novel."

As she said this Wytch looked up glaring at the spectre. He walked over, looking a little annoyed and stood face to face with Ophelia.

"The size of you love you didn't enjoy Exercise in life so I'm sure you wouldn't enjoy being Exorcized in death." He looked exceedingly proud of that threat. Ophelia laughed.

"You can't threaten me Archir, I reside in the place between places. I know your kind. Plus that's another example of your lazy ass writing. A cheap pun as a threat. Get out of my way and stop interfering in Elis Ascension. Those rules apply to you too." She smiled at him evilly.

"Alright woman, I'll fix you later."

"Anytime Archir just not teatime." She replied.

Wytch backed away and resumed his place overseeing the proceedings, glaring at Ophelia scathingly. She turned back to Eli and the last orb moved to him sinking into his left hand this time causing the sensation of a summer breeze as the Rune branded him painlessly. Ophelia moved forward and hugged Eli.

"A lot will happen, but the Forge and your family will always be here for you. My time is up I'm afraid. This lot need to deal with the Storm Bitch, and I need rest. It takes a lot to be here without resurrecting. We will meet again bonnie lad." With a quick kiss, her form faded, and the Dark-Gate slammed shut. Leaving Eli with tears flowing freely.

CHAPTER EIGHT

BATTLE OF WILLS

Elijah stood for a moment reigning in his emotions and then he wiped away his tears before turning his attention to the Storm Queen and her Shada who were still frozen in place. He surveyed her regal features and alabaster skin, her steel-grey eyes though frozen still held the promise of pain. That promise was aimed directly at him, yet he did not feel afraid, he felt sorry for her. That she was so insecure that she had to come after him during his weakest moment spoke volumes about her. The Shada though, something did not sit right with him. The Queen's guards circled her as though she were prey, were they her guards or her jailers? Either way, Eli decided that he did not want them near his family. He wracked his brains for the correct way to do it, then it came to him. The direct route was best. He couldn't risk a general banishment as it would destroy the Gaergohl and any protection they may offer. Before anyone could stop him he levelled the staff toward the Queen.

"Unfreeze them."

"Eli what are you doing? You can't attack the Storm Queen. She would easily fry you." Emily asked confused.

"Probably but I'm not aiming for her. It's the unwanted guests I'm getting rid of. Something doesn't sit right with me about them."

"Ok, I'll unfreeze them but do not under any circumstances hit the Queen. You know the laws as well as I." Wytch replied. A warning in his tone.

"I know, I know. Just unfreeze them."

"Hold on a sec. There." Wytch gestured to the frozen figures. The Shada began howling and circling again and the Queen began to Holler."

"You boy, you're a danger to us all. You must be dealt with as must your family for stealing what's mine."

"Shut Up!" Eli roared causing the Queen to Shriek. Before she could do anything, else Elijah gripped the staff, the owl on the end opened its wings with a crystalline ring and he shouted. "Ordaím duit imeacht Shada."

A flat curved blade of silver power exploded from the crystal tip of the staff and soared through the air before splitting into two and slicing into the two Shada. Immediately both creatures let out unearthly screeches and froze in place. Silver light lanced out of both of them before they exploded into ash which was whisked away on the summer breeze. Everyone stood silent, looking back and forth between Eli and the Queen. The Queen herself seemed to be in shock which lasted a few seconds before she rapidly went red and inhaled.

"How dare you, this is all the proof I need. I shall have your head on a spike boy. You attacked the Monarch of the Throne below. TREASON! That's what this is TREASON! I..." She roared.

"Pipe down ye auld besom, the boy defended his family and dispelled your demonic lapdogs. Now stop shouting before these fine people have to replace windows or the dogs go deaf." Came a regal yet worn voice. On the path behind the Storm Queen, another Queen stood. She was dressed in a flowing red gown, her skin slightly tanned. Everything about her was a stark contrast to the Storm Queen. This was the Monarch of England, the Queen above. On her head sat the Imperial State Crown which sang with power and authority as such things do. In one hand she held the Sovereigns Sceptre, the Great Star of Africa glittered and shone even in the low light, in her other hand she held a Scroll bearing the current Royal Seal.

"How dare you speak to me that way I..."

"Are on my turf. You have interrupted an Ascension, even for a Monarch is against all of our laws. If there was a suitable replacement for you, I would call the Archir for your removal." She stressed the last word.

"Well lucky for you there isn't a suitable replacement for me. As you know my daughter vanished nearly a century ago and I have not gotten around to producing another. Now I have business to finish here." She turned to Eli.

"You boy I name you Thorn and will have you hunted to the ends of the Earth until you are nothing but a memory." She spat toward Eli who just flipped her the bird back.

"Silence your tongue Queen of the Under Throne. Thou wilt not harm an innocent. By the power of the Throne Above and the ancient accords of the

Empire. I grant the child Elijah William Duskphizer a Royal Seal of Protection. He will be hidden from your sight and the sight of any Agent you enlist in any way. This protection extends to all he calls family for One Year and One Day hence." Spoke the Imperial Monarch firmly. The Seal in her hand glowed and a wash of vibrant pure pink power exploded outward in all directions until it had circumnavigated the globe.

"NO!" Roared the Storm Queen shifting back into her true form as she began hurling lightning at the Ward barrier. The Monarch raised the Sovereigns Sceptre as the Great Star of Africa glowed with a soft pink light which caused the Ward Barrier to strengthen.

"One would suggest getting the child out of here, sadly the seal will not activate fully until dawn. The night is that one's domain. Inquisitors, control the Fae."

"Owlighter, grab the bag and the boy. GO!" Roared Wytch.

Thedas didn't need to be told twice; he knew the only way that the Storm Queen would calm was when Eli was away from this place. She would have no reason to linger as the seal would rob her of any prisoners and leverage, they may gain her. But until the Seal came into effect, she could do a lot of damage. Some of which the Archir may not be able to repair. Eli was being hugged by Jason, Emily, Sarah and Hollie as he approached. Emily looked distraught, as any mother would be. Thedas quickly retrieved the bag from behind the Dark-Gate and stood near the family. Something in him stirred. Something which he had long ago buried so he did what any reasonable person would do and ignored it.

"Come on Eli. Time to go."

Eli was gently pushed by Emily toward him. When he was stood beside him, he handed him the bag and grasped his arm tightly.

"Don't try to pull away and don't use any power you'll hurt us both. I will transport us, but I think I'll go the long way round. To throw off any tracking spells." Wytch caught his eye as he said this and nodded. Damn Archir seem to know everything. "Last tip, breath normally."

With that last piece of advice, Thedas began to focus his power and begin the travelling spell. This was one of the few pieces of Magick to still be called a spell as it used power from all five of the pillars. Eli gasped as the world began to spin and blur around them as though they were stood in the eye of a hurricane of reality. He felt a wind whipping around him as though he himself were moving at great speed. A second later the blur cleared for a moment and they stood in front of the Sydney opera house then reality blurred again, and they were stood in a market in Morocco. Again, the world blurred and spun almost unhurriedly, and they were stood by a canal in Venice. Then the top of the Eiffel tower. Then Eli recognised the dock of the Ullswater Steamer. With one final blur and this time the sickening impression of rapid deceleration and a small jolt as though they had been floating slightly off the ground, they appeared a few meters away from the bank of the River Esk, a few miles from his home.

CHAPTER NINE

BRB

They had landed in front of a small playground behind a hedgerow. It was dark and a little cold. Thedas was panting with the effort of sustaining the travelling spell over such a long distance and multiple jumps. He peered around the side of the hedgerow toward the bridge and swore under his breath. Near the bridge, several figures could be seen using Magick to search the area systematically. They would eventually work their way this way.

"Well, I screwed the pooch royally on that one. I should have fully materialised during one of the jumps to activate their tracking Lenses. I'll have to go soon and lead them off. I hear darkest Peru is nice at this time of year." He chuckled. Thedas rummaged in his pockets and pulled out two objects. The first was a long strip of leather which had golden symbols stitched onto it all along the length and the second was a silver chain. "Give me the compass."

Eli fumbled around in his pocket until his fingers closed on the cold metal of the brass compass. He retrieved it from his pocket and handed it to Thedas who placed the silver chain on top of it in his hand and closed it. Immediately a silver light began to shine in his hand and Thedas muttered under his breath rapidly for several seconds. When he opened his fist, the compass was gone and in its place was a shimmering stone that kept shifting between mineral types, wrapped around the stone was an intricate copper filigree and the Viking seal Vegvisir known as Odin's Compass was inlaid on the surface. The stone was attached to a new shining silver chain. Thedas turned it over to show that the silver engraving, which Eli had had no idea was even there, which read "kǫlu nigba ti irin naa gbona" or "Strike while the iron is hot." the not so original motto of The Forge which had been on the compass. Eli did not know how to feel about the change...

"I've installed the travelling spell and an anti-theft Lense. It's locked to mainland UK at the moment, can't have you jetting off and getting stuck. Before you use the travelling spell, cast a dispel Lense as strong as you can muster. It should weaken or break any trackers. Just to be on the safe side materialise in another town far from your target, dispel again and move a few streets away before you travel again. That way you'll be harder to track." He handed the compass and chain over to Eli who put it on. The chain shrank slightly, and he felt the anti-theft Lense bind to him. "Now this…" He held up the strip of leather. "… is a staff strap with a self-tying Lense on it strap it diagonally across your body and then put your staff across your back." Eli did as he was told and soon after the ties wrapped themselves securely around the staff and he was able to move comfortably. The staff now rested securely over the backpack.

"Right lad stay safe and follow what you were told by the seer. I better jump now before those idiots get any closer. Peru here we come." Thedas said as he stepped back and power began to wrap around him. Reality warped slightly around his form which began to rapidly fade. Within seconds he was gone, and reality snapped back into place.

"They've jumped again they're in Peru. Mike stay back in case it's a trick and the rest of us will follow." Came a shouted instruction from the people searching near the bridge. Eli peeked around the edge of the hedgerow and watched as there were five rapid localised flashes of light similar to camera flashes. Only Mike remained now and he didn't seem especially keen on searching for anyone as he sat on one of the benches overlooking the moonlit water and pulled out a bottle.

"If you're out there lad take the road less travelled. So long as I don't see you, I don't need to call the others." He said idly taking a long pull from the bottle.

Eli pulled his staff off and held it in front of him. Carefully calling up his power so as not to attract any attention. "Ceilt Orm" with a whisper of power he felt suddenly lighter if a little colder. He looked down at his hands and noticed that he was spectral. "Nocht" he flicked his staff as he focused on where to go next and the end began to glow with a faint silver light. On the ground, he could see heavy footprints shimmering on the ground leading him toward the river and off to the left. Slowly he followed the footsteps down the muddy path and onto a well-worn sandy path. The footsteps led him to the place he knew as The Crusher. In reality, it had nothing to do with crushing anything, it was just what the town called it, it was actually the remains of the railway bridge.

Eli followed the footsteps until they ended to the left of the stone structure, he sighed he didn't know when the Night Train was due so he decided it would be better to get off the path. With the assistance of his light, he scrambled up the slick angled bank until he reached the top. He let out a small burst of power and dried off an area off on the top wall so he could sit after he planted his staff in the ground, so the light stayed steady. Quickly he removed the backpack and sat down on the mossy yet surprisingly comfortable sandstone. As he sat there his stomach rumbled so he reached down and opened the bag.

"Shut the flap there's a bloody draft." Came and all too familiar nasal voice.

"Ben Bear?" Eli asked tentatively. The mouth of the bag widened and out popped Benjamin Bears furry crumb covered head. In his paw, he held a tuna sandwich which he happily stuffed into his face finishing it off.

"BeBe and I were put in here earlier, well apparently eight years ago. You've aged little man."

"Benjamin, it's cold, it's cooling my soup." Echoed BeBes voice from the depths of the bag.

"Gotta go little man, we found a pocket of picnic-space in here, entrance to someone's pantry. Here have a packed lunch, your stomach's been rumbling sommat rotten." Ben said quickly.

As the bear disappeared a small brown paper bag was ejected from deep inside. Eli caught it and watched as the bag closed itself firmly. He opened the packed lunch and looked inside, the bag contained a small bottle of orange juice, a bar of chocolate and a corned beef sandwich. standard school lunch I suppose. Elijah looked at the contents of the bag dispassionately, he knew there had to be other nicer things in the bag, but he also knew that both Picnickers absolutely hated corned beef. With a sigh, he worked his way through the contents of the bag and had just drained the bottle of juice when there was a rustle from above him as a voice yelled.

"Look out below." Seconds later Eli was knocked unconscious by a bright pink flask covered in white daisies which had fallen from the sky. From somewhere above, there was the sound of an old engine which got louder and closer. Down from the sky, the source of the sound appeared, a woman on a strange-looking broomstick which was letting out a stream of thick black smoke. When she landed, she immediately went to Eli, dropped her broom and after rummaging in a small bag which was clipped around her waist. From the bag, she removed a small bottle of fizzing orange liquid, pressed the cork to his arm and shook the bottle before she poured it into Eli's mouth. The effect was instantaneous he began to cough and splutter sitting up as though he had been shocked.

"What happened?" He coughed.

"Well, I was flying over and a gust of wind made me bank off to the side and my flask wasn't as secure as I thought it was and err... you know the rest. I gave you a pick me up potion. It'll keep you going for a while." The woman says quickly and apologetically.

"Oh, that makes sense." He picked up the flask and passed it to her. "This would be yours then Bess." He smiled shakily.

The woman Bess was wearing a lime green tracksuit with white stripes down the sides, an army helmet, a pair of leather aviation goggles and a pair of thick high heeled hobnailed boots which were covered in a thick layer of mud. Under the helmet, she had long black flyaway hair. When she smiled, she had a slight snaggle-tooth. Bess was best known around Crosstown as Barrel-Rolling-Bess or BRB as she never said goodbye she always said. "Be right back."

"Little Eli, all grown up now. What are you doing here?"

"It's a long story." He groaned.

"Well lad, I ain't got many places to be. Tell me. I could murder a cuppa though." She smiled.

As soon as she said that the top of the bag opened, and a box flew out. As it landed, it opened and there on the surface was a flask of tea and a full service including a few cakes. While they sat and enjoyed the tea service, Eli relayed to Bess the story of his Ascension and the Storm Queen's threats. When he had finished. The usually calm demure woman seemed to be radiating anger and power.

"That, that evil old crone if I ever see her, you watch lad I'll show her a thing or two about pain. Since I missed your ascension, I have a gift for you."

"You don't have to do that Bess." Eli said shyly.

"Nonsense Eli, your ascension is important to you Leanai, and I only missed it because old Gertrude..." She motioned to the broom. "conked out over the Crow Wood and I had to walk back. That was the longest walk of my life, felt like it took years."

Bess squatted down to sit on a chunk of sandstone that was sitting at an odd angle, it must have been uncomfortable as she sat back up and with a flash of multicoloured flame a soft comfortable cushion appeared on top of the stone and she sat back down. Once she had shuffled to make herself comfortable she dragged the broom over and began rooting in a black bag attached to the back of a lawn chair.

Perhaps it would be best for me to explain the Wytches broom, using Bess' as an example. Every Wytch must make their own broom as it is not possible to mass-produce them and allow them to fly. The act of constructing the broom is what infuses every part of it with the power of the Wytch. (Yes, they are named for me they were my original project before the Leanai appeared.) Every Wytches broom is unique and speaks of the personality of its creator. Take Bess' broom. It has thirty-nine Willow twigs which have been braided into Thirteen groups of three, around which Thirteen dried ivy vines sit, looking like decoration. The main shaft is also Willow, giving it the springiness and durability to survive frequent high-speed contacts with the ground. Bess is a brilliant if unlucky flier. In the centre of the shaft sits a gyroscope which helps keep the broom correctly oriented. Mounted to the shaft is a worn but comfortable looking lawn chair on which the bag is mounted. Near the chair is a set of rusted bicycle handlebars which she fished out of the river just last week after her last set was mangled irreparably. The handlebars even had a small bell attached. Finally at the top of the broom had a small funnel which had a screw cap on it. Overall the entire thing seemed lifeless and dusty.

Finally, Bess pulled out a well-used notebook which was marked with multicoloured sticky notes. She began muttering rapidly, and the book was consumed by glittering white flames. She held her other hand out flat and glittering white flames began to spiral, forming a smaller almost identical book. The Magick was over a few seconds later and she handed Eli the smaller book which now had his name in a rough looped script inscribed on the cover.

"I've edited out the more dangerous stuff and the things that I created myself of course. There should be enough in there that you can use that side of your power." She smiled kindly.

"Bess, thank you so very much. I was wondering how I could learn the Wytchcraft side." Eli gushed happily, already thinking about what he might learn.

"Not a problem, l'il man." She smiled.

"What is it about everyone calling me little man?" Eli huffed.

"You're a child of Crosstown, we all saw you grow up. You'll always be the towns l'il man." Bess grinned impishly.

"Bess, what is the Night Train? I thought that no trains came this way anymore."

"The Night Train is a Ghost Train that long-distance ensorcelled mail is sent. It passes through the town at Three oh Seven in the morning. Every day. So you have..." She checked a travel alarm clock that had fallen out of her bag. "Just over two hours. That's ok I can give you a preview of how a broom works. First I'll tell you about the brew."

"The Brew?" Eli asked genuinely curious.

"The brew is a mixture that is created to an individual recipe by each Wytch, it allows the broom to fly. It is also what the flask I beaned you with contains. My recipe is in the book, but that'll only give you some success. It is more of a guide for you. Now watch as I refuel it and see what happens."

She pulled the rest of the broom, so it sat on her lap and began unscrewing the cap on the funnel. Then she grabbed the flask and clicked off the plastic cup which had a black marker line. As she tipped the flask and clicked the button and began pouring the liquid up to the line. The liquid that poured out was black and fizzed as it filled the cup, the smell that hit Elis nose was pungent, to say the least. It smelled like a cross between manure and paint thinner. Once it was poured, she looked to Eli and chuckled at his wrinkled nose.

"You get used to the smell after a while, of your own brew at least. Now the maximum fill you should use of any brew is One Hundred and Sixty-Nine mil. It's all about the numbers you see."

Bess poured the contents of the cup into the funnel and the broom began to shudder. Life seemed to return to the aged looking wood, the braided twigs became more supple and buds appeared bursting into leaves and pretty blossoms. The ivy leaves became green and grew into thick vines which wove themselves into a basket of ivy around the braids. She flicked the gyroscope, and the broom began to shudder. When Bess placed the broom in the air it hung there motionless, it looked like a totally different object. All the dustiness seemed to have blown away even the lawn chair, and the handlebars looked at least cleaner. As it sat, there in the air it purred like a quiet engine emitting a small

"I'm going to head off soon sweetie. I'll leave a communication Rune active so we can talk until I arrive at the party I've been invited to. Try the..." she snorted. "Faemiliar out. What a name, whoever came up with that needs their head looking. It'll at least keep you company."

She sat in the seat of the broom, which sank slightly but bounced back to its original height. Bess handed Eli a flaming Rune and pinned one to her chest before holding out her hand and with a whispered word a hand-knitted green blanket flew from the underbrush. Twisting the handlebar she caused the brooms engine like sound to increase as with a flick of her head the goggles dropped onto her face.

"Be right back l'il one."

"Catch you later Bess and thank you."

With that, she kicked off the ground, and the broom shot forward and she cackled as she zoomed into the night performing her signature barrel roll.

"Can you hear me Eli?" Her voice emanated from the flame.

"Yeah Bess, I can hear you."

"I can see Neil running across the churchyard. I swear if he rings the bell..." The night is silent for a moment before the church bell rang out across the darkness. "Damn it Neil, every time...." She laughed as she fell from the sky. Eli could hear the wind rushing before the flame winked out.

CHAPTER TEN

MATT

Eli sighed, alone again. The warm summer wind rustled the trees and carried the sound of Mike's drunken singing up to Eli who chuckled. He decided that he would take Bess' advice and try the Faemiliar summoning. He felt out the Rune on his hand in his mind and read the instructions for want of a better term. He had to focus on the Rune and meditate on himself before pushing his power through the Rune and the Faemiliar would appear.

He focused on the Rune and began to think about himself and started to call his power. He didn't know how long he had sat there with his hand outstretched before something within him clicked. As soon as he felt the click, he pushed his power through the Rune which immediately began to glow with a beautiful blue light. The ground in front of him began to ripple and shift before a small head appeared. Eli watched with rapt fascination as a creature formed out of the rippling ground. It was a cute perfectly formed racoon made from nature. It seemed to be formed from grass and flowers. The black and grey areas were made from various shades of green grass and the white areas tiny pink and blue flowers. Eli thought they might have been Forget-me-knot. It chittered at him excitedly and bounded over burying itself in his lap. Absently Eli stroked it and was surprised to find that though it looked to be made from nature, it felt as soft and real as the mundane creature. The small green and white trash-bandit chirped happily as he continued to stroke it.

As they sat there lost to thoughts Eli did not notice the passage of time until a distant rumbling sound was heard. Eli whipped around as the long grass and nettles parted and a spectral track seemed to materialise in thin air laying itself as he watched. The track began to extend out over the expanse of the river a faded memory of the old Iron rail bridge materialised. Off in the distance, a trains whistle can be heard, each blast getting closer accompanied by the thunderous sound of dozens of iron wheels passing over the fish plates. He could see the lamp on the front of the engine lighting its way. Beneath him, the ground shook as the spectral train raced down the track and out across the bridge. It was an absolutely stunning engine from the brief glimpse he caught of it. The last car was rapidly approaching as there was a brief squeal of the brakes.

From the back of the train, a shower of spectral letters flew off into the town as well as into a rusted pillar box which was obscured by the overgrowth and trees. A tall ghostly man swung off the back of the train, pulling a bell cord twice as he did. The train sped up and rapidly faded from view, the bridge along with it.

"Alright lad, suppose you're Eli? The one the crazy woman told me about?" He asked kindly. Eli quickly took in his features, he wore a pair of muddy overalls, heavy boots. It was his face that caught Elis attention, he didn't look much older than Eli himself. He had a kindly face which was peppered with a soft-looking facial hair. His deep blue eyes were looking at Eli quizzically.

Side note – Ghosts are technicolour, not the classic grey and see-through. They are solid while they are manifesting and only the tiniest bit see-through, most people don't even notice their insubstantiality.

"Sorry, yes I'm Eli. What's your name?"

"I'm Matthew, Matt for short." Replied the man.

"Nice to meet you, Matt." Smiled Eli a little shyly.

"Come on then lad grab your stuff and climb back down to the bottom, we don't have long before we run out of time to open the way." With that, he faded from view and appeared again at the bottom on the path near the corner of the bridge. Eli put on the backpack and strapped the staff back to it before picking up Bess' book and walking down the slippery slope cautiously. Though he wasn't cautious enough as he slipped and fell, sliding rapidly down and impacting rather harshly with a tree.

"You ok lad?" Chuckled Matt moving over to help him up.

"Yeah. Thanks." Mumbled Eli, embarrassed.

"No problem. Now step over here." Matt motioned to the corner of the wall. "I hope you're not squeamish."

Eli stepped forward and watched fascinated as Matt reached into his chest and with a crunch of bone, he pulled out a key. He gave Eli an apologetic look, expecting to see him revolted at the action, he was however shocked to see Eli looking interestedly at the key and him.

"Thought you'd be squicked out by that lad." He said quietly.

"No, it's interesting and cool." Eli replied. "I assume it's a skeleton key?"

"How'd you guess?" Smiled Matt.

"Our world can be rather literal." Eli snorted.

"True, True." Grinned Matt as he moved toward the wall. The key began to glow eerily and as it did, a keyhole shimmered into view on the corner of the wall. Matt inserted the key and twisted it repeatedly counter clockwise. Thirteen times to be exact. When he had made the last turn the wall split along the mortar and the walls along the wall split open one brick deep on either side. The opening revealed a hand-dug pathway. "Come on then."

Without another word Matt led him into the confines of the tunnel, the only light for a moment was provided by the staff. Slowly with a deep grinding sound that was deafening for a moment in the tunnel. Seconds later it was over, and they were sealed in the gloomy tunnel. Eli shuddered a little, ironically it felt to him like being closed in a tomb. Matt chuckled.

"Lux." He said softly and instantly the tunnel was filled with a warm golden glow which seemed to seep from the walls. "Everyone feels like they're being entombed. It's the pressure difference both Barometric and Seid. That's why everyone has to use one of the entrances their first time to adjust to the pressure difference. Though I can warn you now, do not under any circumstances activate that travelling spell down there you could bring the whole place down. The structural Magicks down here are old and nowhere near as well made as those in the Warren."

"Duly noted." He touched the staff and said. "Raot." The light from the staff faded out.

"Come on then. That command wasn't in Irish was it?" He asked confused.

"Anything is viable it's mainly intent."

"Ah."

They walked in silence for a few moments, Eli thinking all the while. Matt was visibly bored with the silence already he sighed audibly.

"Sorry did you say something?" Eli asked.

"No, but you haven't said anything for fifteen minutes now."

"Really? How long is this tunnel?" Eli asked confused.

"That's what I mean about getting used to the pressure. My job is to lead people down the path which allows them to adjust to the pressure. If you were to apport straight down into Glight or a similar place you'd pass straight out. The walk down is another fifteen minutes but we could sit at the entrance and talk for a bit if you like?" He finished hopefully.

"Yeah that would be nice but how can we get to the door?" Asked Eli confused.

"That's simple..." Matt replied impishly. "We walked the length of the tunnel in the first five minutes. In actuality, the tunnel only goes about five hundred meters. Not even in a straight line we've turned at least a dozen times. The next bit is a little disorienting as the illusion is ended." He clicked his fingers and the corridor rapidly shrank. Eli had to choke down the contents of his stomach as they threatened to come up. Matt chuckled.

They were now stood in a small circular cavern that Eli had to duck slightly to avoid hitting his head. He hadn't realised that Matt was about a foot shorter than him. Then again, his head had apparently been elsewhere for a while. Behind him, the tunnel curved away upwards and in front of them were two doors. One door looked welcoming, and the other was a mesh door that looked as though it led to a lift.

"This way." Matt said.

He led him to the welcoming door and opened the door. Eli was a little confused, couldn't he just walk through it? Matt seemed to read his mind and smirked.

"Two reasons..." He said.

"What?" Eli asked confused.

"That I don't just walk through it. First, it's Cold Iron all the doors in Glight are, they made it that way in case the river ever breaches. Unlike the Barrow, Glight is physically situated below the Esk. Secondly, it would be impolite for me to phase through a door when you can't." He grinned and winked at him before he motioned for him to enter.

Eli walked past Matt through the door accidentally brushing against him and enjoying the coolness of the encounter. Inside was a small bunkroom, a comfortable looking metal frame bed, a pair of chairs with a table between them in front of a fireplace filled with charmed fire and finally a dresser at the far end of the room. Strangely at the far end of the room behind the dresser was what looked like a pile of rocks, a cave in perhaps. Dotted around the room were multiple beautiful drawings of people, places and flowers. Matt walked in and pulled the door shut with an audible clang, he smiled knowingly as he saw Eli looking around awed.

"Not what you expected? Especially for a ghost."

"Well... I wasn't expecting a ghost to need somewhere to sleep."

"This is where I live, I hate discarnating."

"Discarnating?"

"Fading, when a ghost is unsummoned most go back to the space between spaces and wait. Sit down, this could take a while."

"Thanks, I'm not in any hurry to go anywhere." Smiled Eli taking a seat in front of the fire which had just turned pink before starting to fade through the spectrum slowly.

"Drink?" Asked Matt.

"Yeah please."

"Alcoholic or non?"

"I wouldn't mind wine if you have some. Rose?"

"Coming right up." Matt replied, pulling two sparkling glasses and a frosted bottle of Rose wine from a trapdoor under a rug near the fire. He sat in the opposite chair and began pouring the wine. He handed the first glass to Eli and took the other for himself. They sat for a few moments in silence.

"So, where was I? Explaining about ghostly stuff." He chuckled. "When most ghosts fade after being summoned, they return to the space between spaces. That's the place where Artefacts like the Hekataion Arch, the Dark Gate and many others open into. It's also where a lot of Travelling methods, though not the travelling spell, pass through. When there it's peaceful and they can think and wander to other places. Before you ask, the Afterlife is Death for the Dead, when you go there, there ain't no coming back."

"I didn't know any of that, no-one taught me about death." Eli stated, awed.

"They wouldn't it's not really talked about. Then again since the Victorian Era death isn't an end, it's just another part of life. People hold down jobs, still live with their families and many other things after being interred. The forever box isn't really for forever anymore." Eli snorted. "What?"

"The way you said that as if it's an everyday conversation." He clarified.

"Honestly, this is the first conversation I've had in over a hundred years. No-one talks to the tour guide. I only speak in the way I do because I've learnt it in passing. Do I pass for someone who died in the last decade or so?" He asked, genuinely curious.

"The only reason I knew it was longer was the overalls. Can't you change clothes?"

"Nope, ma body is still dressed in them." He stated matter-of-factly.

"Your body is still in your grave?" A surprised Eli asked. "If you don't mind me asking how it hasn't you know..."

"Rotted away?" Smiled Matt. "Let me quickly give you my Death Story, if you don't mind?"

"Nope, not at all."

"More wine?" He asked happily.

"Please." Eli replied. Matt poured the wine and then continued talking.

"When the railway bridge was built in 1860, I was adding this entrance so that there was an escape route from Glight if something happened that breached the dome. My speciality was demolition Magick. I was blasting a tunnel off to the side when the tunnel collapsed because of an explosion from above. Now that wouldn't have been so bad, but the entire area destabilised, and the recovery team couldn't use any Magick. You see, the tunnel collapsed for several hundred meters, with Magick a few hours but in the 1800s it would have taken weeks. I don't know whether you want to hear the rest." Matt trailed off quietly.

"I'm want to hear it if you want to tell me." Eli replied quietly causing Matt to smile.

"Well." He cleared his throat. "Since I dug the tunnel, I knew exactly how far back I was buried and how long it would take to clear manually so I did the only sensible thing, well the only sensible thing to my injured mind at the time. I overdosed myself with the bottle of Laudanum and drank the several bottles of whisky I had stashed at the end of the tunnel. You know to keep me warm." He chuckled darkly. "Thankfully, the Laudanum mixed with the Alcohol did what I had hoped and allowed me to fall asleep and die from a cocktail of Alcohol poisoning and suffocation."

"Wow. I'm sorry."

"Don't be, I died but had enough conscious mind to hold on to this plane and not move forward. So when they cast the preservation charms and stabilisation charms on the tunnels they affected my body too."

"I wish I could hug you." Eli whispered.

"You could but neither of us would feel much, I'd feel the warmth, and you'd feel cold. That's about it. I miss human contact and sadly for me, I haven't seen the outside world in over a hundred and sixty years. You see even though I can speak to you and drink with you I see the world as it was when I died. The town looks as it did that day, this tunnel looks the same, except for my drawings."

"They're amazing." Eli replied.

"Thanks." Blushed Matt. "As you've guessed I died back there behind the dresser."

"Yeah, I guessed."

"You're not weirded out?" Asked Matt.

"Why would I be? We're all different." Replied Eli, kindly.

"True."

"So the way you see the world, is that why some ghosts don't seem to see people?" Enquired Eli.

"Precisely. Sometimes people either don't believe or realise they're dead. Or sometimes they block out anyone, not from their time. Either way, they become wrapped up in that little pocket reality of death. I'd love to see what Crosstown looks like now, I was born here and died here. You know, I can't even see photographs as you do; I see fields if the area wasn't there and what it was like for me if it was." Eli could see that Matt was getting upset at this.

"I'll find a way to show you, I promise."

"I'll laugh and shrug off a promise like that. But something about you resonates with impossibilities. I believe you might pull it off."

In the distance, a bell tolls five times which caused Matt to startle, having not heard the previous set at four o'clock."

"Better get you into Glight and someone'll get you settled."

"I wish you could come with me. I'm a little scared, to be honest."

"I don't know why you're scared of ghosts yet my corpse doesn't freak you out. Tell me your story next eh?" Matt asked hopefully and yet something about his demeanour said he thought that hope was in vain.

"Sure. When can I next visit?" Eli asked.

"Whenever you like, I only got on the train today because I was getting instructions from Belladonna."

"Tonight then?"

"Get settled and come back when you can..." He trailed off standing up. "Come on I'll get you onto the lift. Then I suppose I'll sleep."

"Cool."

Matt led Eli back out into the corridor and opened the creaking gate to the lift. Eli grabbed him into a hug not caring that it felt like being submerged in ice. As Matt hugged him back for a second which seemed to stretch for hours, the glow from the walls faded.

"That's my cue." Said Matt sadly, standing back.

"Tonight ok?"

"Sure thing Eli." He replied as he shut the door and pressed the control. Something in his blue eyes rang Eli's heart like a bell. Matt didn't think he would ever see him again. He'd show him he was wrong. The lift juddered and moved down as Matt faded into darkness, waving and smiling sadly.

"Goodbye Eli." He said softly, to nothing and no-one but his own long entombed corpse.

"He'll be back, I hope for your sake that trapdoor does food." Chuckled a voice from the darkness.

Matt jumped and began looking around the darkened chamber which was lit only by the light spilling from the bunkroom door. He couldn't see the source of the voice and he was surprised to find that it unnerved him. Another new feeling, he hadn't experienced since before he died.

"Down here genius." He looked down to see that BeBe was stood impatiently at his feet.

"Who or what are you?"

"I'm Bernard Bear or BeBe for short. I jumped out of the bag to keep you company. Eli would have come back eventually but this way he'll come back quicker. Now food?"

"Come on then, do you want carrying?"

"Well yeah, my legs are tiny."

Matt picked up BeBe and carried him into the bunkroom ignoring the bears muttering about coldness.

CHAPTER ELEVEN

SAEVA ALLIGATUM

The juddering lift slowly descended, giving Eli his first view of Glight. The town was a lot larger than he ever thought possible, steel beams supporting the vaulted dome roof disappeared off into the far distance. High above, part of the roof, at the far end of the cavern looked to be made from crystal. Above which the sky could be seen through fast flowing water. Glight itself was a mass of rusted metal buildings, a maze of pipes some rusted, corroded and leaking while others gleamed in the rippling early morning sunlight. People of all kinds packed the narrow streets on the many levels of the town. Each level was colour coded, if the faded and chipped coloured paint on the buildings was anything to go by. On the blue level as he came level with it one of the buildings there was a group of twenty or thirty people in neoprene hoods that were shaped like animals. On the wall behind them was bright red graffiti which read: "FreeYourAWOO." As he passed, they all rushed to the edge of the balcony and raised their glasses and howled. Eli smiled at their antics.

Slowly the lift reached the bottom of the shaft, the red level. At this level he noticed alot of... seedy establishments. These shops had adverts for XXX this and illicit that. There were lots of signs to blood bars and rare steak houses. Eli felt that he shouldn't lose his way down here or even linger long. The lift shuddered and rattled to a halt and immediately every eye locked onto him hungrily. He knew he was in trouble, and moreover he was trapped. Quickly he scanned the area looking for an escape route. An empty alleyway a few feet away could allowed escape. But there were three older, stronger looking men blocking his escape. He stepped out of the lift. Silently he prepared several Lenses ready to defend himself just as the first brute began to speak. His voice was deep and growling which caused every hair on Elis body to stand on end in fear.

"Well well... what we got 'ere Stan. Fresh meat." He said lasciviously.

80

"Looks very, fresh Abe. Maybe we should take him down to that rent by the hour hotel near Coltsfoots. You know use him for a few hours then maybe sell him off to one of the blood banks." The other man chuckled darkly.

"Perfect, could do wid a bit of cash to be honest. Wife's spending faster than I can grift it."

Eli didn't like this direction; it was his first time away from home and he wasn't about to let it end with him being used or sold. He thought back to his defence lessons with Sarah and Jason before he rapidly called forth several Lenses. One created Magick Armour around him, another a shield encompassing him and the final one burned anyone who grabbed him. All in all, a good all-round defence or so he'd been told. Thankfully, he had never had to use them in a real situation until now. From his lessons the Lensing should have been undetectable but apparently it wasn't. The first man, Abe began to laugh darkly.

"Little thing thinks he can defend himself. Defence Magicks that are taught to babes. Well I'll fix that boyo..."

From somewhere in his ragged clothing he pulled out a set of shackles, five heavy iron bands connected by a macabre chain, each link had sharp bladed spikes. The entire thing reeked of an official-feeling yet dark power. Eli immediately recognised the item, or Artefact as he corrected himself mentally, from his history lessons and visits to the Bailey Museum. They were a set of Saeva Alligatum or Cruel Confinement bands; a medieval tool from when the Inquisition was a lot newer and more, barbaric in their methods of capturing prisoners. Saeva Alligatum were now illegal due to the damaging effect on the victim... I mean subjects, life force, access to Magick and even their mental faculties. When applied the bands suppress all access to power and any thought of escape, calling power or even bad thoughts to the captor caused the bands to tighten and each barb to dig into the skin. That wasn't the worst part, each barb would then begin to emit a stimulus to the nerve endings causing them to fire the message of pain. It could easily break a person very quickly.

"I see you recognise them, no need to bore you with the details. You're coming with us lad. You'll fetch a nice price." He said, throwing the device at Eli faster than he could blink. It whistled as it sliced its way through the air, the dark energy rippling to life as it began to reach toward him. Abe was still talking. "I, was once a member of the Inquisition, but my attitudes were apparently a little too medieval for those bleeding hearts. No issue though, once ya broken; I'll be minted."

Shockingly, the deadly looking bands froze in mid-air and seemed to disassemble themselves explosively as they froze. "What the f..." Abe begins before an unseen force sends them both rapidly pissing off into the distance. Their feet never touched the ground once. When they were gone Eli got his first look at his saviour. He gaped slightly. She was a short, pleasantly plump looking woman who wore what had once been a fine Victorian mourning dress but now the front was open showing ripped and tattered jeans and crumpled leather high-heeled boots. That is not to say that the dress was ripped or torn, the front panel had been cut away in an arched shape as had the bustles and then they had been stitched together expertly and edged with fine, expensive white lace. Instead of a standard bodice top the garment resembled a blazer. The whole outfit was deep green with white trimmings. Over it she was wearing a crisp white apron.

The strangest thing about her was not the outfit though. She was pleasantly plump. She was also covered in tattoos, over her Draiohba, though it seemed hers were fading, perhaps they only showed when she used power. Some people were lucky that way. She had long black hair streaked with blue which was tied up in what must have been a ridiculously tight bun. A few strands of hair hung either side of her face, framing the soft yet fierce features and her blue eyes which burned with cold fury. From the corner of her pristinely lipsticked mouth a hand-rolled cigarette hung precariously. The actual strange thing about her was that she had an ancient looking Colt Repeater Rifle strung across her back and what looked like a Glock barely concealed by the bustle of the dress. She caught him looking at the guns.

"Sometimes Magick don't work lad." She said in a gruff voice. "I'm Madame Marigold Coltsfoot, bin telt tae keep an eye oot fer ye an' gie ye board." As she spoke, she expertly took a long drag from here cigarette before spitting it on the ground and scrubbing it out with her boot. "Folly me lad." She said before turning and walking off without actually waiting for an answer. Eli followed her. The denizens of this area of Glight seemed to avoid her like the plague as they navigated the streets passing one amoral shop after the other. Finally they reached a crossroads next to the cavern wall. One of the crossroads was signposted "Country Roads" which seemed to lead into a tunnel of sorts. She stopped in front of that road and turned to Eli while rummaging in her apron pocket.

"I've the key 'ere somewhere. Apartment 313. Paid up fer 6 month, after that ye'll pay yerself or move owt. Payment includes 3 meals an' cupboards stocked wi' snacks etcetera. When you arrive ye'll find a copy o' the house rules, your stuff brought by a weird guy and his pet and a blank Journal, ye'll ken whit that is I s'pose?"

"Yes, Thank You Madam." Replied Eli with a shallow bow.

She found the key, an old Iron type thing that had the number 313 inside a scrolling pattern on the top. Eli took it, it was a weighty thing, and he was surprised to find that he could feel the warm summery feel of Magick interspersed with the chilling wintery feel of Cold Iron. Cold Iron usually totally nullifies Magick.

"There's a crystalline substance mixed in with the Molten Iron during the forging process which allows it to hold a small charm or two for a long time. The charms key the room to you and also allows you to travel that route." She said jabbing her chin in the direction of the route ahead. "All you have to say is take me home and step forward. Every town in t' UK 'as one o' these roads if ye know where tae look. For reference the one in Crosstown is located in the Shades. Dangerous place to be at times but also a quite interesting place. Permanent shadow hanging in the air... bloody alchemists." She finished with a snort.

"Cool, that's good bits to know."

"That it is lad. Now bugger off to yer new apartment. I'm off to pay some unfortunate people a little visit." She said. Her tone promised that these visits would not be pleasant for subject. Eli grasped the key and turned to face the pathway. As he stepped past the sign that read Country Roads he said in a firm voice: "Take me home." The world lurched just as Coltsfoot snorted and walked off humming a familiar song.

CHAPTER TWELVE

NEW HOME?

The lurching of the world caused his stomach to roil in protest as his vision became dark for a moment, when it cleared he was stood in a dimly lit wood panelled corridor directly in front of a door which held the number 313 in the same script as the key. He slipped the key into the lock feeling the Magick slip out into the door and they seemed to become colder and heavier in his hand. The key spun in the door unlocking it and locking it again without him doing anything before it stopped at its original position. Eli grasped the key again and felt it was warm again the door glowed and vibrated momentarily. His name painted itself onto the door. As soon as this happened Eli clicked open the lock and depressed the handle allowing the door to swing freely open.

He had to admit to himself he was a little scared as he had never lived alone. He supposed that he would have had to at some point like everyone else. Does everyone feel this way when they enter their first home? Nervous, excited, scared, alone? Mentally he shook himself. He was probably being silly. As he stepped over the threshold, the lights came on softly by themselves. The room was spacious, one wall was dominated by a long very thick looking window which had a submarine like metal door in the middle which led to a wide, open roof terrace. He approached the window and looked out. Only a few dozen meters above was the crystalline cavern roof above which the river flowed. Examining Glight he realised the scale of the place; he could vaguely see the lift shaft a few hundred meters away, but the town stretched into the distance curving around the corner. The town stretched off into shafts in three directions or so he could see. He looked to be many floors up on the top level, but the cavern was also indeterminably deep. He didn't really know how far above that street he was.

Eli stepped back and surveyed the rest of the room. Directly in front of the window a small two-seater dining table was set up. On top of the table was the Journal Madame Coltsfoot mentioned, he would come back to that soon. There was a copy of the house rules such as they stood. They were handwritten in a tight looped script and they said:

Coltsfoots Bar and Board

House Rules

1: No swearing in the public areas – This will incur swift retribution.

2: Keep your room/apartment clean. - Inspections infrequent and unexpected.

3: Decorate how you like - Just hit the reset button when you check out. – Room design book located on shelves.

4: Mealtimes are set - But food is sent to the rooms of those who do not attend group mealtimes.

5: Do your own damn dishes – If you do not attend a group meal.

6: Rules for group dishes will be explained on first attendance of meal.

7: NO-ONE from red section is to be brought back to your domicile. – I have standards and a reputation to keep.

8: If you borrow something from one of the marked storerooms follow the guidelines posted there.

9: All external apertures are to be kept closed – This is a rule of Glight and for all our safety.

10: ABSOLUTELY NO DISCRIMINATION – I run an inclusive establishment – Breaches of this rule will be corrected, painfully.

FINAL NOTE: No one may enter or leave at Daft O'clock – I will not be liable if you breach this rule and are disfigured.

N. B – Daft O'clock is 00:29 – 00:31 every day. Read the flyers in the lobby if you really are curious.

With that the note ended and Eli placed it back on the table. To his left there was a spacious if dated looking kitchen/diner, all open plan. The wall across from him was dominated by two long full-length bookcases, in-front of which was a warn but comfortable looking brown recliner and a tiny side table which held a stained glass lamp. The lamp was designed to look like a tree, the stand was carved into a gnarled tree trunk shape. It was complete with a small hole which had an owl's head poking out. Stood on this was a beautiful glass lampshade, the coloured glass made to look like a tree canopy. There were only several books per shelf leaving plenty of space for more. Good he thought to himself. To his right there was a small seating area which had a TV mounted to the plain grey walls. Near the seating area were two more submarine like doors.

He walked over to the nearest one and figures out after a moment he had to turn the heavy wheel and pull the door. It opened onto a fastidiously clean white bathroom, well more of a wet room actually as it had a drain in the centre of the floor. Unlike a normal wet room, it had a clawfoot bath as well as a shower and a utilitarian looking toilet and sink. On right he found a small cupboard. He assumed towels and things went here. Tucked behind this was a hamper. To his left, another door. He assumed it led to the bedroom as it seemed to be on a right angle to the other door. He closed the door and tried to turn the locking wheel, but it wouldn't budge. After quickly examining the door Eli found a switch. When pressed it caused the wheel to spin sealing the door shut.

On opening the final door at least part of his theory was correct in that the other door was present on its correct wall. So that meant, he could get to the bathroom bypassing the main room. Strangely the bedroom door led into a corridor which was about the size of a small walk-in wardrobe and the other door was on the same wall as this door. He stepped in and realised that the metal walls were warm. He wondered if they were heated or possibly the water pipes. Behind him the door clanged shut and this doors lock spun shut itself. Eli walked to the other door and opened it before stepping into the room. He pulled the door shut causing it to lock itself.

The bedroom itself was divided in two, as a thin metal wall divided everything in two. To one side, there was a small office and as he moved forwards past this, the bedroom moved into view. Both rooms were sparsely decorated. The bed was a large double with black and white sheet set. There were two bedside tables each with a matching lamp. The far wall was overtaken by three dark wooden doors, one of which was open showing that it contained wardrobe and drawers. He moved backwards to examine the office area. The desk was built into the wall and a comfortable looking office chair. There was space for a computer and all that would entail. On the desk was a CD in a case, it's golden face catching the light. Beside it was a small domed device.

CDs or Compaction Disks were a device where using the combination of Magick and Technology, items can be changed into data, meaning the contents can be viewed as an inventory on a computer. There were many other facts about this device that came to Elis mind, but he shoved them away as irrelevant until needed. He moved the reader onto the bed and then picked up the disk and inserted it into the hinged top of the device. The moment he pressed the Decrypt/Decompress All button, he stood back as a silver circle expanded out three feet in each direction. Whirring could be heard as well as the sound of a laser scanning rapidly before with a metallic/digital sound that sounded like something out of an old series of sci-fi programs, his stuff materialised in a flash and a slightly pointless special effect. On the bed and the floor where bags and boxes out of which spilled food, books and many other items all of which came from Elijah's rooms at home.

He unpacked all the boxes over the next hour or so, the adrenaline from the previous night showed no signs of subsiding, once he had finished this he looked at the room design guide after checking his balance via his Journal and realising that his mother had sent enough for him to live somewhat comfortably without working if he needed to. He would find some way to earn his own income soon he hoped. He read the instructions and selecting some things to be purchased and installed for him, including an office space and an actual computer unit instead of just his laptop. He checked the time and saw that it was only One in the afternoon and decided a shower and at least fresh underwear was in order, he really liked the new clothes. Maybe he would explore Glight's upper level clothing stores at some point. The book had informed him it all changes would take effect once he left next time, but he would have to lock the door from the outside and then be away a minimum of six hours. He placed the Journal in his bag.

Eli sat for a moment before getting up and heading to the bathroom where he had unpacked towels and other toiletries. Once he had used the loo he jumped in the shower, fully enjoying the feel of the hot water on his skin. He couldn't wait until he got back and had a full-length mirror in her and the bedroom as he really wanted to examine his Draiohba. After a fairly long shower which lasted over twenty minutes, he wrapped a towel round his waist and walked over to the "air-lock" door as he had dubbed it. A few minutes later he got into his room and was just about to drop the towel until an almost familiar voice spoke from behind him.

"Took you long enough."

CHAPTER 1

BASIC HISTORY

At the sound of the voice Eli whipped around to face the source, almost losing his towel in the process but just... managed to hang on to it. He was about to sling a Lense to incapacitate his intruder until he met their eye. It was the man that had dropped him off on the riverbank above. Eli realised that he didn't even know the name of the man who had saved him and who was currently sat on his bed and looking fairly comfortable at that.

"S@!t you startled me. Wait why can't I swear?" Eli asked.

"Madame Coltsfoot has a blanket Moratorium on foul language even when company is visiting in your own room." Chuckled Thedas. "My name is Thedas North, an Owlighter and I have been asked to teach you some things."

"Nice to meet you, give me a second so I can dress." Replied Eli.

A quick thought and Eli called up a privacy Lense which caused a screen which was, unknown to Eli, almost identical to the one his mother had conjured earlier today. He summoned his underwear which flew cleanly out of its new living place. Ironing and cleaning charms on his new clothes and they were as good as new. Within a few minutes he was dressed and dismissed the screen. He looked over at Thedas who was still watching him smiling slightly.

"So what are you going to teach me?" He asked Thedas.

"So much, but we are going to start with some history in the form of a memory and then a little trip. Do you like lime?" He asked casually.

"Lime? The colour isn't bad I suppose." Elijah said.

"I mean you're not allergic to it are you?" Thedas pressed.

"How can you be allergic to a colour?" Elijah replied confused.

"Oh B@*&^£%d I totally forgot it's not a fruit here..." He trailed off clearing his throat several times. "Got anything to drink? That Moratorium is annoying, makes my mouth feel as though it's been washed out with dish soap and dried with cotton wool. It is funny to hear the word bleeped out and see someone's mouth blur for a moment."

"Erm... Sure. I have Blue cola in the drawer next to the bed.

"Not usually what you find in someone's bedside drawer." He said with a slight leer which worsened when Elis eyes darted to the drawer on the other side of the bed. Thedas barked out a laugh. "I won't go snooping this time... least I know which side of the bed you prefer." He chuckled again as Eli blushed fiercely. Thedas reached into the drawer and pulled out two glass bottles of luminous blue cola, not really caring that it was unseemly to go through a younger person's drawers. He held out the bottle with one hand and patted the bed with the other.

"Sit here so I can show you a few things." He said smiling.

"I hope it's not anything rude." Eli said causing Thedas to chuckle and grimace at the same time.

"That would be wrong on so many levels. Anyway sit. We have to get this bit out of the way in the next twenty minutes or I'll miss the Lightway window, it'll make the run longer."

"Erm... what?" Eli replied confused as he sat propped up against his pillows next to Thedas.

"One thing at a time. Now the nineteen eighties were a time of Great Upheaval for the United Kingdom, what with the Miners Strikes, rubbish uncollected in the streets and rolling blackouts. But what people don't often talk about are two events which are pertinent to what you will witness later. The first was The Great Storm of 1987, which spanned two days October 15th to 16th, this storm tore through the southern portion of the United Kingdom causing the most damage we had seen since the Blitz and killing 18 people. But the part of the damage I want to discuss happened in Kent, a town by the name of Sevenoaks. You see in 800AD there were Seven Oak trees on The Vine, which today is a cricket ground. Whenever these trees died, or they were always replaced as they were firstly part of the towns heritage and secondly oak is a natural conduit for power. This was used to the advantage of the towns founders as there was a Seidhr Vault on-site. The trees helped shore up the protections suppressing the entity in the Vault." As he spoke a screen of light appeared and began playing news reports and other footage.

"A Seidhr Vault? I thought they were myths."

"All myths have a basis in truth. This one a firm basis. There are 101 Vaults, 88 for Minor Seidhr and 13 Major. Now the storm ripped six of the seven trees from the ground and a few eyewitnesses claim to have seen a cloud of darkness exploding from the ground and flying into the storm. There now stand eight trees but the vault itself is empty, sealed from the outside but nothing remains within," The screen showed the area being talked about and a close up of the door to the vault.

"What's the second event?

"A month later on the 18th November 1987 the escalator serving the Piccadilly line at Kings Cross St Pancras Station caught fire killing 31 people. During the clean-up and removal of the workings of the wooden escalators the machinery began to malfunction, and the construction workers began to feel ill. As per protocol there was a Field Agent from the Royal Society for the Research and Recovery of Seidhr Knowledge also known as the R.S.R.R.S.K. Now neither of those mouthfuls will ever pass my lips again I will follow current convention and refer to them as The Guild. This field agent scanned the area and promptly passed out, when he was brought round a few minutes later he bolted all the way from the station and to the London Field office below Tower Bridge. You see, he had never encountered a Seid Rating like that before. You know about Seid ratings?"

"Yeah, they're how Magick is measured and on a scale of the same name how peoples levels are measured. The Magick rating is 0 to 1000 the personal level is 1 to 13 each in decimal increments." Replied Eli.

"An almost textbook answer, I wouldn't expect any less. But perfectly correct none-the-less now what is the highest publicly recorded Seid rating discovered?"

"Erm... I think it was the Hekataion Arch with a Seid Rating of 391.93sr."

"That's the one. An interesting Artefact that one. It can only be entered if an object known oh so creatively as a Hekataion Alignment is used. The alignments are extremely complex puzzle boxes, contained within is a small Mobius dimension about the size of a small village. Fields and forest land are all there is and a small shelter. They are used by the Bailey to contain anyone who can be rehabilitated but needs long term imprisonment. It is usually for anyone twenty years and up, The Pit can't be used on a person for that long you see. Leeches them dry. Anyway, back to my point. the rating that that Field Tech picked up broke his scanner at 888.88 recurring. What you're about to witness is the after-effects of that Technicians report.

"Witness?"

"We're going on a little field trip. On your roof terrace there is a QEX point keyed to the key. Select the Crusher and I'll meet you there." Before Eli could reply his form blurred and he faded out.

"F$£k sake. I hate it when people do that it's plain bloody rude." Eli grumbled but headed to the roof terrace through the airlock, its doors sealing behind him. When he exited the roof door, it clanged behind him and immediately a six hour timer showed on the windows. He snorted, maybe he was in a video game and had no idea. He rid himself of that thought he examined the terrace. There was a set of black and marble patio furniture and what looked to be a grill of sorts. Over the edge there was an exceedingly long drop into the mass of metal boxes and pipes that was Glight. Eli pulled back he had a spot of vertigo at that moment. Ironic considering, he had inherited wings. The last item of interest was a jet black crystalline dome with a keyhole in it. Below which was a typewriter with an enclosed strip of paper. Eli Typed The Crusher onto the strip of paper and inserted his key and turned it. Nothing happened. He sighed and mentally slapped himself before pressing the return key and then turned the key again. Instantly his world lurched, and he vanished from the rooftop with almost no fanfare.

CHAPTER 2

LIME JELLY AND ELI

To say that Elijah's stomach did not react well to unexpected and jarring transport across space was a slight understatement, the moment he phased into existence it decided that housing what little food he had eaten was no longer an option. A wave of nausea overtook him, and he was violently sick into a nearby bush. When he finally was able to regain his composure, he took stock of his surroundings. He stood across the sandy path from the bottom of the old bridge. Daylight shining through the dappled canopy. A few feet away was Thedas who was leaning against a tree beside a small pebble beach looking out onto the river. He was trying extremely hard not to laugh.

"Travel that defies physics doesn't sit well on your stomach? That's a shame as there's more of that today."

"If there was a countdown, it would probably help." Thedas snorted at Elis grouchy statement.

"You want the parent and toddler mode then." Thedas said smugly. "Now I want you to focus on Kings Cross Station and use the Travelling spell to get there. At least two stops. Materialise, run fifty feet and take off again got it?"

"Yeah. I know two places I can stop along the way." Replied Eli.

"Good, don't be too long, we have twenty minutes before the Lightway shifts and we either have to Run further or wait until next week. See you soon." With that he travelled away just like before. Eli Sighed and went to stand on the small pebble beach, mentally preparing himself for his first use soloing a travelling spell. He clasped the stone in his hand, not really a necessity but it made him more comfortable and less likely to drop in on someone having sex, and began calling his power. This in itself was difficult as he had received a monumental boost to power the day before. It wasn't that the power wouldn't come it was that it was all too eager. The moment he touched the stone with intent he was wrapped in a maelstrom of reality warping power, he couldn't see the familiar river now he was getting flashes of places at an almost seizure inducing rate. It was taking all of his willpower not to be blasted in a thousand different directions. The result of an accident like that was never pretty.

'Canal Street, Manchester,' He ordered mentally.

Immediately he was there, it was just as he remembered it when Sarah and he had passed years ago. A riot of colour and people of all personalities. He had heard that Anthropomorphic people were quite popular here. As soon as he felt the power wash off him, he ran to the nearest shop and bought a pre-packaged sandwich, ducked into an alley and started the process again. This time he ordered:

'Smeatons Tower, Plymouth.'

The power whipped around him and he landed outside the red and white light house in a crowd of people, some of whom screamed at his sudden appearance. Somewhere in the crowd he heard the word Heretic spat in his direction. He took off down the hill and as he neared the harbour wrapped the Magick around him again.

'Kings Cross Saint Pancras Station, City of Westminster.'

He landed outside the station in a panting heap with a small boom that sent crowds of people running screaming. London had had a spate of terror attacks of late and everyone was jumpy. He had panicked when he heard the word heretic and allowed too much power to funnel around him when travelling. Eli was pulled roughly up from the ground. He looked at the assailant and was relieved to see Thedas.

"Move, that entrance will have the Inquisition here in seconds." Thedas whispered harshly.

He pulled Eli into a small alleyway in the side and directly into a patch of shadow, immediately there was a crushing pressure all over Eli for a moment before they stepped into now blinding light on a platform. The signage showed they were on the Piccadilly line at the base of the escalators. Before Eli got a chance to speak a small lantern was draped around his neck and Thedas was muttering. An unfamiliar sweet and zesty smell filled Elis nose and everything around him began to slow, taking on an acidic green hue. Eli looked down and saw that his lantern was glowing with the same light.

"Take three even and measured steps toward me. Slowly, one at a time.

Breathe normally." His voice sounded far away and underwater at the same time.

Eli took a deep steady breath and choked on the overpowering sweet yet bitter taste in his mouth. He took a step forward heel to toe and gasped as everything shifted around him. Faces of commuters, dress styles, posters and other details like mobile phones. Again, he stepped and again everything changed. One more step and the scene changed to the charred wreckage of the escalators he had seen in reports. Each step he had taken had felt like walking through slimy cubes of who knows what. Eli began to wipe the unseen gunk off himself which caused Thedas to chuckle. The rich sound was right next to him this time, yet the world still had the lime green hue.

"We're woven in the Lightway which will keep us insubstantial and invisible here. When an Owlighter is woven inside their Lightway, they are able to observe a moment in history without physical interaction. Therefore, negating the possibility of accidental interference in what could be a critical juncture in time. Now you see that guy over there?" He said pointing across the hall to an official looking man.

He was a tall muscular man who looked to be in his late thirties. He was wearing the official uniform of The Guild, a vibrant Royal Purple flared jacket with a golden runic brocade pattern. Nobody ever said The Guild was subtle, but they certainly made an impression. His cropped blond hair shone in the artificial light. Across his chest was a bandoleer which held potions, crystals and other esoteric looking tools. In his hand he held what looked like a Geiger counter but the tube at the end had been replaced by a long multiplexing crystal wrapped intricately in copper, silver and gold wire. He moved it slowly back and forth as he stepped forward toward the burnt-out husk of the escalator.

"That is your Aunt Belladonnas husband, Count Geremiah Hawthorne. He still is today the Highest-Ranking Guild member." Said Thedas. "Now watch what was to be his last day."

Geremiah began muttering readings to seemingly nothing until a notebook floated in front of him and began recording the readings. This went on for a while until Thedas sighed and muttered something about forgetting how boring parts like this were and with a gesture the scene began to fast forward. Eli watched fascinated as Geremiah cleaned out chunks of debris with Magick until he finally reached a Thirteen-sided door. The door was covered in switches and buttons. Geremiah flipped through his notebook and started to experiment with the door his notebook dutifully recording each combination he tried. Again, Thedas became impatient and sped everything up.

"Look, solving the door took him most of the night. I mean that's not a long-time, this door was generating an energy field to confuse him and scramble the combinations on the door. It's a relatively simple door compared to some of them. Which still surprises me..."

The fast forward stopped as he keyed in a sequence and the Runes glowed an eerie blue light before the door split and opened like a flower inward. They followed him down what appeared to be a heavily warded tunnel into an antechamber. The room like the door was thirteen sided and seemed to be a dead end. In the centre of the room was a podium on which sat a spherical object. Geremiah ignored the podium for a moment and started rapidly photographing everything. Strangely every flash of the camera revealed what appeared to be an ancient and complex web of wards. Eli couldn't even begin to guess what ninety percent of the seals and symbols were supposed to do. Once he had photographed the room, he hung the camera back on the bandoleer and moved to the centre of the room. Once stood in front of the podium he looked at it from all angles.

On the podium the sphere was made from metal and crystal. Both the spheres poles were made of a black gemstone and there were five metal bands each a different colour, Pink, Blue, Purple, Green and Orange. The poles and bands were covered in symbols. They both watched as Geremiah began spinning the metal bands and poles until after several minutes the sphere rang like a small gong. Geremiah placed the orb back on the podium and the effect was instantaneous. Lines of power roared out of the podium and struck the walls, which proceeded to melt away revealing another chamber.

This chamber was cavernous, the floor was inlaid with copper lines and circles. Inside each circle was an Artefact that radiated cold power. Power that spoke of death and malice. The podium still stood in the centre of the room, but the sphere had melted away just like the walls. In its place was a spiky crystal formation which pulsated between blue and green and emitted a palpable heat. So much so that Geremiah immediately began to perspire. He moved to the wall as something had caught his eye, the entire wall seemed to be rippling and dust seemed to fall slower near them. He noticed that the entire cavern was covered in sandy silver light which on closer inspection turned out to be what was probably millions of moths. Moon Moths to be exact. As soon as he realised this his eyes widened and took several steps backwards as he knew the legends of those moths and how they affect time. This hunt had just become much more dangerous.

What he had not noticed was a curvaceous woman with dressed very similarly to him, but she wore a simple leather jacket. Her eyes held a hungry light as she looked at the crystal formation in the centre of the room. She stood in the shadows watching as Geremiah's eyes glowed silver and he began looking around the room starting in front of him. Like a cat that had spotted a mouse he zeroed in on something that everyone else could not see. Holding out his hand he spoke something under his breath. With a small flash of light and a shift in the air a small polyhedral shape appeared floating near his shoulder. It immediately began emitting a multicoloured light which revealed the outline of a large Rune. This seemed to be the cue for the woman she sent a blast of power toward Geremiah.

"Crap, so that's what happened." Thedas said.

"What?"

"Mage combat. Watch..."

So, they watched, the moment that power impacted with Geremiah, who at the last second had managed get a rippling shield to encompass himself, a circle of black energy sprung up around the edge of the room. Mage Combat had been initiated. Two had entered but the law of the world stated that only one could leave, alive.

"Zinnia Mandragora, I should have known you would rear your deadly head." He snarled, hurling a razor-sharp blade of energy back at her. It exploded as it impacted with a curse which she had thrown back at him.

"The Guild needs to be stopped Hawthorne. You privileged fools hoard away the knowledge of the ancients. It belongs to the people; I will share this discovery with everyone."

"You foolish woman the people are, you know what we could do the whole badly scripted argument while we fight or we can just fight."

With that he threw a jet of raw power at her just as she responded in kind. The two jets collided and immediately reality began to palpably warp around them. This seemed to agitate the moths as the walls of the room seemed to ripple and the moths began to emit an agitated whispered scream which caused a rippling interaction with the energy of the Mage Combat. Suddenly with a clap of thunder a very disgruntled looking Wathelbury appeared in the periphery of the combat.

"Lucky I wasn't in the bloody shower who summons someone..." He trailed off as he looked around the chamber, realisation entered his eyes as he seemed to recognise the location. As he looked around, he noticed the combatants' energy interacting with the moths and the crystal on the pedestal which seemed to be soaking up the excess energy as it was pulsating faster and faster.

"Oh, hell no..."

He threw up his hand and let a Rune fall into the air where it hung for a moment and let out a blast of power causing everything to freeze. Wathelbury breathed a sigh of relief for a moment but panicked as the Rune began to stutter and emit a mechanical grinding sound. The gem on the podium released a blast of energy which literally smashed into the Rune which immediately exploded into three separate Runes. Zinnia was hit by the first Rune and immediately winked out of being. Geremiah took the second to the chest and his movements seemed to accelerate before he seemed to blur and phase out of reality. The final Rune hung in the air and the energy left from the combat was drawn into it. Everything slowed to an almost imperceptible pace.

Wathelbury stood gaping at everything that happened, panic blossomed on his face. Just as his panic was reaching a crescendo there was a flash of static electricity and a small puppy that seemed to be made of electrical sparks appeared. It began yipping excitedly. Wathelbury calmed a little.

"Good we got him. Why do I recognise this place?" He asked and received a yipped reply. "Shit, what? Not her. Owlighter I know you are here. Get out of here now, this is one of the thirteen."

Before Eli could question what was going on, he was yanked from behind and dragged into the darkness and had to run to keep up with Thedas who was dragging him by the hand. Both lanterns were red. Seconds later there was the sound of a church bell in the distance. As they heard that they were struck by a wave of energy and thrown onto cold, wet grass.

CHAPTER THIRTEEN

A BOY NAMED TABITHA

Eli was overcome with a shiver that had nothing to do with the water from the wet grass rapidly seeping into his clothes or the unnatural coldness of the summer evening. Without even looking up he knew exactly where they had landed. They had landed just beyond the Churchyard of St Michael and All Angels Church outside Crosstown. Every time throughout his life that he had been near the beautiful serene building he had felt the same cold, the presence of death and the power of the consecration. That is not to say that the consecration was uncomfortable, in fact they were the exact opposite. They were warm and welcoming and restful.

He sat up and noticed that Thedas was doing the same right down to the shiver. Eli had never really liked churchyards or barrows or any place that held an association with death. For some reason, his sensitivity to death was higher than the average Leanai and no matter how many tests he had been subjected to, there had never been a satisfactory explanation. Thedas had pulled out his diary and was flicking through it muttering to himself. While he did Eli watched the last of the sunlight disappear past the horizon, they had been gone a whole day.

"Nope, I really can't be here for this." He said scrabbling up and straightening his jacket. Eli called up a warming Lense. the moment he did so Thedas' eyes widened. "That's my cue." Before Eli could reply he was gone. Eli stood up leaning against the wall, he spat onto the grass verge trying to get rid of the strange sweet taste. He wasn't sure that he liked it. Steam began to rise from Eli as he intensified the Lense. He closed his eyes and tried to make sense of everything he had seen. A wave of tiredness threatened to overwhelm him but that didn't last long as a wave of fear tore through his body. The reason for this was a sharp, bitingly cold, metal point was digging into his throat.

"What are you doing here? Make a sudden movement or lie to me and you won't get a second chance." Came a soft yet dangerous masculine voice.

Eli opened his eyes and his breath caught in his throat. The man that stood in front of him had vibrant bleached blond hair with flashes of blue. His steely silver eyes complimented the shining blade he was holding to Elis throat. He wore a pair of thick heavy black boots that came to his knees over a pair of torn stone-washed jeans and a pastel rainbow t-shirt that said "Live life 'til you die from it" in bubbled letters. If Eli had to guess, the sword wielding maniac wasn't far from his own age. His eyes held barely checked anger.

"Come on speak up."

"I... I... just got thrown out of transit by the church bells. My friend bolted and left me here. Since when does the church have people guarding with swords?"

"Since people started digging up graves and stealing the bodies."

"That's... sick." Grimaced Eli going green at the thought. The man sighed and was about to speak when a voice echoed from what seemed to be everywhere and nowhere at the same time. It was a languid almost bored female voice.

"Tabitha darling," The voice said in an almost sigh, drawing out the ar in darling. "either skewer the Duskphizer boy or don't either way I brought lunch, I packed extra dear in case you decide to let him live." In a very cinematic spiral of glimmering black/purple sparks a picnic basket appeared on a nearby bench. "But, I would move a few feet away sweetie. Your boy is about to blow."

"He's not my anything." Snapped Tabitha but stepped back rapidly as Eli burped loudly and doubled over, retching. "Oh my god, why is it green and what is that weirdly sweet smell?"

"That my dear proves the boy is no threat." Came the invisible voice.

"How?" Tabitha asked confused.

"That smell is unnatural to this world, it is the smell of time Magick. An Owlighter was here. The blast of power we detected was their arrival, maybe when Neil rang the bells it interfered with their travelling."

"Weird and eww he's still going." Said Tabitha with mild disgust.

"Yeah that can happen believe me." Replied his mother's voice almost wistfully.

"Mum how would you know?" Tabitha asked.

"Well we all have pasts dear; you know that." Replied his mother, a blush evident in her tone.

"Yeah well..." He replied. "Feeling better sick boy?" He said to Eli.

Eli looked decidedly green, no pun intended, he had by this point stopped throwing up and was leaning against the wall of the churchyard. He dabbed his mouth with a soft silky handkerchief that he had not physically placed in his pocket. His stomach was roiling, and he would be glad if he never smelled that scent again. Tabitha went over to him and grabbed his arm which caused Eli to jump backwards and smack his head off the wall. He groaned and Tabitha grimaced.

"Smooth going Tabitha, stand back." Tabithas mother said. Immediately he stepped back as Eli made a gurgling sound and doubled over again. "If he carries on like that, I'm going to join him. Screw etiquette, I'll heal him."

"Mum no, you know how risky that is what if his body takes it as combat initiation?"

"You think I can't take him?" Came the amused reply.

"I'm more worried about a vendetta after."

"Fine dear. Get him to the bench, Nana sent one of her brews. She saw this." The voice said.

"Of course, she did, doesn't miss a beat that one." Snorted Tabitha.

"Why do you think we weren't shocked when..." Replied her mother mischievously.

"That's enough Mother." Tabitha lightly snapped, suddenly serious. "Not in present company."

"Ashamed dear?" His mother seemed to be enjoying this back and forth.

"Not at all, but it's family business. Now shut up and let me deal with that mess."

Tabitha moved back toward Eli and touched his elbow. "You're safe. Follow me." He put a bit more pressure on Elis elbow and led him towards the bench. A step to the side every so often as Eli puked again. A minute or so later they were next to the bench, and he encouraged Eli to sit. Once the other was seated Tabitha turned to the basket and opened the lid. Rummaging around inside he smiled when his hand made contact with a large cold glass bottle. He removed the spherical bottle and examined the liquid within. The liquid was a thick white liquid with a thick orange sediment layer in the bottom. Tabitha shook the bottle until the liquid took on a slight orange hue. He was struck by the thought that this almost sounded like shaking a tin of mushy peas, he shuddered. Eli looked up and grimaced.

"Mushy peas?" He said almost balking.

"Yeah that's what it sounded like to me." Chuckled Tabitha.

"Gross. What is that anyway?" Asked Eli.

"One of my Nanas healing concoctions. Like every potion you'll need to key it."

"Okay gimme it, I hate doing this. It's weird."

"I know, a little draining. Here." Tabitha handed him the bottle.

Eli took it, clicked his thumb onto the top and hissed slightly. When he had pressed the top of the cork, the tiny needle embedded within pierced his skin. Several drops of blood slipped down the cannula and into the mixture. He shook the bottle where the liquids mixed and became a rosy colour before it flashed a yellow colour for a moment. Immediately he popped the cork.

"Ower the hatch." He grimaced and upended the bottle draining the contents.

The mixture tasted like a sickening combination of cinnamon and peppermint. As he drank it, he thought it had the texture of runny icing, a little bitty and thick. Eli burped loudly and blushed immediately sending a sideways glance to Tabitha.

"Happens to everyone, believe me. How was it?"

"Thick. on the upside it killed off the last of the sweet flavour mixed with my barf and I don't feel in immediate danger of throwing up now." Replied Eli quietly, embarrassed.

"That at least assures me that it is working. I'll be off then." Said Tabithas mothers voice.

"See you later mum."

"I'll be around sweetie. Nana packed plenty for you both and some other bits in the second compartment." The trees nearby rustled and parted as she Walked away. Tabitha opened the basket again and pulled out some food items. He handed Eli a sandwich and unwrapped one himself. They sat in silence eating, Eli had ham and cheese while Tabitha enjoyed tuna and cheese, his favourite. The basket provided two premixed alcoholic drinks; Eli was sure his contained rum.

Eli sat for a while contemplating a question while Tabitha watched, amused. Eventually he cleared his throat.

"So, your name is Tabitha? A strange name for a dude." Asked Eli tentatively.

"Dude? You don't say that often, do you? It doesn't suit you." Laughed Tabitha.

"Well I don't know what to say. I've never met a man called Tabitha before."

"That would make an awesome book title huh?" Laughed Tabitha.

"Yeah. Are you avoiding the question?" Eli chuckled in return.

"Trying, Unsuccessfully." Snorted Tabitha. "Long story short my Mum wanted a Girl."

"Yeah, I wanted a girl." Came his Mother's voice solicitously from nowhere.

"Leave it Mum, don't go there. I'm enjoying waiting for moonrise with my friend." Tabitha snarled lightly.

"Do you even know his name?" She laughed.

"I was getting there. Leave us alone, please." He almost whined the last word.

"Okay Sweetie. I'll let you have your fun. Buh-bye." She said fading away.

"How do you know she's gone?" Eli asked a little unnerved.

"You don't." Snorted Tabitha. "Anyway, I'm Tabitha, nice to meet you. Sorry for the misunderstanding with the Sword." He smiled and offered his hand.

"Elijah." He replied taking the proffered hand. "And it's okay, maybe I enjoyed it."

"Maybe you did." He said lightly. "Anyway, Elijah it's nice to meet you."

"Eli, and it's nice to meet you too, Boy named Tabitha." Said Eli.

"Demoted to boy now?" Tabitha raised his eyebrow.

"More sellable book title." Smirked Eli before he burst into laughter, Tabitha joining quickly.

In the distance neither of them really heard or paid attention to Tabithas mothers chuckles on the breeze. "Mother you old bat, are you ever wrong?"

CHAPTER FOURTEEN

PLAGUE BEARERS

The moon rode high in the sky as they both finished off their sandwiches and drinks. They sat in companionable silence both lost in thought, neither could really place why they felt so comfortable with each other. Eli watched in wonder as the moonlight illuminated the scrapyard in the distance and as the wisps meandered through the cattle fields below. Never had he sat outside in the moonlight and just watched as the world passed by as the light played on the scenery. Also never had been as poetic in his head, or anytime for that matter. Tabitha seemed to be having similar thoughts as he sighed wistfully in the cool night air. They had sat there for about twenty minutes, neither wanting to speak as neither of them quite trusted that Tabithas mother was gone.

In fact, she had left earlier to take tea with her mother by the fire, projecting for extended periods these days chilled her to the bone. Her own mothers' uncanny knack of being right about the most obscure things, unnerved her. Though they had never been unlucky in a horse race. Currently they were both watching the goings on at the periphery with great interest, on an old out of tune crystal ball.

Tabitha began to pack away the rubbish from their small impromptu picnic, while Eli drained the last of his drink. Both were nervous and slightly saddened that their short meeting was drawing to an end. Eli was feeling better thanks to the potion and Tabitha had to get back to his job. They sighed simultaneously.

"I'd better get on with the patrol." Tabitha said sadly.

"Yeah, I'd better get back home, I suppose."

"Where do you live? The Forge?" Tabitha asked curiously. Hope laced his voice for an answer.

"No, I live in Glight. Long story." Smiled Eli.

"Cool, you'll have to tell me sometime."

"Yeah, I mean I don't have to be home until before Daft o'clock, whatever that is."

"Coltsfoots then." Grinned Tabitha, "Woman unnerves me."

"She saved my life yesterday."

"Yeah that sounds like her. Hold on." Tabitha said as a messenger Lense dropped a note in front of him. He opened the note which read. "Take him with you and make sure he get's home. I'm freezing sweetie. Nana says I have to stay home. Love Mum." Tabitha snorted. "Never subtle as usual mum."

"What?" Asked Eli genuinely confused.

"My mother was projecting, and it's hard on her. She suggests that you keep me company and that I get you home safe after."

"I'm game." Eli said smiling.

"I'm starting to get that impression." Smirked Tabitha grinning. "Come on then. We will pick the basket up on the way back."

"No problem." Eli said as he reached back to release his staff. He checked his watch it showed 10:35. "Plenty of time."

"Yeah. The gate at this end is locked at night so you'll have to lowp over it," Tabitha said.

"Accent slipped." Giggled Eli.

"Shut it rich boy, it happens." Tabitha snorted without heat.

"Come on then prince Tabitha. Lead the way."

Tabitha smiled at the nickname and led Eli over to the long metal farm gate at the back of the churchyard. He mounted the gate with a practiced ease, painfully aware of the cold bar beneath him and Elis eyes on him. Eli followed him clumsily a moment later and fell to the ground. He narrowly avoided a broken nose by virtue of Tabithas quick reflexes and soft, toned arms.

"Thanks." Blushed Eli. "So, what do we do?"

"We have to wander the churchyard, check. For signs of Magick use and that's about it. It'll take about an hour."

"Okay." Eli said, he flicked his staff in front of him. "Nocht" He intoned, and the staff illuminated the immediate area, only slightly brighter than the surrounding moonlight. Tabitha looked confused as he could see no effects at all from whatever Eli had done. Eli reached out and took his hand for a moment gently and wove him into the spell, he gasped, whether for the contact or the effects even he didn't know. As they looked around, there were no obvious traces of power. Both men stowed their weapons loosely so they would be easily accessed if they needed them. Slowly they walked past the newer graves and toward the kissing gate that led to the road at the rear of the church. As they entered the older part of the graveyard movement caught their eyes and both were armed in seconds. Tabitha seemed to be muttering under his breath while holding his sword in the ready position.

As they scanned the dark graveyard in front of them, staring blankly into the night, Eli notices a small figure behind one of the nearby dilapidated graves. The figure was a small boy dressed in clothing from a time gone by, the sight of him sent a shiver of sorrow through Eli. No matter how many ghosts he had seen in his life, the ghosts of children still saddened him and also chilled him more than any other. He reattached the staff to his straps and knelt down a little in the damp grass. At the end of the day if anything was powerful enough to disguise itself and hunt in a cemetery then he probably wouldn't be able to ensorcel fast enough to not end up joining the inhabitants of this place. The children looked nervous as he came down to their level.

"Hi." He smiled. "I'm Eli."

"I'm David." Said the young boy closest to him, his voice reverberating slightly.

"What you guys doing?" Asked Eli keeping his voice light.

"Hide and seek, Geoffrey is over near the toilet at the back end. He'll be coming soon. I'm gonna go hide again, mister." He smiled a little before turning to the others. "Come on guys, he's bound to be at ten by now."

With that every child's form shifted into orbs of energy and zipped off into the graves. Just as an echoing giggle and the words "Coming ready or not." Seemed to come out of thin air all around. Eli stood slowly huffing with the effort. Tabitha snorted and held out a hand.

"How Old Are You?" He said slyly.

"Twenty-One, yesterday." Eli replied blushing profusely.

"Ah that's why you're groaning worse than a ghost... Grandpa." Tabitha smirked.

"What the? I'm not that old. How Old Are You?" Spluttered Eli.

"Twenty, my birthday is August 30th." Replied Tabitha smugly.

"Fair. Just call me daddy not Grandpa lol." Eli smirked until suddenly his eyes widened and he realised just what he said. As soon as his expression changed Tabitha burst into a peel of laughter.

"Ok Daddy." Snorted Tabitha. "Let's wander back over to the bench and have a quick cuppa, it's chilly."

"Okay."

They walked around the side of the church and stopped as they heard the droning sound of a Concertina being played from above. After they had stepped back onto the grass far enough, they saw a man dressed somewhat like a pirate playing a beautiful concertina. As he sat on the church roof, he was playing sea shanty's and singing along in a deep gruff voice. Every so often he paused to take a long pull from a bottle of what they assumed was rum. They watched and listened for a few minutes until he seemed to have drained the bottle as he threw the bottle to the ground. Instead of smashing it seemed to sink with a dull splash before bobbing back up, where it stayed bobbing on none existent waves. Finally, Tabitha tugged on Elis sleeve and led him to the back of the churchyard near a small building labelled Gents. They passed through a kissing gate and turned left where there was another bench. The hamper had somehow moved to this bench.

Eli immediately went to the hamper and after a quick glance at Tabitha who nodded he opened it and pulled out a plastic thermos labelled tea/two and two plastic cups. As he read it, he smiled slightly thinking how nice it was to have someone else who liked tea the same, his mother liked it with no sugar and usually booze. He chuckled lightly, now he was wondering how Tabitha liked his tea, Eli liked his tea strong but a little milky. Tabitha was watching Elis every move with interest and detached amusement. He shuffled on the bench to allow Eli room to sit on the bench facing him slightly. The creak of the bench and the slight rustle of a light breeze in the bushes were the only sounds in the area as Eli sat down.

Tabitha took the offered plastic cup and held it steady whilst Eli opened the thermos and poured the strong, sweet and steaming liquid. Several small drops splashed onto his hand and almost immediately went ice cold in the night air. Soon both men had full cups and sat nursing them, relishing in the company and the heat of the tea. As they sat, both thought long about their companion and in those moments the seeds of a long-standing friendship were planted. No words were spoken while they drank their tea and relished in the warmth running to their cores.

From where they sat, they could see the outline of the crooked and rusted iron fence in the pale moonlight. It was quite a distance but still visible. The fence surrounded the Well of St Michael a holy spring that people flocked to visit. It was a simple well made from sandstone which had been mined from the river a mile away. Now at that time of night the well should have been silent, but it was not. On the path to their right, a few feet from the fence, there was a loud roar of power and two figures appeared. In the moonlight they looked to be wearing long hooded cloaks. The colour could have been black but then again it could have been any colour in the semi-darkness. As soon as the power receded the figures began to talk. Their conversation went something like this:

"Those interfering Graveminders are here." A young female voice growled. "What do we do? The spell needs to be done by midnight."

"Cleo, shut up they'll hear us. Besides it's the BG, he's useless, come on we need to get to the well side." Said the first voice, a male.

"Hah, yeah the BG hasn't caught at the last two sites. Silly little bitch, playing dress up as a hero. Right across the boundary. She gave me a sapphire class Charmstone and a new Gieldr to try. She won't accept failure this time." The one called Cleo said in an authoritative tone.

As they hurriedly walked down the path and through the metal gate, a metallic screech was heard as the rusted gate was opened and closed twice. While the figures had been speaking Eli had caught sight of the hurt that had flashed over Tabithas face, whatever the comments had meant they had hurt him. A small spike of rage surprised Eli, he had only met this boy, at sword-point earlier but he seemed to have claimed him as a friend. They both stood as they felt power starting to rise at the call of a song sung by the woman's voice. Eli stepped forward, his form blurring, though he did not know it and he seemed to streak between places, a few steps away.

"ELI NO!" Shouted Tabitha in a panicked warning.

But it was too late Elis form blurred and shifted place, once, twice, three times and impacted an invisible barrier. Immediately he was thrown backwards and upward with great force, a few seconds later he hit another invisible barrier above the churchyard. Around him sparks danced as the consecration tried to say tangible to hold him out. Eli reigned in his Magick knowing that it was bad form to damage consecration. The moment his power was contained the sparking stopped as the consecration once again became inert. Feeling this and realising he was a good thirty feet in the air Eli panicked for a moment as he began to fall. His fall lasted all of a second before he stopped in a jarring manner. As he stopped, he felt an unfamiliar sensation in his back, when he opened his eyes, he saw that his wings had come out and they seemed to be holding him up.

Power emanated from them causing him to hover. This time the consecration did not react. Instinct took over part of Eli and his wings moved to allow him to descend, the moment he landed he drew his staff. Tabitha ran to his side.

"Are you okay?" he asked breathlessly.

"Yeah, shocked is all. You know about the hole bouncing and flying thing." Snorted Eli. "Figures the first time I'd use these would be accidental."

"You've never flown before? It'd be the first thing I did if I inherited them." Said Tabitha.

"Nah, I hate heights." Eli muttered, blushing.

"Ironic." Replied Tabitha with a chuckle. "What do we do about those two?"

"Follow my lead, put your sword away." Said Eli, turning toward the iron kissing gate that led to the well.

CHAPTER FIFTEEN

MIDNIGHT CHORUS

Tabitha stowed his sword while Elijah put his staff back over his back. They looked down into the well site and saw the hooded figures, one stood at the edge of the well holding a flashing blue stone at the end of a chain. The other, the woman stood, hands clasped in front of her. She sang in a falsetto voice; the words of the song were in a language not known to any human tongue. It was guttural and seemed to stick in her throat. The longer they watched, her mouth began to smoke, and her eyes began to bleed. She looked as though she was panicking and could not seem to stop speaking. Her companion seemed startled for a moment then a smirk can be seen from under his hood. Eli turned to Tabitha who looked all at once fascinated and disgusted at the scene. Tabitha gasped which drew Eli's attention back to the figures. The female, Cleo, was now sprouting oozing pustules all over her face and hands, probably all over her body. Her eyes showed panic and pain through the film of blood. The males hood had now fallen away, and he was now covered just as she was, his voice was suddenly added to hers.

"Crap, Eli that's Plague Magick. We need to get help."

"Right hold on." He thought back to the first ever piece of Magick he had officially been taught. The summoning of the Inquisition. His power began to rise, and he spoke into his cupped hand which slowly began to glow blue and red. "Plague Casters, Send help. Tripnine." The last word held power, and he immediately threw his hand into the air. The pulsating Lense launched from his hand like a rocket and hung high in the air.

It hung there flashing rapidly between blue and red for a moment before it exploded into multiple smaller identical orbs which blasted to the ground. Seven figures all dressed in the Grey and black almost robe like uniform of the

Inquisition. One of them, the one that had appeared closest to Eli turned to them.

"You better have a good reason for summoning us. I was on lunch." The woman said. "I am Lead Inquisitor Iudex."

"Down there in the well, those two called up a Plague Spell. I was joining my friend on patrol."

"Patrol?" Iudex almost sneered.

"I am Tabitha, latest in the line of the Graveminder Clan." He said stepping forward.

"Ah, that explains it. My apologies for my tone. Plague Casting you say?" Her eyes widened, and she turned to the other robed figures. "Right cap it and burn everything biological inside, create an illusion before it comes down, so the public doesn't know what has happened. This is a tourist spot, can't have it damaged."

She stepped forward and raised her arms to the air, her motion was copied by the other six who by now had properly encircled the well. They began to chant a long litany of words in seven different languages. It became an echoing cacophony. A second opaque bubble appeared over the first and a moment later there was a flash of fire from within which was accompanied by two brief screams before everything returned to normal. The domes both fell, and the well looked like nothing had ever happened. The other six Inquisition members immediately vanished and Iudex turned to them both.

"Well that's that. I'll be off and you two stay out of trouble, it's the second time this week I've seen you young Duskphizer. Do not make it a third. Your rewards will be sent into your accounts now." With that she vanished in a blue and red flash of light.

"Well that was exciting. What time is it?" Asked Eli.

"Eleven fifty-nine." Replied Tabitha looking at a pocket watch. "We had better leave soon."

"Yeah."

Unexpectedly in the churchyard the bell tolled once, the tone echoing in the night. For a moment all is silent until a white glow appeared for a moment before it faded and a voice began to sing, loud and deep. They ran to the gate and saw that the churchyard was full of semi solid people. In the distance the source of the voice sat in an armchair in the newer section. The source of the voice was Wytch, though Eli and Tabitha could not make that out from where they leaned on the gate. In the distance Haru also ran beneath the moon on all fours in canine form. The song was an old one, Amazing Grace. Mainly because it is public domain. Soon bagpipes and the concertina joined the chorus as the other figures sang along. The power and emotion behind the tune made both men feel small in the grand scheme of things and brought a tear to their eyes.

"I've heard rumours of this from my family. It's the midnight chorus." Tabitha breathed to Eli.

"The what?"

"The Midnight Chorus is a phenomenon that's said to happen only for those who need to see it. Possibly to fortify them for a journey or some, time of trouble in their lives. It can only happen where an Archir is in attendance. I think the guy on the chair is one? If we approach, it will force them by lore to leave."

"Oh, what about the wolf? Could that be Haru?" Asked Eli.

"Could be, he is the Archir whose pillar was lost. He was the Archir of the Nagual - Shapeshifters." Replied Tabitha.

"So this show is for us?" Asked Eli.

"Unless someone else is around, then yeah..." He trailed off. "Feel that?"

"Yeah, a cold energy. Behind us."

They turned and saw a soft sapphire blue glow was coming from the area of the well below. With a quick glance at each other they moved forward as one. Neither made a move to draw their weapons as the power seemed almost benign, natural even. The kissing gate screeched as they passed through it, squeezing through it together. Below them the glow was emanating from the murky waters of the well. The glow cast odd shadows as it was obscured by the undergrowth. Eli led the way down the uneven sandstone steps until he stood where the male had been. He shivered at the memory.

"What's going on?" Asked Tabitha.

"I don't know but something inside me is resonating with that glow."

"Nana always says go with your gut."

"Far be it from me to argue with Nana Graveminder." Joked Eli.

Tabitha snorted. "You'll fit in well if you ever visit our home."

"Maybe one day?" Smiled Eli.

"Yeah maybe. Anyway, get on with it, it's cold, and the silence is deafening now the singing has stopped."

Indeed, it had stopped and now the only sounds in the air were the rustling of the wind in the grasses and the lone hoot of a far-off owl. Eli closed his eyes and thought back to Aunt Ophelia and her gifts. She said she had given him a gift called the Seight. He focussed on this and felt a tingle of almost static electricity wash over his eyeballs below his eyelids. As he opened his eyes he gasped, so did Tabitha at the same time.

"Elijah your eyes, they're glowing silver." He stated, awed.

"You think that's weird? You should see what I'm seeing."

"Describe it to me."

"I'll show you in a memory when we're safe. I have a feeling we'll have company soon."

"Okay, I trust you." Said Tabitha confidently.

Eli examined Tabitha through his new outlook on the world. He looked breath-taking, he had power wrapping around him in an almost lazy serpentine manner. This version had long attractively cut hair, it was still blue but now had streaks of many other colours through it. A pair of wings that looked to be made of pearls shimmered behind him, though they were transparent, maybe he didn't have them yet. His eyes shone and crackled, they looked as though someone had taken a thunderstorm and made two eyes from them. Behind his head a spectral outline that looked like a pentagram filled with Runes hung in the air. His sword was planted in the ground, it looked bigger and more powerful but yet it seemed to be the same sword. Both hands rested on it. Three spectral children stood behind him, a tall girl and twin boys. Overall the picture was striking.

He tore his gaze away from the vision before him and began surveying everything else. The surrounding ground was lifeless and charred but everything else outside the wells enclosure glowed softly with life. As he turned his gaze to the well itself he nearly passed out due to the wave of power he was hit in the face by. Above the water two Runes hung in the air, raw and in their natural forms. Shapes of pure energy. Eli had heard of this from his mother's friend Gerard who was a Seidhunter working in France. He had once told Eli that Raw Runes of this type were known as Wyld Runes. Spelled with a Y to differentiate between those and the Wild branch of Runes and animals. Gerard had explained that these were incredibly rare and hard to capture, the capture Lense would need a lot of power to capture the Rune. He had also told Eli that he would need to listen for the Runes name in order to capture it. Wyld Runes did not hide in the scenery like others they were blatant, but also paid the second highest amount under the type known as Nitid Runes as they were the most powerful.

Eli began to listen carefully to the night air for the names of the two Runes. One of the Runes looked spectral, and the other was almost elemental. As he focussed on the spectral Rune, he began to hear excited whispering. Words on the air described the effects of the Rune in first person, as though it was telling him itself. He listened as the ghostly voice told him its story. A story of ghosts and people who could walk anywhere there was not iron. Ghosts who were able to live as though alive again. It told of many things it had seen and could do until finally it told him its name.

He had not dared think this would happen as Seidhunters witnessed Runes all the time but without a name they usually faded or had to be left. He thought of the capture Lense which immediately sprang to life and formed a three-dimensional Polyhedral shape with thirteen points which sat in the air near his head. He focussed on the Rune again and felt a shift in the power as though it were watching him, waiting. He held out his right arm and commanded the Lense to begin.

"Phasmastis.." The word rang with power and a sound like a gong. it was a word that had not been spoken in hundreds of years. "Rune of Phantoms."

Immediately the Wyld Rune began to shift places and try to fade from existence but it was caught in a beam of containing power by the Lense which had moved in front of his outstretched hand and had begun to draw power from him. The Rune seemed to scream as it shuddered and blurred trying to escape. Eli felt the tug on his power and his mind. That was what he was missing, he had the name of the Rune, he had the power over it.

"Phasmastis." Eli thought firmly. "Stop struggling. SUBMIT."

The effect was instantaneous, the Rune stopped and hung in the air solid as the capture Lense surged forward and engulfed it. As soon as it did the Lense expanded and then seemed to contract. With one last power pull the Lense shot back to Elis hand and he closed his hand around a smooth hexagonal stone. The capture Lense returned to his shoulder level in the air. He opened his hand and looked at a clear glasslike stone which bore the Rune encased inside and radiated power.

"Eli what was that?"

"Hold on there's another. Hold this." Eli handed him the Rune.

He turned his augmented gaze back to the other Rune which seemed to be on high alert. It seemed to be on alert, watching him like a deer about to flee. Eli listened again this time to the new Runes story. This Rune told of secrets heard in ways that no-one could know. Of learning, teaching and absorbing knowledge. Again it went on to tell of many other things for what felt like hours but had only been a few seconds. Suddenly he heard it, the whisper, quieter than all the rest, its name. the Rune seemed to realise it had slipped and tried to fly off but Elis capture Lense was faster and the Rune was held in its beam like before.

"Studis." Eli said. As before the Rune froze and Eli swore he almost heard a cussword on the wind.

"Studis keeper of knowledge and things best hidden. I command you to submit."

Why his thought command had been wordier Eli was unsure, but it seemed to work. Again, the capture Lense snapped forward and engulfed the Rune. Though this time the struggle was longer and took more out of Eli but he held fast and he felt the Rune submit with a muttered fine. So, this Rune could communicate, strange. What was even stranger was that his capture Lense seemed to have become more solid. When it sprang to Elis hand, it felt actually solid. It deposited the Rune and did not dissipate as he cancelled the command for it.

"Nope, staying here." The Lense actually spoke in a tinny voice.

"What the f..." Eli started.

"Oi language." The Lense snapped.

"Raot." Snapped Eli. This time it was the Lense that swore as it was drawn back into his hand.

Eli looked at the object in his hand, this time the Rune was made of a grey gemstone that was shaped like a book. Like before the Rune was encased in the gem. Tabitha was in awe. He silently handed over the other Rune and looked at Eli who swayed visibly as he pocketed the Runes. In a flash he was at Elis side holding him up. His hand accidentally dipped below his jeans onto his ass, the moment he did, his face flushed in the night and he moved his hand.

"Come on. We need to go back to your apartment." He glanced at his watch. "It's twenty past twelve."

"Okay, hold on." Slurred Eli. He pulled the Phasmastis Rune out and squeezed it in his hand. "Phasmastis" He muttered and told the Rune to leave a copy of itself to continue supporting the ghost populace. As he did so another figure appeared. I was a curvy woman who was hooded and robed.

"Give me that Rune boy. My idiot acquaintances failed to get it but it's mine."

She began charging a sickly looking curse in her hand. Eli summoned the basket which materialised in his hand and pulled Tabitha into a tight hug.

"Breathe normally." He said.

The travelling spell wrapped around them and they were gone as the sickly curse struck the spot they had been. The woman screamed with rage but vanished again as an Inquisitor appeared.

CHAPTER SIXTEEN

TORI

As soon as the spell wrapped around them both Eli knew he would pass out soon. he had to jump to Gretna and Luguvalio before he aimed back for crosstown. Instead of the riverside he changed his destination to the Hotel his mother had taken him to as a child to meet Gerard. The hotel had an international QEX point in room thirteen for over one person and one for single users in the old-fashioned telephone booth in the hallway. He aimed them there, and they appeared in a whirl of power in the middle of the hallway. The woman behind the desk looked like she was about to let rip at them both for breaking social courtesy. Even for a hotel it was bad form to use any Magickal travelling method to appear in the lobby unless you had paid to do so. The woman held her tongue when Eli passed out cold and fell to the floor. She hurried over.

Tabitha looked her over. She wore a dark grey business suit and a Daffodil yellow shirt which offset her dark blond hair and the yellow spiralling Draiohba that covered her exposed skin and the edges of her face. A pair of golden spectacles rested on top of her hair. The woman leaned down and looked at Eli critically.

"Is that Emily's boy Eli?" She asked as she looked to Tabitha. "Oh It's you Tabitha, your gramps is in the bar, messing with my fire again. Even in the summer they want it on." She smiled fondly.

"Yeah, Tori it's Eli. He's drained. It's been an interminable night." Tiredness evident in his voice too. "I need to get him back to Glight, he's staying at Coltsfoots."

"I'll get her to come get him, are you going too?" Tori asked?

"Thank you, Tori, lifesaver is what you are."

Tori snorted and got up, brushing herself down and walking back over to the small office that looked out onto the lobby. She moved her hand over a communication sphere. It flashed and resonated with a crystalline sound. There was a dial tone and then Coltsfoots voice sounded from the sphere.

"Coltsfoots bar and board, lady of the house speaking."

"Lady my eye, Marigold it's Tori." Snorted Tori and Coltsfoot chuckled.

"Hello, my dear, how are you? Bit late for a call."

"I have Elijah Duskphizer and his friend here. Eli just passed out in my lobby."

"Ooh and so close to daft o'clock. Tell them to hold his key. Can I keycall them from your lobby?"

"Of course. Sorry to be a bother."

"Never a bother Tori, never. I'll see you and your mother for poker next week?"

"Happily. Speak soon Marigold."

"Speak soon Tori."

The call ended with a single crystalline tone. Tori looked up and saw that Tabitha had already gotten Elis key from his bag and was clasping his hand with the key firmly between.

"Stay safe and hold tight Tabitha." With that she tapped the orb twice.

A split-second later the room seemed to fold in on them and a moment later they were in Elis room with coltsfoot standing over them.

CHAPTER SEVENTEEN

COLTSFOOTS PLAN

Madam Marigold Coltsfoot was not a patient woman at the best of times but when one of her guests had to be Keycalled a scant two minutes before Daft O'clock, she was not best pleased. she watched the clock on the table by the door, she liked what the boy had done with the place. The seating area looked better across from the door, his changes to the kitchen to include a brewers station and a small spellcrafting workbench showed her that this boy was studious and very much worth her time. The grey tartan carpet and mustard tones of the furniture and drapes made the space feel clean, tidy and open. He had even spent a great deal of money stocking up the bookshelves and upgrading the TV. She was confident that even after the term that was paid up that he intended to stay longer. A small chime came from her pocket and she watched as the two minute spot between twenty-nine minutes and thirty-one minutes past the hour slid open and a golden two hour slot opened. She looked outside and a bat that had been flying by was moving very slowly past. Daft O'clock had begun.

Coltsfoot turned to the two boys on the floor in front of her and sighed. Looks like she'd need another key. Annette Graveminder had warned her that this would happen, the old bint was never wrong. She sighed and moved over to the pair, from her apron she withdrew two bottles of pick me up potion.

"Here, one each. We all need to talk, and this will allow you both to have enough energy to finish that. It's weaker than most but should give you a boost for three hours." She said handing the potions to Tabitha. Tabitha did as Eli had earlier before necking the potion in one swig. He bristled as energy poured through him. He looked at Elis arm and saw a small puncture, he pressed the bottle to that and shook it before pouring it into his friends' mouth. He put his hand over Elis mouth and massaged his throat forcing him to swallow before he moved to the side. For the second time that day Eli sat bolt upright coughing.

"Pick me up potion?" He grimaced.

"Yeah, the travelling spell took the last of your energy." Tabitha said softly.

"You'll have plenty of time for that later." Said Coltsfoot her accent still had a Scottish lilt, but it was nowhere near as broad.

"What happened to your accent?" Eli asked confused.

"I ham it up in public. Image is everything." Coltsfoot Grinned. "Now up and invite us into your lovely new sitting area, I'll send for tea."

"Okay." He struggled to his feet and bowed slightly. "Take a seat both of you. I wouldn't want to be remiss as a host."

Both Coltsfoot and Tabitha snorted at this but took a seat in the seating area. Tabitha took the sofa and Coltsfoot sat in a comfortable armchair. Eli sat on the sofa at the other end. With a lazy gesture from coltsfoot a fine china tea service appeared with a clink. The teapot steamed and the cake stand groaned under the weight of thick slices of cake and sandwiches. She looked at Eli. He rolled his eyes, she had provided tea, but he was the host so should serve. For the next several moments, Eli poured the tea and handed the plates out. They all began to fill their plates and prepare their tea how they liked it. Eli noticed a newspaper on the coffee table, the title was The Anvil in looped script. A wave of sadness washed through him, that was the newspaper which his mother owned. He didn't look at the newspaper again.

"Now," Coltsfoot said swallowing a large chunk of chocolate cake, crumbs falling from her mouth as she spoke. "I need to talk to you both about living arrangements. I have been contacted by both your parents and told to expect that you will end up residing here. I have no problem with that, but I have also been told by your Grandmother, Tabitha that you will both need to leave the area in the next few days. It is safer you are not here due to the Storm Queens antics. She and her court may not be able to see you but unbranded assassins can. That's a way around the Decree."

"So, I can't live here?" Eli said sounding quite upset.

"Yes and no. Tabithas Grandmother is almost never wrong, she says that the threat appears in about three days and the oversight will be corrected within a month. She advised that you both travel the UK until Tabithas birthday in two months. After that you'll be able to see your family again safely Eli."

"How?"

"The Monarch of the Over Throne will be advised to lift the Decree, by who I don't know. She will instead redo it saying that no harm can be incited by either

119

throne for the remainder of the original term. This will happen on television in a rare meeting between the two thrones."

"Sounds interesting. So, what do we do just wander?"

"Grandma Graveminder says that you'll have plenty to keep you busy, and you'll earn money along the way. She also says that if she needs you to go anywhere, she has her ways of getting in contact with you."

"Yeah she definitely does." Chuckled Tabitha.

"Now Eli on the subject of money read this." She handed him a newspaper. "I couldn't give you direct contact, but I gave your mother a piece of advice and she took it. Open to the personal section."

Eli did as he was told and opened the newspaper flicking the broadsheets until he came to the Personal Messages section. He looked down the rows until he came to a box labelled, Little One. It read.

"Little One, miss you so much. All family safe so don't. The terror misses her big brother. Found out she's been dating a local shop owners' son. Remove all funds from bank account ASAP. Too easily traced. Give close and clear form signed to the Scottish Thistle. Do not go yourself. I expect a reply to Anvil 13 ASAP so we know you're safe. Bank account should be closed within 48 hours. All my love Mum x,"

He breathed a sigh of relief; his family was safe. His mother was not angry at him for having to leave and she had told him how to move forward. He opened his satchel which he still had draped over his shoulder and pulled out his Journal and flicked to the banking section. He read everything on the page seeing that all balances were in normal accounts which he could close with no issue. The list for Journal balance was zero. He realised that the back page of the Journal had a pouch in it which he could store money and it would record the balance. In the spine of the Journal was a slim silver pen. As he clicked the top, he felt a small sting as the pen filled itself with blood, a security measure to make sure only he could amend anything within the Journal. He began to write out the close and clear instruction as his mother had told him to, next to him Tabitha was doing the same. Eli had been plainly aware that Tabitha had been reading over his shoulder, close enough for him to be able to feel his breath in his ear. After a few moments they tore out the signed slips and handed them to her.

"I'll do it at opening time."

"Could I ask a small favour Madam Coltsfoot?" Asked Eli cautiously.

"I suppose." Coltsfoot said, smiling slightly. She already knew what was coming.

"Would you be able to order me some fresh clothing from the shops on this level? Until we figure out what's going on, it might be best if we stayed here and planned." Eli said cautiously.

"That has already been arranged. You can thank Grandma Graveminder. She saw your measurements and also forwarded enough money to cover both of your clothing. In return your mother is paying for supplies and other odds and ends to make sure you are able to be comfortable wherever you go."

"Okay... so we're leaving one way or another." Snorted Tabitha.

"Looks that way yes." Smiled Coltsfoot. "Now I will drop by at eleven to bring the clothing, supplies and money. Get some sleep both of you. And you young Duskphizer, I expect you to be a gentleman." She smirked.

"I will ma'am." He replied.

"Good. Now do you mind if a frail old woman uses a wee bit o' Magick to get tae her rooms?" She asked innocently.

"That's perfectly fine Madam. Goodnight." Eli said kissing her hand which smelled of stale smoke.

"Charmer that's what you are. Goodnight to you both."

"Goodnight Madam Coltsfoot." Said Tabitha as she popped away.

The moment she was gone they burst out laughing. Mainly at her antics.

"Frail old woman my ass." Said Tabitha between giggles.

"I know, nothing frail about her." Replied Eli. "Come on, I'll show you to where you can sleep. Bathroom first though."

Eli led Tabitha across to the bathroom door and let him into the room. A new sealed toothbrush lay on the sink. Tabitha went in and shut the door. Eli tidied away the tea service and straightened the cushions. Several minutes later Tabitha came out of the bathroom and went over to the patio doors where the basket had laid forgotten. He grabbed some clothing out that Eli knew hadn't been in there earlier and looked apologetically at Eli holding up the clothes. Eli nodded tiredly. He finished what he was doing and went onto the bedroom.

Against all habit he put a pair of green tartan pyjamas on (They were a gift from his own grandma who lived on the Orkney Isles.) and went to the bathroom passing Tabitha in the corridor. He performed his ablutions and went back to the bedroom where Tabitha was stood looking at the bed. Like Eli he wore pyjamas, though his were blue with spots. Both were too tired to make fun of the pyjamas.

"You take the bed and I'll take the sofa." Eli said going to the cupboard to get some covers. He was stopped by a gentle hand on his arm.

"Stay?" Tabitha said quietly, almost pleading. "Don't worry your gentleman status will be intact but I don't want to be alone. I've never been away from home."

"This is my first night sleeping away from home too. Are you sure?"

"Yeah am sure." Tabitha yawned pulling him over to the bed.

They both awkwardly arranged themselves at either side of the bed and Eli turned out the lights with a wave of his hand. He lay there in the silence next to his new friend for a moment, tears threatened to overwhelm him. Eli was scared, he had never been away from the comfort of home and now he had been through multiple stressful situations and hadn't slept for days. A soft sniffle from the other side of the bed brought his attention back to the present.

"Tabitha?" He said softly.

"Yeah." Came the muffled sniffling reply.

"Come here, I think we both need a hug."

"'Kay." Came the hesitant reply.

Tabitha shifted over and curled into Eli who had put his arm out. Once they were both comfortable, they quietly cried themselves to sleep in a matter of minutes. Both were exhausted but more importantly felt safe.

CHAPTER EIGHTEEN

GETTING TO KNOW EACH OTHER

Tabitha awoke with a pair of strong arms around him and immediately panicked. He could barely remember the night before and in his panic fell off the bed with a thud. Eli snorted; he had been awake for a few minutes. He had been trying to figure out what had gone on over the last few days and also how to extricate himself from the bed without waking the other up.

"You were awake the entire time?" Tabitha said laughing slightly though also a little outraged.

"Yeah trying to figure out who the guy in my bed was. Then when you started wriggling to get out from my arms, it amused me. Starting to feel like a bad one-night stand." Chuckled Eli.

"We didn't...?"

"Nope, I'm still a virgin and happy about it."

"That's good. You couldn't be interested..." Tabitha started to say while staring at the floor.

"Hey," Eli said firmly causing Tabitha to stop and look up at him in shock. "That is not, what I meant. Don't start a pity party. if I wasn't interested, I wouldn't say it like that. I meant I'm a virgin in all respects. I have no idea what type of person I like at all yet. I just want friends to begin with. Then, who knows?"

"Oh, right. But you should know..."

"I know." Said Eli softly.

"How?" Tabitha asked fear lacing his voice.

"Adam, had an apple." Smiled Eli kindly before rapidly changing the subject. "Now enough of this. Some people might not like this kind of talk,"

"Who and what do you mean? We're alone." Tabitha said confused.

"Dunno, but someone somewhere." Snorted Eli. "Wouldn't want to offend."

"Yeah wouldn't want to offend someone who is listening in that doesn't really know us." Snorted Tabitha.

"Breakfast?" Eli said quickly, his voice showed his amusement.

"Oh, yes please." Tabitha hissed. Eli blushed. "I'm starving."

"Come on then." Eli went to get up, then stopped. "You go to the bathroom first, you're a guest." He said almost pleadingly.

"Yeah, a guest. I'll pop to the bathroom then."

Tabitha got up, grinning and walked slowly out of the room making Eli groan and throw a pillow. He heard Tabitha laughing as he walked down the corridor. Eli waited until he heard the door open and close and closed his eyes mentally calming himself. Moments later he got out of bed after letting a small Lense wash over him, just on case. He quickly changed into fresh clothing and sprayed some aftershave that had been packed in his bag. As he finished dressing Tabitha walked back into the room already dressed.

"Let me guess Nana Graveminder packs an all-purpose hamper?" Smiled Eli.

"Yeah, that basket has half a dozen situational pockets. They're packed and accessed when needed. I'm assuming that your jacket has one. You looked surprised that you had that hankie last night."

"Yeah, I definitely didn't have one in the pocket. Then again I was given them by an Archir."

"What?"

"Two turned up at my Ascension, at least that's what I think they were and what they were referred to as. Come on we can talk over breakfast I'm starving." Indeed, his stomach immediately rumbling as if to back up his statement.

They both walked through the apartment in companionable silence and went to the kitchen, Tabitha took a seat on a comfortable bar stool at the far side of the bench and watched Eli begin pulling out ingredients from the cupboards and fridge. He also pulled out a large plate of metal from under the range like cooker and placed it across the five heating plates. Eli turned and began preparing a full English breakfast after turning all the heating elements to full.

"Wait, you cook? Should I call a medic now or later?"

"Later." Smiled Eli. "My fare is not immediately deadly, kind sir. It wouldn't do to have the guests perish on the premises would it?"

"This is true." Chuckled Tabitha. "Good job I'm immune to most poisons. In my family it's a survival trait."

"Interesting way to grow up." Smiled Eli. "Tell me about you? What about where you grew up?"

"Okay... there's not really much to tell. I grew up in our family estate Potters Field Sepulchre, it's located in the Grampian mountain range. From the tower window where my room is, I can see the observatory on a good day. Usually it's just snow and fog. We Graveminders are taken to each of the navigational Cairns across the mountain and have to leave a drop of blood on a special stone, only we can see it. Once we've done that, we're able to snap to any of them. You see when the fog falls, or worse when the blizzards whip up, Magick can go a bit well a bit wobbly for want of a better term. So it's safer for us to use the cairns."

"That's kinda cool. What's the Sepulchre like?" Asked Eli. Tabitha could see he was genuinely interested.

"The Sepulchre itself is quite a foreboding building form the outside but on the inside my grandmother and mother have made it really warm welcoming and homely. it looks like a cross between a castle and a cathedral. I love it there. The grounds of the Sepulchre proper are covered in snow most of the year. We're really high up at the top of one of the mountains near Ben Nevis. From my bedroom window, which is in one of the towers, on a clear day I can see the ruins of the Observatory at the Summit of Ben Nevis. It's far away and tiny but I know it's what I'm seeing. Theirs a Cairn at the top and it's one of my favourite places, standing there I feel like I'm on Top of the World. You can see for over a hundred miles on a good day. Sometimes all you can see is cloud immediately at your feet. Did you know that there's what's left of a piano up there? Some charity guys carried it All the Way Up in the Eighties." For a moment Tabitha's face was lost in happy thought before he brought himself around. "Anyway, the grounds of the Sepulchre are a huge Graveyard for The Unclaimed. Those that would normally be given state funerals as they are either unidentified or have no-one left to take care of their final journey. Now women of my family are all natural Necromancers and the men are Ichoromancers. That means they can control the very lifeblood and body of a person. We contact the spirit, assess their wishes and in cases of unidentified people sometimes we can inform their families."

He stopped and took a drink of the steaming cup of tea which Eli had placed on the countertop in front of him. Eli went to the stove and continued to cook, waiting for Tabitha to resume the story. After a few moments of wistful thought, he did.

"All through the Clans land, which is a massive portion of the mountain range from valley to peak, my family live in small groups of stone-built houses, near the cairns but just far enough off the beaten track that no-one will stumble across us. Each location has a cemetery of its own that the residents watch over. Throughout our land there are ancient black barked trees, so old that no-one actually knows their species. these trees all have leaves of a different colour, no two the same, the colours range from blood red to sea blue and beyond. There are legends that if the Clan comes under threat, these trees are able to come to life and defend us. No-one in living or dead memory has ever witnessed this. They are known almost jokingly, but more lovingly but the family as our Bark Guardians." He chuckled fondly.

Tabitha looked at Eli seriously for a moment. "You can't share this with anyone."

"I wouldn't. But also, why not?" Asked Eli his tone somewhere between affronted and confused. Tabitha immediately smiled apologetically.

"Sorry. It's just that our clan used to be persecuted in the dark-ages, during the Witch trials people in the area immediately used us as scapegoats. Even the other Magick users. We were too prominent and easy targets. Strangely not one member of our family took umbrage, we accepted it and walked to our deaths to protect the others. It's why we ended up getting given full Clan status and granted the huge territory we have. But after that it became family law that our secrets are to be guarded. Anyway, I trust you and I haven't been punished by the law so obviously I'm right to. Nana Graveminder is ruthless with breaches. Though we couldn't hide the actual land, I mean who wouldn't notice an entire mountain range vanishing. Instead we have ancient and powerful Wards that were forged...."

He slapped his hand to his forehead muttering "Idiot."

"That's it now I know why I can tell you!" He exclaimed.

"Why?"

"Because our Clans are allied permanently. Your family were the ones who created the Archetype for the Wards. It's rumours that the reason they are so powerful is they were created in something called the Pillar Smithy. What's that?"

"I'll get to that, finish your story first." Eli said sticking his tongue out causing Tabitha to smile.

"Fine," He chuckled. All over our land are kissing gates and other apertures which link to Cemeteries All Over the World. While my immediate family deal with all the United Kingdom's Necropolis' the rest of the family are assigned to various countries. We have agreements with faiths worldwide to take in the dead that they cannot. Now Mr curious dish up food and sit, it's your turn. Same question."

"Fine, fine, Mr demanding. Here." Eli said smiling as he placed a plate full of steaming delicious smelling food in front of him. They ate in silence for a while, the food rapidly going down on their plates. Both men were starving they had been through a lot in the past day or so. After a while and feeling pleasantly full Eli cleared his throat.

"So, my turn, huh. Well there's even less to tell about my Life. I grew up at the Forge, on the outskirts of Crosstown. It is named as such due to the extensive Smiths and Forges which we have across our land around the house. Our family have always been Smiths of one form or another for centuries. We were renowned for making enchanted weaponry and Wards. There's an old Duskphizer tale that we were the ones who crafted Excalibur and later the blade that would best it Cumhachdor, literally Dark Power. Before you ask, we are a totally grey family. Neutral in all wars just like yours. Cumhachdor was wielded by Mordred, Arthurs bastard son. What's not widely known is that he walked into battle side by side with his Father. They were fighting the tribes from the kingdom of Reghed which was ruled by the Fisher King. The Fisher King saw himself as the true heir to Avalon. At the end, Mordred though twisted by his mothers' hatred of Arthur believed in Camelot and the ideal of Magick in the open. When his father was mortally wounded and so was he, Arthur commanded Mordred to slay him, use the power of the sword to heal him and live. Mordred wept as he shoved the blade through his father's heart and pulled out the last of his life force. As soon as he was healed, he went on to slay another two hundred enemy soldiers before following the last part of his father's final decree, he called up a storm and used the sword to ride the storm to safety."

"So that's why there are so many shrines to Mordred?" Tabitha said in realisation.

"Yeah but also why so many of them are vandalised every year. Y'see only certain families know the full legend and the rest know that he was there so they see him as the ultimate betrayer. No-one will listen as there's no real proof. One day someone will find documented evidence."

"Maybe yeah. So, your family created Cumhachdor and set the Wards for my family? Anything else?"

"Oh, loads of boring stuff, we've made Artefacts for centuries. Anyway, the Pillar Smithy is a place underground, we don't know exactly where it is. From what I've heard there's a tunnel under the Mansion that leads to an ancient fixed portal which is accessible only by the blood of the family. I've never been myself you can't enter until after your Ascension. Something about the high Seid rating affecting growth, I dunno."

"I bet it's interesting to see."

"Oh, the Pillar Smithy really is a sight to see." Came Coltsfoots voice from the door. "You didn't lock up last night. Sorry I usually remember to knock but the door indicator was set to open, so I thought..." She trailed off with an affectation of nervousness.

"It is perfectly fine Madam." Eli said smiling. "Take a seat over there and I will prepare tea.

"Why thank you young man. I'll tell you what, you provide tea and I will deal with the cakes. I've just been to the bakery on blue and they did me an amazing deal on plenty of boxes of cakes to keep us going through service tonight."

"If you're sure my lady, I'll fetch the tea in a moment. I know it's lazy, but I don't want the dishes to sit. Does anyone mind if I use a Lense to clean them?"

"No, it's fine." Both replied. He watched as Coltsfoot clicked her fingers which caused a wide three teared cake service to appear, like the last one it was groaning under the weight of thick cakes.

He waved his hand in an almost lazy fashion and was shocked to see his Capture Lense appear and began to clean the dishes rapidly. It caused them to float in the air while it cleaned them, a smell of apple in the air. All the while, annoyed muttering could be heard. Eli shook himself off and quickly prepared a tea tray and took it over to the seating area. Tabitha and Coltsfoot were watching his Lense with shocked interest.

"What is going on with that Cleaning Lense? It looks more like a Capture Lense." Coltsfoot asked curiously. "And why are my Censorship Spells bleeping it?"

"First time I used it last night, and I found two Wyld Runes. One for ghosts and the other a Lense for learning. When I captured the Learning one, the Lense became hard to handle and gave me attitude."

"That can happen with Wyld Runes. A few friends of mine work for the Guild and Wyld Runes can change the capture Lenses' properties. It looks like yours has gained some sort of Sentience and now wants to Learn by doing things. It means that it will probably become many of the Lenses you use. I would suggest that you cast the Rune on the bookshelf and tell it to copy and read them all. It reminds me of the old Legends of the Akashi. They were used by the Sorcerers of old, they functioned in the place of a Familiar. Too obvious you know?"

"I never knew that," Tabitha said sounding interested.

"Not many do, a lot of the records about the old ways were destroyed in the Victorian Era." Coltsfoot said knowledgably. "Keep feeding it knowledge and any Runes of Knowledge you might find. If you could manage to rebuild the Akashi even partially, you'd be made for life."

"Noted." Said Eli quietly, he had always wanted to make a name for himself that was not based of the Family name.

"Now I came here to give you your clothes and money." She rummaged in a large handbag and pulled out two money pouches with their initials on them. Behind them near the balcony doors numerous bags shimmered into existence. Coltsfoot handed them their respective bags and took a long drink of tea, draining his cup before accepting a refill from Eli. "Have you given any thought as to where you'll go for the few weeks?"

"Not really." Tabitha replied. "I'm assuming we'll get some sort of sign."

"Yeah." Eli concurred.

"That is probably the best way. Knowing your Grandmother as I do, she'll have a plan already to make sure you get to where you need to be." She took a bite of cake and a sip of tea to wash it down. "Now, when you leave, I'll seal this room. Meaning when you come back it will be like you never left."

"That's good then. I think I'm going to like it here." Eli said wistfully.

"Good. You seem to have good taste. Anyway, I'll let you two get to know each other. I would advise that you pack a bag. I know you have a Kleiner Bag Elijah so pack that with everything you can think of. Tabitha your Grandmother sent you her own Bag and apparently, she ordered enough food and camping supplies to feed a small army. I'd divvy it up between the two bags to make it easier. I know they weigh nothing when full but if she's gotten you anything Magickal, then the Seid rating will cause extra weight."

"Okay, are you sure you won't have another cup of tea and slice of the cake you so graciously brought?" Eli asked Coltsfoot politely. She pretended to think.

"Well if you are going to so politely twist my arm." She grinned, already pouring another cup and eyeing the last well-stuffed vanilla slice.

Eli inwardly snorted and poured himself and Tabitha a fresh cup. The three sat making idle chatter while enjoying the company now that the business had been concluded. They really talked of nothing in particular, the weather and sports mainly. Tabitha was surprised to find that Coltsfoot was an avid Kettleball follower. Her favourite team was the Scarlet Thunderbirds based in Liverpool. They had been top of the Masters League for nine years running. The biggest attraction at their museum was the Golden Nine, the nine solid gold trophies that they had won. Coltsfoot had said twice during her speech about them that she had always wanted to go to see them.

"You know Tabitha both your Nana and I were Slingers on a division three Team during our youth. Over four months we were promoted from Amateur through Division five and four. We got a new Scholar in our second year on the Isle of Trades, part of the Orkney Archipelago. Managed to hold on to Top of division three for four years after he disappeared. He looked a bit like you Elijah."

"I know very little about Kettleball." Said Eli, feeling a little embarrassed.

"Quick lesson." Said Tabitha. "The scholar is the main player, expert brewers and puzzle solvers. They brew potions in the team's base. Games are played on the Pen, a five sided field. Universities and colleges usually have a Pen which is set in the classic woodland and meadow layout. Masters league Pens have around thirty configurations. Scholars brew the key, a potion specified at the start of the game, we'll come back to that later. They also brew support potions which are loaded into a metal and glass ball called crucibles. They then launch these potions to the Slingers."

"I'll take it from here. Slingers are exceptionally athletic, I know surprising that I was but hey we all age, however slowly." She holds up her hand to forestall their chivalric denials. "None of that, now we Slingers, there are four of us, spend most of our time in the centre of the Pen whipping crucibles at the other teams Goal which is a large Cauldron, the kettle where the key is being brewed, each goal is worth fifty points and it will destroy the key potion. A team can be knocked out if five goals are scored in their kettle or someone manages to shatter the kettle, instant five hundred points. The other team members are two Guardians to stop the other team sneaking up and incapacitating the

Scholar. Three Gatherers to gather herbs and other things to brew the potions. And finally, three Hunters who try to incapacitate the other players. Games can go on for days, but they stop for ten hours for rest. The Pen is placed in stasis."

"There are other parts to the game, like the Scholar having to solve a puzzle to unlock their tools but they would take a while to explain." Said Tabitha.

"I have a copy of the rulebook, a little outdated but it'll give you the basics. Would you like to borrow it?" Said Coltsfoot.

"Most certainly Madam, if it would not inconvenience you?" Eli replied.

"No, no trouble at all. Here." She moved her hand in a spiral motion toward the coffee table and an old leather-bound book appeared. It was very thick, and dusty looking but it exuded that wonderful, to Eli, smell that old books had.

"Thank you, Madam." Eli, though eager to read the book, said as he poured her another cup.

It was nearly an hour, two further cups of tea and three slices of cake later when Coltsfoot finally left. Eli was rapidly finding that he enjoyed the company of the matronly woman. She had a biting wit and was sharp as a tack. He hoped to learn more about her someday. Tabitha and Eli sat quietly once she had left and enjoyed the silence. For a few minutes before deciding that they should pack the things that Coltsfoot had bought them. They began to pack in companionable silence. Eli looked at Tabithas Kleiner bag and saw that it was covered in patches from All Over the World.

"Nana Graveminder sure is well travelled." He said.

"Yeah she travelled a lot with her friends after her time on the Isle of Trades."

"The Isle of Trades is where a lot of Magick users go to learn at University level isn't it?"

"Yeah, usually less, wealthy people. I'd imagine you would probably be able to afford one of the schools in Oxford, Cambridge or even the Capital."

"Westminster? No even we aren't that rich."

"Really?"

"Really, you need at least six figures in the bank."

"And your family don't?"

"Not disposable income anyway." Snorted Eli. "Most of it's tied up in the paper since it went national."

"Sorry if I seemed indelicate."

"No, it's fine. I'm not as uptight about that. If you're curious just ask."

"Same."

They went back to packing for a while, they both noticed that a lot of the clothing was more traditional wear. They were about to question it when a note dropped out.

"Though the style may seem outdated, I have seen that you might one day need them. Nana G."

"Your Nana is starting to make me nervous with all the things she can see."

It was Tabithas turn to snort. "Try living with her. No fun in trying to sneak out when she's stood there with money and a cloak by the time you've climbed down the tower."

"Really?"

"Yeah, when I was fourteen. I didn't bother after that. Just told her to send me a note if I was allowed."

"That is genuinely hilarious."

"Try living it and then tell me." Tabitha said sulkily.

Soon they were finished packing and Tabitha started to feel tired and in need of a shower.

"I need a shower then a nap, is that ok?"

"Sure." Smiled Eli. "Mi casa es su casa. I need to pop out, anyway."

"Is that wise?" Tabitha asked concerned.

"I'll be fine, I just need to run an errand before we leave. I made a promise."

Tabitha pulled him into a hug and whispered. "Stay safe." Before heading into the bathroom. Eli watched him go for a moment and then retrieved a cloak from the bag. It was a muted dark blue cloak with a silver star shaped clasp that opened by splitting in two. He threw it on and picked up his satchel, used the QEX point down to the ground floor and left the building into the quiet late afternoon streets.

CHAPTER NINETEEN

COUSIN MICHAEL

Eli pulled up his hood the moment he stepped on the street. Slowly he began to make his way through the purple section of Glight. He really wasn't in any great hurry, so he decided a small walk around the shops wouldn't hurt. The shops at this level seemed high end, they were primarily clothes shops and other niche boutiques. Idly he wondered if this was where his mother shopped for clothes as he recognised a lot of the styles. He passed a jewellery shop and paused an idea forming. Quickly he entered the shop and picked out a fairly masculine silver cuff. The band itself was only about a centimetre thick and had an ornate pattern engraved in it. In the centre was a medium sized square cut peridot gem, the birthstone for August. When he picked it the woman at the counter looked at him.

"Young man, do not waste my time. That is moon cleansed silver and an enchantment grade gem, it is awfully expensive. Something of this calibre must not be wasted on a flight of fancy."

"Madame," He said with no respect in his voice whatsoever. In fact it was rather harsh. She looked taken aback. His tone spoke of money. "it is you who waste my time. I know exactly what it is that I am purchasing. I have just come into my majority and I have also just captured a Rune which I intend, to enchant onto this bracelet. Perhaps though if you do not want my custom, then I shall go elsewhere. Either way no commission for you."

"My apologies." She grumbled. She was about to say something else when the door behind her slammed open.

"Alison! Go into the back, I will deal with your lack of customer relation skills later. Young Lord Duskphizer does not need your attitude." He glared as she opened her mouth to argue and she closed it again with a sneer to Eli and walked into the back.

"Hello Eli. I apologise for her abruptness, those your age usually want something cheap to impress someone." The man said. Eli knew him immediately.

"Cousin Michael? So this is where your shop is." He said in realisation.

"Yes, it is. Now you want this piece? It's Three Hundred and Forty Pounds. That's without my commission which I'll waive. Did I hear you right? You successfully captured a Rune?"

"Two." Said Eli.

"Come into the back."

Eli followed his cousin into the back and passed Alison as she barged back into the shop. The back room was comfortable, the soft furniture was all focussed toward the fireplace. The room was dimly lit and warm. At the far end of the room was a well-lit workbench, his cousin stood next to that. He made his way across the room.

"May I see the Runes you Captured?" He asked Eli.

"Sure."

Eli rummaged in his satchel and pulled out the two Runestones and handed them to his Michael. Michael turned them over in his hands and examined them.

"The clear one is Phasmastis, the phantom Rune. The Book shaped one is Studis, the Rune of Learning."

"Eli this is amazing. You realise the Guild will come for you soon. The moment the first capture is confirmed you're drafted. I'd like to buy a copy of both. I'll give you the Guilds starting rate, One thousand per Rune as well as the bracelet. As you're family I wonder if you'd offer me exclusivity on any Rune you capture?"

"I can do that? Also, mother says I have to deal in cash as vulgar as it is. You know what happened at my Ascension."

"I agree with her and I also have enough in the safe to oblige. On the desk is a copper bracelet with a quartz gem inlaid. Try enchanting that first to check it works and then do the bracelet. That way I can demonstrate effects to customers."

"Sure, I don't know how to copy the full effects of the Rune yet, only the intent of when I copy it."

"Oi, I can help!" Came a tinny voice from on Elis person, he recognised it immediately as that of his Capture Lense. He flexed his hand, and the Lense materialised. "I'm starting to like being out." It chortled heartily.

"You said you can help." Eli said impatiently.

"Yeah, gimme the Runes you want copied and I'll copy them and if you give me your Journal, I can write them up"

Eli pulled out the Journal from the satchel and placed it on the table and took the Runes from Michael. He put them on top of the Journal, immediately the Lense engulfed both the Runes and the Journal. It writhed and glowed in the air for a second before it spat two Runes out onto the Table.

"Copies." Its tinny voice said as though it had its mouthful. It spat the originals into the satchel. "Merged with the journal, so much easier."

"What?"

"I'm also your journal now kid. That Phasmastis Rune weirdly changed mine and the Journals properties. When I tried to spit out the journal, it wouldn't come out." It said, its voice was changing as it spoke. Becoming less tinny and more natural sounding. It was soft yet male.

"Ok we'll deal with that later. I'll try merging the Rune with a single effect."

Eli moved and sat on the comfortable black tartan stool and faced the workbench. On the bench was a selection of jewellers' tools and various metals and jewels. What interested Eli though was the hollow black stone sphere which was about the size of a lobster float. Two of the sides were open, ninety degrees from the openings was two sliver plates the same size as the openings. Inside the sphere was a cylindrical wooden block which was filled with grooves to hold jewellery. In the top was an indentation which was perfectly circular indicating a possible lid. Inside behind the metal plates was a pair of silver chains which ended in square clips. He picked up the orb which he knew to be called an Ennaorban or an Enchanters Orb. He also knew the name was bastardised from the Yoruba Language which originated in Africa, where the device also was created. Eli picked up the Bronze-Quartz bracelet first and slotted it into the wooden block before pulling the Phasmastis Rune once more from his satchel. He ran his finger in the indentation until he came to a slightly larger node, once he found this, he pulled upwards. The circle at the top opened silently as though hinged. Inside lay a velvet cushion onto which he placed the Rune and closed the top. He placed a hand onto each metal plate and began funnelling power into the device. A metal rustling of chains told him it was working; the top began to glow a soft white light.

"Cumhacht a insileadh ó go dtí laistigh Phasmastis." Eli intoned focusing on allowing matter to pass through matter.

The power surged in the confines of the orb until Eli imposed his will on it and forced it to infuse with the bracelet. After several minutes he felt that it was complete and the light from within died down. A second later the tinkling of the chains releasing could be heard. Eli reached into the centre and removed the bracelet, dropping it a moment later.

"Bloody hot." He grumbled causing his cousin to laugh.

"I did the same thing."

He picked up the bracelet and examined it. A moment later he put it on, and the quartz stone began to glow. Michael though it didn't feel any different or look it, maybe it hadn't worked. He leant on the desk and his hand went right through it causing him to smack his head on the wall. He cursed.

"Well it works." He said to a laughing Eli. "Quit laughing. How do I turn it off?" The moment he said it the gem stopped glowing. "Intent based, right? Better not do that elbow deep in something."

"Very true."

"You do the other and I'll go and fetch the money and the contract."

"Okay, you'll have to send the contract to mother, I'm still under twenty-five remember."

"Oh yeah, I'll retrieve one and send it to her." He replied though Eli thought something sounded wrong in his tone. "Won't be long."

Eli quickly put the second cuff into the Ennaorban and began to enchant it, giving it a few more features of the Rune. This one would be more useful than the one he gave his cousin. The longer he spent with him the more something didn't add up. For example, the front of the shop was well maintained and pristine, yet everything in the back room was threadbare. Perhaps his cousins business wasn't doing as well as he would like people to believe. It would also explain why he was willing to overlook something as well known as Contract law. No-one under twenty-five could sign a contract even one of employment without familial approval. Where none was available, a state appointed Guardian would stand in instead. A few moments later the Ennaorban went dark once more. He waited for it to cool and then quickly took the Rune and the cuff into his satchel.

"Shift into the Journal please, in my bag." Said Eli politely to the Lense.

"Since you asked nicely. I'll hide the Runes too, don't trust the man." The Lense replied quietly as it sank into the Satchel.

Eli had to agree with it at this point, he was starting to feel uneasy. How long did it take to fetch cash? Just as he thought this, Michael reappeared with the money. Eli stood and took the offered envelope which he immediately stuffed into his bag. Michael held out a contract.

"If you sign here, I'll send a copy to your mother."

"No." Eli said firmly.

"What?" Michael his voice laced with venom.

"I cannot put pen to paper until Mother has read through it and signed it first. You know that."

"It sounds as though you don't trust me." Snarled Michael, playing his hand accidentally.

"After that cousin, I don't." Said Eli, power ringing in his voice.

"I'll take my money back then." He said, grabbing for Elis Satchel but instead grabbing his arm roughly.

"That was a mistake." Said Eli angrily. He released his hold on his power and blasted Michael into the wall where he slumped unconscious. His rage still had not abated, so he flung his power out toward the bench. It lanced through the air with deadly precision and split the Ennaorban clean in two. He left the Runes on the desk where they sat but with a thought removed the power he had given up when the Lense copied it. They were pretty trinkets now. He felt a little bad about taking the money, but he then reasoned that the man had tried to force a contract on him and had physically assaulted him. If Michael called the Inquisition, then Eli would hand over the money without comment. He would also send a letter to his Mother via the newspaper in order to fill her in.

Eli hurriedly left the shop as Alison burst in and began shrieking like a harpy. He pulled back up his hood which had slipped at some point and moved out into the crowd. He had a look in a few other shops, picked up some chocolates and nice soaps that took his fancy before he decided to head down the levels toward the lift that he had entered on. As he walked down the steps that linked the levels he passed many interesting figures, people who were part animal yet walked upright as well as those who had decorative animal masks on. When he passed a few of these people, they barked and yipped at him excitedly.

Quickly he wrapped his power around him to reduce the possibility of being noticed as he entered the red level, he didn't want a repeat of last time.

It didn't take him long to reach the lift and call it. While he waited, he kept his back toward the shaft, watching for anyone coming near. After a few minutes he heard it rattling down and stop behind him. Eli opened the heavy door, entered the car and allowed the door to slide shut after him. He pressed the up button and leaned against the wall while the lift slowly rattled and rose upward.

CHAPTER TWENTY

THE NAMING OF RACCOONS

The lift shuddered and groaned as it stopped, Eli hadn't noticed earlier how rusted and rickety the lift actually was. He saw that the cables looked rusty. When he realised this, he shuddered and opened the door and almost jumped out into the cavernous tunnel. A screech and excited chittering made him look around the dark area. He could hear the rapid scratching of claws on the stone getting closer, but the acoustics of the tunnel made it sound like it was coming from every direction. A second later he was knocked back against the metal grating behind him. He screamed and waited for the claws and teeth of whatever monster had accosted him to pierce his skin. Instead he was being licked all over and his nose was filled with the scent of flowers and freshly cut grass. After a moment, his assailant jumped off him and onto the floor. Before Eli stood the Faemiliar he had summoned the other day. He hadn't even noticed that it had wandered off and was not with him, he had assumed it was exploring. He had never heard of them.

The Faemiliar was stood looking at him with its tiny hands on its hips, it looked a little annoyed. It began chittering and gesturing at him as if telling him off. The impression he got from random images that seemed to flash into his head was that the creature had gotten bored while Eli and Matt had been talking and wandered off to investigate some bugs and trash nearby. When it came back, it was alone and scared. Now it was miffed at Eli for summoning it and leaving it. It sat for nearly two days outside then in the tunnel waiting.

"I'm sorry. I didn't realise you were gone. What's your name?"

The small, plump, green raccoon squeaked and shrugged.

"Are you a boy or girl?"

"It looked down at its belly and then at Eli and shrugged again, the pink and blue flowers seemed to shift one minute to all pink, then blue finally settling back on the mix of both colours.

"Okay... I suppose it really doesn't matter either way. Would you like me to give you a name?"

It squeaked and chittered happily nodding fervently.

"Right... Gimme a sec."

Eli studied the small creature and began to wrack his brain for names. He could go for the obvious Bandit, but he was quite sure that he remembered it in the news as a famous Racoon. He didn't want to offend any memories. So, he kept thinking, he couldn't make it too male or female as he wasn't sure which it was. The wilful little being reminded Eli of a forest glade. Then a name came to him Arden, meaning Great forest. It was a popular name a few years ago for both boys and girls. His mother had always said that she would have named Hollie as such, but her cousin had a child about an hour before Hollie was born and took the name. That cousin wasn't often spoken of any more even nearly twenty years later.

"I've got it." The creature looked at him questioningly. "It's a neutral name but a good one, Arden. It means Great Forest."

The creature considered this and then chittered happily, the flowers changing colour rapidly before settling back to their pattern of pink and blue. It then looked at Eli and held up its arms as though flexing its muscles.

"Yeah bud, that's right. Great Forest. Maybe that's what you'll grow to be. So forgive me?"

Arden put its finger on its chin and looked up as though considering whether to forgive Eli. It stayed like this for a moment humming slightly before it looked at Eli and nodded. Eli was relieved and happy even as he was assaulted once again by an armful of enthusiastically licking Arden. After a moment Arden climbed down Eli and settled itself in his bag which seemed to thankfully stretch to fit it, Eli could only feel a slight change in the weight of the bag overall.

"Comfortable there?" Eli asked bemused.

A nod from Arden and a small thumbs up assured him that Arden was not moving. The bag rustled around and Benjamin Bear forced his head out, eyes squinted as though annoyed. Arden squeaked as though surprised.

"If this thing craps in here, I'm not cleaning it up. Not sharing food either."

With that he popped back into the bag and from its depths weird music could be heard. Eli sighed and readjusted the bag turning to Matt's door.

CHAPTER TWENTY-ONE

PHASMASTIS

Eli knocked on the metal door and waited, then waited some more. Before he could knock again the door clunked open. A bleary-eyed Matt opened the door. As soon as he laid eyes on Eli, he brightened and smiled.

"You came back..." He said softly.

"I promised I would, and I might have something that can help you."

"Help me?" He questioned, clearly confused.

Eli was about to answer when Matt jumped and looked behind him, he bent down and picked up something. When he turned back, he held BeBe in his arms.

"I told you he'd come back, BeBe is always right." Said the bear smugly. "I wanna go back in before my steak gets cold."

"Steak!?" Came Benjamin's voice. "Move you fluffy cretin." The bag rustled once again causing Arden to squeak indignantly as Benjamin almost exploded from the satchel. "Come on then, in we go."

"Bloody Picnickers." Sighed Matt as he stepped back to allow them to enter his lodgings.

Nothing had changed since he'd been away. Benjamin went over to the trapdoor where BeBe was stuffing his face with a steak dinner. He tried to get to BeBe's food but was batted away. BeBe seemed to be showing him how the trapdoor worked. Eli looked away to where Matt had already moved to the chairs and was indicating for Eli to sit. Once they were seated Matt poured them both glass of wine.

"So what's this discovery that could help me? And in what way?" Matt asked curiously.

"I found a Rune called Phasmastis. It might allow you to see the world properly. Each time I think about it I know that I need to use the Rune on your body. You said it was in the tunnel?"

"Yea but the way is blocked."

"The Rune will let me walk through the wall. Any tips?" Grinned Eli.

"Don't stop, Relax and Breathe normally."

"Breathe normally? Everyone keeps saying that."

"Good advice I suppose when you need to do it to survive." Snorted Matt.

"Want me to try?"

"Yeah go for it, not like you can kill me again." Smiled Matt.

Eli stood and unhooked his satchel, dislodging Arden who scampered over to the bears and chittered at them insistently. Benjamin looked at it.

"You want some too? Well okay then I'll ask for you." Benjamin caught Eli watching, amused. "What? The cretin has taste. Now go an' sort ghostie out." Waving his paw dismissively.

Eli did as he was told and picked out the Journal, he threw it in the air and it shifted back into the Lense. A second later he picked out the clear Runestone and held it in his hand.

"Eli wait..." Said Matt. Eli turned to him. "If this works, I'll probably look different, what you see is a glamour rooted to my skin."

"It's fine I could feel the almost static feel of a Glamour in here, but I thought it was something in the room. Now I'm going to go before I lose my nerve." He squeezed the stone out of habit and it felt reassuring to him. He focussed on the effect he wanted and intoned. "Phasmastis."

The sensation of cold static washed over him, he looked down and laughed internally that he had become totally intangible and colourless just like the classic legends about ghosts. Since he wasn't sure how long the effect would last, he stepped forward and walked through the dresser and into the pile of rubble beyond. As soon as he did so, he realised what Matt had meant about not stopping, he could feel his insubstantial body trying to change into stone. It was truly disquieting. He pushed on and began to feel as though the air was being squeezed from his lungs. Breathe Normally he thought. He relaxed and breathed normally and slowly. He kept on forward until he felt like he was trying to walk through a barrier of cling film. Don't stop he said to himself firmly in his head and he pushed forward. With an audible pop he stepped out into the chamber.

It was dark in the small chamber, pitch black. With a flash of power and a whispered "Lux." a soft golden light lit the chamber. What he saw made him almost cry. Matts body was pristine as though he had died only minutes before, he was lying in the foetal position in the dust. Around him there were several bottles and a syringe. In the dim light something odd caught Elis attention, he bent down and saw what looked like sweat on his brow. He mentally prepared himself for his first literal contact with a dead body. After a second he reached forward and felt for a pulse. Matts skin was not warm but not the ice cold of death he expected, then suddenly he felt it, a single beat followed several minutes later by its counterpart. Matt must be on the edge of death and when they had cast the preservation and stabilisation charms on the rest of Glight, he was probably caught in their web and held safely on the edge of death.

Eli focussed on the Rune, demanding its properties to see if there was any way to safely merge Matt back with his body to save him. Flashed images went through his head about merging spirit and body. The body would fade from this time and be sent back to the point of death, if done correctly he may be saved if someone got to him in time. If not, he would pass on or repeat the cycle. Eli thought it better than residing in a bubble. He stood up and held the Rune in his left hand and held out his right hand toward Matt.

"Phasmastis." The power rose enthusiastically to his call and immediately funnelled toward Matts body. As it contacted him, his body began to glow blue for a moment before it rapidly aged and crumbled away. Eli thought it was a little anticlimactic until the entire tunnel began to shake and crumble. He was about to run when the rocks to his side of him where he had entered began to shift and move. One minute it was a circular pile of rubble and the next it was a squared out nicely tiled tunnel. The floor was slate, and the walls and ceiling were tiled in deep green almost reflective diamond shaped tiles. Now the light only surrounded him in a band which emanated from the tiles. Then as he watched the same tunnel extended into the distance and around the corner. Eli quickly moved toward where he had entered and stopped at a seemingly solid wall. For a moment he thought he would have to walk through this wall until he noticed the lazy ripple of an illusion. he put his hand through it and immediately stepped through, shivering slightly at the wash of cold static across his skin.

He entered a room that did not resemble the one he had left. The floor was tiled in slate like the tunnel, but several rugs covered the floor. Both chairs became more comfortable looking, and the tabletop held a mosaic. On top of the table sat two glasses and a permafrost'd bottle of rose wine like they had been drinking, the fireplace in front of him was more ornate. Everything, the bed and other furniture appeared more elegant. The Bears and Arden still sat eating at the trapdoor in the floor. A small envelope shimmered into being propped

143

against the bottle. Eli stepped forward and picked up the envelope which had his name scrawled over the creamy coloured paper in green ink. He pulled out the thick velvety paper and unfolded it before beginning to read:

Eli,

> *As I hope you have gathered, this letter comes from Matt. When you sent my soul back to my body, it shifted me back in time to the point I would have died under the preservation charms had I not been shifted into a ghostly form. Luckily for me, or unluckily I suppose that would have been several weeks later. The healer informed me that I had slipped into a deathlike coma and that slowed my heart-rate enough that my Magick was able to burn off the poisons. As luck would have it as I awoke in the tunnel the healers were standing over me using their Magicks to try to retrieve me. From what they told me afterwards they had been trying for nearly an hour when my body glowed blue and I awoke.*

> *Before you panic, you have not actually changed time, your memories will adjust, I left a copy of myself in the tunnel to guide and chat to you and the room revealed itself as to how I crafted it for you once my body was sent back. That way time all matches nicely. For fifty years this room was sealed, until you arrived. Yes I visited often in my past, I am still living in your time and we will meet again. Now the point of this letter. The door will respond to only you. Follow the tunnel and solve the puzzle on the door, when I dug the rest of the tunnel out I discovered a chamber that had been cut in the bedrock by an unknown force. I told you that the tunnel was meant to be an escape route and I think that the contents of the chamber might actually provide that.*

> *I know that you will probably need this room several times during your life and hope that it will serve you well.*

> *Your friend*
> *Matt*

> *P.S. - My real name is Matthias Grav'Mindar. I just thought you should know that, show this letter to your travelling companion someday. They will understand.*

His name seemed somewhat familiar, but he put it to the back of his mind in favour of investigating the chamber that Matt had alluded to. He stepped back through the illusion and walked down the corridor. The wall lit up, and the light followed him as he walked up the slight incline of the corridor. After about a minute he came to a stone wall. There was an inscription on the wall. It read:

In legends I could show you a faraway place,
In reality I show your Soul and your Face.

Eli thought about this for several minutes, re-reading the clue again and again. Finally, it clicked, and Eli slapped his forehead with his palm. The answer was so obvious. He squarely faced the wall and called up a Lense that he had been taught when he started shaving. The mirror hung static on the wall, before expanding to the size of a door. He reached out and touched the surface of the mirror which rippled, and the view shifted to show a dark chamber. Slowly and carefully he walked toward the mirror and stepped through. It felt like stepping through thick, clinging, metallic liquid.

When he stepped into the chamber, he was almost overwhelmed by the sheer volume of power that the room was filled with. He could almost taste it. Light emanated softly from the walls giving everything a green hue. The room itself was tiled floor to ceiling with the same green tiles that the corridor outside had on the walls. Eli gasped as he looked at the marble pillar on the far side of the room, hovering above it rotating slowly in mid-air, was the most beautiful Rune he had seen so far. As it rotated, it caught the light with a multicoloured metallic sheen, this was a Nitid Rune.

Stuck to the wall behind the Rune was a piece of what he thought was vellum which had his picture inscribed on it. Eli walked over to it and examined it. It was too detailed to have been done by hand unless they were an artist. Carefully he removed it off the wall and turned it over. A short note was hastily scrawled on the back.

E,

The Rune on the pedestal was discovered when we dug the tunnel. The doorway was as it is now. A Guild representative attended the scene and tried to capture the Rune but was presented with a vision of the only one the Rune might surrender to. As soon as I saw it I knew it was you. The representative said that if you manage to capture it, then you will be held among the Elite of the Guild. This is whether you have captured One or One

*Thousand Runes. He also said that it is some sort of Transit Rune.
I have ensured that once you leave, the Room is only accessible
to you and your trusted.*

Good Luck with everything Eli.

M.

Eli smiled after reading it. Momentarily he was lost in thought. He shook himself to face the problem at hand. He called the capture Lense, and it appeared at his shoulder. It turned toward the Rune and spoke:

"Nope, you'll have to do it manually. If a Wyld Rune can change my programming that much then this could destroy me. I kind of prefer living. Besides this Rune wants you to capture it, properly. It's a test of worthiness I suppose." With that it floated back into his bag.

Eli sighed and focussed on what the Capture Lenses seal looked like and infused the memory with power. The moment he focussed the Lense on the Rune Eli's world exploded around him. The Runes power shattered the world into shards. Eli fell into one of the Shards. Then another and another. He caught glimpses of numerous places, some recognisable to him, others looked Alien and dangerous. There were numerous Biblical hellscapes.

One that stuck in Elis' mind for the rest of his days was a room with a view. A view of where he thought he called home, from the cold depths of space. Though it wasn't the view that had captured his attention, but the room itself. This room was filled with the buzzing; clicking, and whirring of machines he'd only thought possible in the realms of science fiction. Behind what Eli thought must be a ward, stood a man with his jaw hanging. This steely eyed man spoke with authority. "Who the F..." Eli did not hear the rest of the man's demand as he was thrown back into the vortex by an unseen force. He was sure that this time it was not the work of the Rune.

At some point the twisting and turning through the Air Eli lost the meagre contents of his stomach, he heard a roar and something that sounded like swearing. He realised that the Rune would hold him falling like this forever if he did not dominate it.

This Rune was not whispering about itself it was screaming from within the roar of power that he was swept up in. He could tell the Rune would cooperate provided he was decisive. Otherwise it would do exactly this throw him forever between every place it had ever been and also would ever lead to. He desperately listened out for the Runes name, it kept alluding to it but not revealing it. Instead the Rune constantly went over where it had been or would be, the fact this it could bridge worlds and fold space. Then he heard it, whispered softly under the chaos. Its name was Drucapaturam. Thinking back to the metallic room he realised that he had managed to influence the Rune already.

"Drucapaturam, the Bridger of Worlds." Eli intoned, his words causing ripples of power in the vortex. "I command thee to Submit. Take me where I command." He concentrated on the woodland near the Churchyard in Crosstown. The effect was instantaneous, the vortex shattered around him and he fell from a great height toward the ground. In panic he spread his wings and managed to soar clumsily to the ground. He landed and pain lanced through his right leg. Eli sat in agony for a moment as the Rune hung in the air, almost taunting him. Using the meditative techniques, he had learnt as a child to focus his power he adapted it to allow him to distance himself from the pain. He looked down at his leg and nearly passed out anyway he had snapped the bone which was poking out of his skin.

"Lense find any bone fragments while I deal with the Rune please?" He panted.

"Fine, fine. Catch the thing or call for aid."

"I know." He replied as he turned his attention to the Rune which now seemed to be on alert. Without even bothering to call the Capture Lense fully he thrust his will at the Rune and ordered it to submit. It fought tooth and nail but eventually Elis pain fuelled surge of power managed to dominate it and he felt it form into a cool, sharp metallic object in his hand. The Rune did not seem too happy about being captured but it felt compliant. His Capture Lense returned a few seconds later and spat out a few fragments of bone before it retreated to where it now seemed to call home, his satchel. Eli pocketed the fragments and then focussed on the balcony at home. Power roared from his hand and seemed to strike the air in front of him. Where it struck the very air cracked with glowing green lines of power before shattering like a pane of glass.

Coltsfoot sat on the sofa in Elis apartment sipping tea and eating a particularly mouth-watering slice of moist apple cake. She had been there now for twelve hours after Tabitha had woken from a nap to see Eli had not returned and he had immediately run to Coltsfoots room for help. Not long after they had gotten back up to the apartment the two annoying picnickers and a weird little green racoon creature had tumbled out of one of the food cupboards and said the Eli had vanished in an explosion of power. The three little creatures were distraught, she had had to order a separate tea service to place on the kitchen counter for them. For all the loyalty a picnicker showed to their charges, they really were ruled by their stomachs.

Now as she sat waiting for any word from her contacts and comforting the young man before her she wondered what had possessed the boy to go out with such great risk to his own safety. Oh, she would be having a harsh word or two with him when he returned. Though something about the entire situation rang in her memory as familiar. Before she could voice this, she felt a wash of power coming from the balcony and she could see purple lines of power.

"Shit," Coltsfoot swore vehemently, breaking her own rules.

She grabbed Tabitha and hauled him off the sofa. Tabitha yelped indignantly as he was thrown behind the kitchen counter just in time to avoid the spray of glass as the windows blew inward. They looked up a second later and gaped at the sight. A portal had shattered open, shards of reality floating dangerously around the aperture. The power was palpable form it and the sound of it was deafening. It sounded like a low thunderous jet engine. Eli could be seen on the other side, his leg bleeding profusely. Tabitha surged forward in an attempt to reach Eli.

"Tabitha, NO!" Shouted coltsfoot over the thunderous noise of the portal. "Look at the outer edge of the portal, its purple. That's an incoming portal you'll be ripped apart by the dimensional distortion."

"We need to get to him."

"I know but he'll need to reverse it. Hold on."

Coltsfoot stepped out from behind the counter and walked to stand beside Tabitha in front of the glass covered seating area. She planted her hands on her hips and looked determined. Tabitha wondered what Coltsfoot would do. When she spoke her voice rang with power, allowing it to be heard over the racket.

"Elijah, if you want us to help you're going to have to reverse the polarity of the Portal. They're unidirectional idiot boy. Magick you don't understand can be deadly. If that's what I think it is just order it to reverse. Luckily, the splash zone won't hurt you."

Eli looked to be mouthing something but they couldn't hear him. He gestured toward the portal and seemed to pull. The shards of reality retreated into the portal and the edge turned green.

"Fetch the fool here. There's only one group I'd trust to help him now so I'll call them."

Without a second thought Tabitha jumped into the portal and after a jarring moment which was accompanied by a feeling like being thrown through a tunnel, he stood next to Eli in the field near the church. Tabitha looked at his injury and was nearly sick at the sight of so much blood. He made a complicated gesture at Eli, hoping the other boys power did not react badly. Seconds later his wings had retracted.

"One more time Eli, get us home."

Eli groaned and switched the portals polarity once more. A sheen of sweat broke on his brow from a combination of the pain and effort of using so much power. Tabitha rushed to his side and dragged him bodily through the portal mumbling apologetically. He left a spell behind which gathered the blood the other boy had lost. It seemed that going through a portal backwards was infinitely more jarring than his first journey as when they landed in a heap on the balcony, he felt dizzy. Both he and coltsfoot watched in awe as Eli called out "Raot." In a single heartbeat the portal sealed itself, leaving it as though nothing had every been there barring a line of crystalline dust which shimmered on the floor. What startled them more was the glass returning to its former place and everything that was damaged seemed to repair. Eli coughed, blood.

"I wouldn't trust the cakes." He gasped out, before fainting dead away.

CHAPTER TWENTY-TWO

THE GUILD

"1... 1... 2... 3... Space....5... Hell... Albuquerque... 8... Rigel... New Orleans... Home..." Eli muttered in a semi-conscious pain fuelled haze.

"What's he going on about?" Tabitha asked Coltsfoot as she joined him next to Eli. Concern laced his voice.

"I have no idea at all. I think maybe he's dreaming?"

"What or where is Albuquerque?"

"We don't talk about Albuquerque..." Coltsfoot almost snapped. "Don't mention it to our guests. They will not react well."

"Okay... Who are our guests?" Asked Tabitha clearly confused.

"Well as I said earlier, they are the only people I would trust not to attack Eli, I have had to invite... The Guild. He's one of them now."

"If I am to travel with him, will I be protected by them as well?" Tabitha asked, worry lacing his voice. For the first time he had begun considering the ramifications of accompanying the ginger boy on his journey.

"I can answer that..." Came a soft female voice from behind them.

They turned to see two people in the purple and gold long, hooded, leather jerkin of The Guild stood in the doorway, at their head was a tall lithe woman. The uniform was updated to a more classical, practical style several years earlier. She had long black hair with purple streaks, braided very tightly. She was Leanai, they could see that from the beautiful deep purple, flowing, thorn like Draiohba that decorated her skin. They couldn't gauge her age as obviously Leanai age differently to humans. Her jerkin was different as she wore red and gold with golden braiding around the arm holes.

"I am Lieutenant," Pronounced with an F. "Augusta Kisaven. You may refer to me as Kisa should you wish."

She stepped forward and removed a yellow flower shaped Rune from her pocket and looked to be slotting it into a fingerless glove she wore on her right hand. Once it sat securely in the palm of the glove Kisa, (As she really did prefer to be called) held it out over Eli. A soft buttery yellow light radiated down on Eli and seemed to soak into him. After a moment ribbons of words made from darker red light began to flow out of Eli and back into the rune.

"Before you ask, Runic Magick interacts with ones Ontogenic Field differently to regular power. His Auran will not perceive this action as a threat, I am merely assessing his condition in order to help him." Her tone bored as though she had said this several times before.

"What's an Auran?" Queried Tabitha.

"Ach they're a children's story laddie." Coltsfoot said. She winked as he noticed her accent was full force again.

"Actually, they're not." Kisa said, not breaking eye contact with Elis prone form. "Trainee Daniels. Show them."

A young man with cropped mousy brown hair and green eyes stepped forward from behind the others. He was dressed in a paler purple jerkin with silver stitching. From a leather box around his head he produced a battered, old fashioned camera. He unfolded the top and passed Tabitha the camera.

"Look at Elijah through the top. It'll be upside down, but you'll see."

Tabitha did as he was told. He lined up the camera so, Eli was lying at the top of the viewfinder. He gasped. A faint shimmering replica of Eli was staring intently at Kisa, watching her every move. Silently he passed the camera to Coltsfoot who looked through it.

"Huh, neat." She said before passing the camera back to Trainee Daniels.

"So, you see, it will allow me to heal him as he is in need of help." Kisa stated.

They watched as she began muttering under her breath and a stream of golden words flowed into Eli. His breathing which had been slow, became almost like he was sleeping. Tabitha had to swallow bile as the light tore open the wound in his leg slightly and the bone snapped back into place audibly. He watched in almost sick fascination as the light wrapped the bone slightly and the wound knitted itself back together. The blood that had crusted on his leg, rapidly vanished. A cast formed around his leg. The plaster was wrapped a rainbow wrap, the colours alternating with each strip.

"The blood is destroyed before you ask. I'm not in the habit of practicing black or white Magick or for that matter Ichoromancy." She said giving Tabitha a pointed look.

"Good to know." Muttered Coltsfoot. "What's wi' t' cast?"

"Ah, the severity of the break would normally take about a week for the Magick to repair fully. If he stayed off it for that time. I've already heard of this boy and know that he won't have that luxury. He will need a cane for several months, but I've added a spell into the cast that will destroy it after twenty-four hours. The extra power of the cast will be added to the healing charm in his leg. I've put him in the cast as for the first day. Charms like that are exceedingly fragile. If he so much as bumps his shin it would shatter them."

"Tha's cutting it fine. It's doable though."

"Now can you help me get him into his bed? Then I'll give you a breakdown of his injuries."

"Can he be transported Magickally? I could shift us all through there."

"Yes, and that's fine."

Coltsfoot snapped her fingers, the sound echoed for a moment and the room faded around them and they stood in Elis room. The two purple clad Guild members who had been until this point for decoration, carefully lifted Eli onto the bed. One of them, a woman removed Elis satchel and placed it at the end of the bed. Kisa had taken out a notebook from somewhere and was scribbling notes.

"He had three broken ribs, minor spinal damage, a minor fracture in his neck and his wrist as well as internal bleeding. He'll be in a bit of pain for a while but that'll fade. Im assuming he fell while flying?" She asked.

"No idea, we need to get the story out of him when he awakes. He's been missing for over half a day now."

"I'll wake him. I'll need the story to justify using the Rune on someone unconscious." With that she waved her hand toward him and he gasped.

"Where?" Eli croaked, shuffling painedly to sit up. He glanced at his leg. "Well s%&t."

"Oi, I'll cuff ye one lad." Snapped Coltsfoot. Relief in her voice. "Explain why ye blew me windaes oot wi' a portal."

"Portal?" Said Kisa sharply. "He can create Portals?"

"Haud yer wheesht woman. I wan' ma answers first." Snapped Coltsfoot, daring Kisa to argue. Kisa had the good sense not to argue.

Coltsfoot made comfortable chairs appear for everyone, they were gratefully received. Eli coughed a little and started to speak, Kisa took notes in shorthand as he did so. He explained from the beginning, going into great deal about his Cousin Michaels actions, Coltsfoot made some comments under her breath. About how he had kept the money and destroyed the Ennaorban. Numerous snorts came from the assembled people. Eli glossed over his journey through Glight but went into further detail about Arden, who appeared at the mention of his name and snuggled int Elis leg. Finally, he reached the crux of his day, Matt. He explained why he had gone back there and the results of the use of the Rune. When he mentioned Matts true name Tabitha gasped and Coltsfoot snorted. Both shook their heads at him to get him to continue. As he explained the chamber, Kisa inhaled sharply at his description of the Chamber and the Rune. Once he had finished the description of his arrival in the churchyard he stopped and waited for the onslaught of Questions. He did not have to wait long.

"These Runes, let me see them." Said Kisa.

"Your Guild credentials, let me see them." Shot back Eli. Kisa actually snorted.

"Good Lad, here." She fished out her credentials and handed Eli the leather wallet.

He flipped open the credentials and his eyes went Silver for a moment. Once again there were small gasps around the room, in response Eli rolled his eyes as they returned to normal. Kisa took the credentials back from Eli and waited for him to retrieve the Runes from his Satchel. She gasped as she saw the pair of Wyld Runes and the Nitid Rune. Yes, she had seen them in the Great Mosaic but never up close. The boy in front of her now outranked her. A lesser person would walk out with the Runes there and then and claim the office for herself. She on the other hand was not that sort of person, she had sworn her oaths and would uphold her duty. Once she had completed her notes about the runes and had a completely unnecessary hold and close look at them. Kisa turned back to Eli.

"Well Young Lord, that is Impressive. You've outdone your Great Uncle Geremiah. He had numerous captures of standard and Wyld Runes but never did he capture a Nitid Rune. Willing or not. Now there are a few bit's of paperwork for you to sign and a small Spell we need to cast."

"Spell?" Eli asked a little confused.

"Well in reality you now outrank me. The spell we need to perform is the

Spell of Gilding. It changes your Draiohba to reflect the Nitid Rune you caught. Basically, it makes your markings shiny. It's painless but tingles a bit so I'm told. You'll be one of I think fifty-four people across the world. Part of the Gilded Council. It also means you along with two others will control the Guilds actions in the UK."

"Wow, that's a lot of responsibility." Eli sounded awed.

"Don't worry we mostly manage ourselves. The Gilded council is a bit like Internal Affairs and Policy making. Like everything else in the Guild it's all paperwork." She smiled.

"Okay... Shall we get the Ritual and stuff done? Can I contact you for help if I need it with things about the Guild?"

"Of course, I would have had Madam Coltsfoot discuss a proxy for you. I can act in that capacity. All paperwork would be shared with your mother of course if you like but after the Gilding you will legally be an adult. The one other time someone your age became Gilded they had a proxy for the first few months. How about if I can reach you, I will bring the paperwork to you and discuss it, otherwise to your mother?" She asked.

"That'd be perfect Kisa."

"Okay, open your shirt please." She stood up and picked up the Drucapaturam Rune and placed it on his heart. "Nitidum Gildicarum." She intoned. Eli felt a cold shiver run through his body. Everyone watched enraptured by the sight of his Draiohba changing until every line changed, until they all shimmered in the same multicoloured metal hues as the Rune. Now his Draiohba were uniform, no longer desperately coloured but all many hued. "I have never seen so many colours on one Gilt person. They're usually a single metallic colour, two at most. Your Draiohba are stunning Lord Duskphizer." She bowed slightly.

"Eli please. My Grandfather is still *The* Lord Duskphizer and I don't like pomp." He chuckled.

"Eli then. Now we will be off shortly. Stay off that leg until tomorrow, you'll drift off to sleep soon anyway. But before I go, I need help answering your friends' question. Will you offer him protection as you are a member of the Gilded Council now?"

"Of course, I want him to have all the same rights and protections as a full Guild member. Should he want it I would also like his granted the Capture Lense and Seight, should you test him as being proficient." Eli said without a thought. His voice held a reserved authority which made Kisa and Coltsfoot smile.

"That's perfectly doable Eli. Tabitha will have the rank of Guild Initiate until he captures a Rune, but that still provides him everything you requested." She turned to Tabitha. "Do you agree with Elis' request?"

"Yes." He replied feeling relived.

"Then I will need to take your hand for a moment ." She held out her own which Tabitha took. Her eyes turned Silver and her breath hitched as she saw what Eli had seen. She immediately found the propensity for the Seight. "The test is positive. You must return to the Sepulchre before Midnight Tabitha. The gift Eli is bestowing upon you will bring about a chunk of your Ascension early. You will still need to have a full ceremony on your Twenty-First birthday."

"Okay, do I just need to stay there tonight?"

"Yes, only your family may be present." She replied knowingly. Both Eli and Tabitha looked a little crestfallen. Kisa let out a small burst of power as she muttered the incantations that would gift the Seight to Tabitha. She almost coughed during the incantation and her breath imperceptibly hitched. She just carried on and thought nothing of it. A Whisper of power washed over Tabitha. He didn't feel any different, but he assumed he would feel something at midnight. "When your power comes, use it to look for any Runes at the Sepulchre, if you can catch one we can promote you to any rank Eli wishes."

"Isn't it fairer for me to Earn promotions?"

"You'd think so, but you'll find that the Guild is a semi-noocratic organisation. Noocracy being the old concept of Rule by the Wise. But we are ruled by the Gilded. Basically, it's part that and part Nepotism. The Gilded can promote or demote a person. The colours in Elis Draiohba say that he is high on the chain, I don't know how high, but he is high."

"I'm nervous about having so much influence." Eli murmured.

"You'll be fine and have plenty of help. Oh, and your eyes will reflect your Draiohba during Seight."

"Weird." Said Eli.

"Well, we will be off. I will leave a calling card for you. It will allow you to get in touch with me should you need to." She pulled out an elegant calling card and slipped it into his satchel.

"Thank you. I don't have one yet..."He whispered.

"Actually, you and Tabitha both do. They are in holders on the desk. One second." Coltsfoot Said.

She walked into the alcove and returned moments later with two sleek black calling card cases. As she handed them to each boy, they noticed they were both monogrammed and had a diamond-shaped jewel on the front.

"They have a five hundred card capacity for your own cards and the same capacity for those cards people give you. It works like a Rolodex. The jewel contains a communication Lense. They're gifts from me."

"Thank you, Madam." They said in unison.

"You're both very welcome. I'll show your guests out. Eli I'll be back with some food and to check on you later."

Eli and Tabitha handed cards over and received cards in return from She guided the others out as she could see that Elis eyes were starting to close. A small smile came to her face when Tabitha sat protectively in one of the conjured chairs next to the bed, falling asleep almost instantly. Coltsfoot removed the other chairs and left. The lights in the room dimmed.

CHAPTER TWENTY-THREE

COLTSFOOTS VISIT

Madam Marigold Coltsfoot did not usually pay such close attention to the lives of her guests. But on this occasion, she felt justified, she had ties to both boys. That is not to say that she did not know anything about her guests. She had a struggling writer, a travelling salesman, a *recovering* alcoholic and several more unsavoury people that she didn't like accommodating, but they paid. In Glight money was all that really mattered. Marigold sat heavily in her favourite, well worn, overstuffed armchair by the enchanted kitchen fire which she had turned up the heat so now the room was like a tropical country. A chill had taken root in her bones, the source of which she could not quite lay finger on. She lit a cigarette and watched as her latest cup of tea poured itself. It had been a little over two and a half hours since she had left the boy, she had seen off the Guild and had immediately been set upon by several guests needing things done.

With a thought an old memory album floated across the room and landed on her lap. She flicked it open and started looking through the pictures. Something about the boys upstairs were familiar to her. When she thought back to her *youth,* she knew something wasn't right. It was as though a huge portion of her past was missing. Finally, she came to the memory she was looking for, the memory showed her Kettleball team. There in the back of the still image stood two almost familiar men, different hairstyles but the look was the same. She tried to get the image to shift and allow her to view the memory, but it would not. Only one or two things could turn a captured memory into a still image. Still images were outlawed in the Victorian Era after people's souls were proven to be damaged by them. The images in front of her should have submerged her into the Memory, allowing her to investigate it in detail. When she looked closely, the Scholar leaned on an intricate cane. Wait, she recognised that cane.

The album fell to the floor as she stood up and strode hurriedly to the cupboard marked Lost and Found. She opened the door and ignoring the boxes on the shelves she pulled out a large carboard box that once held a wallpaper she now hated. This box currently housed numerous walking canes, a sword, half a dozen umbrellas, and Coltsfoots emergency shotgun. Marigold picked out the cane she was looking for instantly. It was made from striking black wood which was beautifully carved with Runes and the top of the cane was a highly detailed silver wolfs head. Once she had replaced the box, she stood the cane by the fire and quickly put her boots on. As she was about to leave the building by the kitchen door, she was smacked clean in the face by a letter.

As she looked at the front of the envelope, she noticed that it was addressed to Eli, she looked at the senders' address and noticed that it was form Michaels store, Glitz and Glamours. Immediately a protective streak overtook her. She copied the envelope and its contents, sending the original to Eli and opening the magickal copy. She knew she could get in trouble, but she would take any reparations that Eli asked. She read the contents and swore internally. Not a chance. She wasn't going to let this fly, first stop The Forge then. She had a few visits to make today.

She was in that much of a hurry she didn't even bother with her QEX point, her form wavered leaving the kitchen empty. A second later she stood at the Gates to The Forge which stood open waiting for her, or so the floating note intimated. Though it was vaguely sunny a light mist of rain fell from the sky. She walked up the long drive and took a left as instructed. After a few more minutes the small cottage that the family had build Sarah nearly a decade earlier. A more quintessentially British cottage she could not imagine. Whitewashed walls and a thatched roof. It had a vegetable and a potions garden all surrounded by a white picket fence. In the front garden as far from the door as the plot of land would allow stood a large hexagonal gazebo. On the deck sat Sarah and Emily around an iron table enjoying a light lunch.

"I do apologise for arriving at Lunchtime Ladies."

"Nonsense Madam, please join us."

Marigold offered no further argument just as the other two had expected. You see Madam Marigold Coltsfoot was well known in Crosstown. No matter what time she left her own home she would always manage to arrive for a visit when food was being served. This wasn't by mistake on her part, however. She had long ago decided that when she wanted information or wanted something done it was always best to arrive around a mealtime. Never hurt that Leanai were exceptionally polite and would often invite her for some sort of usually delicious repast. She sat herself primly on the chair and waited as her hosts served her some tea and a small plate of sandwiches. For a moment her demeanour showed her to be every bit the Lady her tattoos belied her to be.

"Thank you, Ladies. I did not mean to intrude upon your hospitality." She said out of formality.

"Think nothing of it Madam. Now what brings you here on a day that cannot seem to make up his mind?" Emily asked.

"I'm here to have a chat about young Eli."

"I thought as much. Not giving you too much trouble, is he?"

"Aye sendin' me grey afore me years he is. Seriously though he's fine, well broken leg and extensive healing but fine."

"What?! I have to see him." Emily exclaimed starting to get up only to be restrained by Sarah.

"Emily, no. you know we can't. That man that helped Eli escape said that we must stay clear of Eli until the Storm Queens spies are dealt with. She may not be able to get to us but she can still hire people. Madam Coltsfoot was picked to guard him as people are terrified to go against her."

"I'm sure I don't know why." Marigold snorted.

"It doesn't have anything to do with how heavily armed you usually are. I wouldn't be surprised if you had a few offensive items on you now."

"A lady never reveals the contents of her garter Sarah."

"Quite. So, Eli is ok?" Asked Emily in a quiet voice.

"Sleeping like a baby with his new friend at the moment."

"Friend?" Asked Emily confused.

"Yes, he's made fast friends with the Graveminder boy."

"Oh, really? Perhaps I'll have to invite Mina over for tea sometime." Emily said thoughtfully. Plans already forming.

"That might be productive. Now, I don't suppose you have anything a little stronger for my tea Ladies? It pains me to ask but I have a chill in my bones I can't shift. Somethings going to happen." Marigold asked, both other women heard the genuine embarrassment in her tone. Neither missed the shiver that ran through her, as she paled. It was easy to forget that this formidable woman was quite a lot older than she looked. As they watched her eyes seemed to sink, her skin and hair became soaked with what they assumed was sweat and her lips took on a blue hue. Honestly, no-one really knew how old she was. A second later she looked normal but was shivering violently. Sarah ran into the house and pulled off a knitted pink comforter she had knitted a few months ago and headed back out. On her way through her small kitchen she spelled a fresh pot to brew and move to the table outside when it was ready. Finally, she picked up a small bottle of whiskey she kept for *emergencies* and headed into the garden once more. She wrapped the comforter around the older woman as the tea arrived. She poured a decent dram of Whiskey into her teacup before she played mother for everyone. Neither woman missed the fact that Emily topped her own cup off from a silver hipflask, though neither commented. For a moment, the only sound was a soft cough from Coltsfoot at the burn from the tea. This sound was suspiciously absent from Emily.

"At least Eli is ok, does he need anything that we hadn't thought of?"

"A solicitor." Marigold said, almost back to her normal self.

"WHAT!?" Both women exclaimed, Emily spraying her tea to the side.

"Your cousin Michael has decided to sue your son for Twenty-Thousand pounds."

"What the bloody hell for?" Emily almost screamed.

Marigold recounted the story from the beginning as to what Eli had told her of his day since he went to visit his cousin, then Matt, then the visit from the Guild. By the time she had finished the tale both women were shaking with rage.

"That... That bastard. I'll kill him." Emily swore vehemently.

"He's been looking for easy money for years. His business has been failing for a while and that wife of his... less said about her the better." Sarah said, her voice was calm and dangerous.

"Alison? Spends every penny. I'll sink them both."

"He tried to screw Eli with an illegal contract, assaults him and then sues when Eli rightfully takes the money as compensation. I know Eli he would have sent us a message today and asked if he should keep the money, which he should."

"I'm going to have to get the solicitors sorted. Actually, you said he was Gilded?" Emily asked, an idea presenting itself. "This Kira is she his Proxy?"

"Yes, thankfully. I ain't got the chops for politics." Marigold said sounding relieved.

"Did she leave you a calling card?"

"Several. Here." Marigold reached into her bosom where she had stored a small wad of cards and removed two, handing them to the women who took them with an internal chuckle.

"I'll go and speak to her in a moment, I think. Madam will you be okay in Sarah's capable hands?"

"Of course, mi'lady. Dae whit ye must tae protect that boy."

"I will and thank you for caring."

"Always lassie. I'll sort ye a safe way tae meet him at the Blue Moon Market."

"That would be wonderful. Thank you." Emily smiled as she stood.

"No problem at all."

"Stay safe madam." Emily said kindly.

"You too love. Now Sarah how about another slice of cake?"

Emily snorted quietly as she pottered off up the path humming in a slightly menacing manner as she did so. She didn't notice the concerned eyes of those she had left behind at the table. Their concern was justified as she was not walking in exactly a straight line, it proved to both women that she had been drinking a lot more than a snifter in a cup.

"I think it's time I leave lassie. Look after her. She seems to be hitting the bottle again." Marigold said to Sarah almost conspiratorially.

"I will Madam, can I see you out?"

"Would you mind if I transited out?" Asked Marigold almost apologetically.

"Of course not, where are my manners." Sarah waved her hand in a complex manner and a small ring appeared around Coltsfoot who felt the oppressive feeling of the Wards lessen slightly.

"Thank you for your hospitality Sarah, bring her tae mine next week. We might need to step in."

"You're welcome Marigold my dear. I will see you on Tuesday at Eleven AM."

Marigold smiled and thought of home, something about today had taken it out of her. Her next victims... *hem* guests would have to come to her. A second later Sarah say Marigolds form waver and she faded out. Immediately she snapped the hole in the Wards closed and got up to follow Emily. A wave of her hands and the tea service and blanket began to float towards the house where she knew it would all clean and pack itself away.

CHAPTER TWENTY-FOUR

EMILY

Her throat burned as the vodka made its way to her stomach quickly followed by several dispersible mints to mask the scent. She sat on the chair next to her dresser slumped slightly. Emotions warred within her about everything that had happened over the last week. Her son was now basically on the run and had been only a few days. When she looked back over the last few years something didn't sit right. Her memories, they were there, but they seemed hazy and very perfunctory as though badly written. To her she felt as though these memories were proof that she was sick, something was seriously wrong with her. Over time she had come to rely on alcohol and her *medication* to stop herself totally losing it. Alright relying on alcohol probably wasn't good for her. Leanai or not a liver was a liver.

She wasn't blind and the looks her friends gave her stung but she had to deal with everything herself, her father had been missing for eight years since he went off looking for her sister and his body. It fell to her to make sure the Duskphizer name remained as it was, *mostly* unblemished. Before she realised what she was doing, she had poured herself another drink and thrown it back. Something within her broke and the tears came. Her mind was overrun with a wave of melancholy and dark thoughts. Her grip on the glass tightened and a moment later the glass shattered in her hand. Emily did not even flinch, her mind didn't register the pain nor the stream of blood which was pooling on the carpet. Magick would even struggle to remove the stains soon. Despair is a powerful stain.

The door to the room opened slowly after several knocks went unanswered. Sarah peeked her head tentatively and gasped as she laid eyes on Emily. Despair rolled off the woman in waves, to Sarah it was palpable. She began to slowly let healing energy fill the room hoping to heal her without triggering a defence reflex. There, she could feel a connection to Emily's wounds, but they were not responding, her emotional state seemed to be keeping them open. Sarah, in her desperation did something she had never done in her life. She silently prayed to the Archir.

The world slowed to a halt, blood hanging in the air like a ruby jewel.

Hiya, you know who it is. I swear I'm not always hanging around this family. Honestly, I just was passing through the Aether nearby looking for a half decent bar. You have no idea how hard it is to find a decent bar in the place between places. I mean there are some good ones, but the travel time is ridiculous. Especially when you are supposed to be managing a world such as this. Now what have we here? I heard a prayer on the wind.

What the... maybe I need to assign someone to permanently watch this family. Let me look back, crap I knew that hasty re-write would come back and bite us in the ass. I really should have sat with Haru afterwards and we should have gone over it properly. It's hard to do a general re-write live, they need the threads of a story to weave together like a complex tapestry. What we did was more like taking the threads and throwing them on the floor. Nowhere near our best work. Sorry about that.

Emily has been surprisingly sensitive to us since she was pregnant with Eli. Still don't know why. We had to change a couple of things and she carried on talking one of her friends, who had been written out, for six months. There's only one person I can think of who could sort her out properly and that's Richard. He went off before the time change and seems to have been lost in the wash. Well I'll be back soon, here, have some music.

Music begins to play, you know the type that really annoying hold music you get. Not the songs that are any good but something like overused royalty free classical or a really bad jazz tune that you only ever hear on phone calls like utilities and those catalogues you get in magazines. This goes on for a while longer than you'd like but not long enough to grate on your nerves seriously. The music thankfully stops.

Phew. I'm back took me longer than I thought. He'd been shunted to the edge of another worldline and was stuck there. Thankfully, he had managed to regain his body and had been running toward the Awakening when we changed time. I better slot him in, though I'm not really supposed to interfere, well I had to or we could lose her.

Richard materializes near the bed and immediately looks around at the frozen scene.

"Archir unfreeze this so I can clean up your mess."

The power behind his statement just made my ears ring. I certainly need that drink now. See you around. The world resumes.

As the blood began to flow once more, leaving its mark on the custardy yellow skirt, Sarah became acutely aware of the new presence in the room and gasped. For a moment she gaped at Richard as he smiled with a never forgotten warmth.

"Richard?" She whispered with evident disbelief. "How?"

"No time for that you foolish girl, I trusted you to take care of her. You should have seen this." Replied Richard with no heat to his words just cold disappointment. He sighed as he saw the hurt his words had caused. "I'm sorry, I shouldn't have taken it out on you. Been a while since I've had to deal with emotions."

"I've tried to curb this downward spiral but, something about the last decade doesn't feel right. Almost like everything I remember is scripted."

"I know exactly what you mean, maybe now isn't the best time to discuss this. Considering she is currently re-colouring our rather expensive carpet"

Richard turned towards his daughter tears pooling in his eyes, they held unspoken regret. For a moment he seemed lost in thought, though in fact he was trying to mentally communicate with her. When this failed after he felt like he was brushing against cotton wool he ceased this course of action. Sarah's eyes widened as the room became heavy with Richard's almost treacle-like power. She felt it slowly rolling off him, feeling its way around the room. Shock lanced through her as the full extent of his power became manifest. The room before her was filled with a disorienting lemon-yellow aura, that clung in an almost sticky manner to everything around Richard. He focused his Magick and moulded it to his will, Richard's gruff voice broke the silence speaking only one word.

"Ameliora."

The thick power seemed to come to life, launching towards Emily encasing her in it's healing warmth. Any remaining power dissipated leaving Emily encased. Sarah's first thought was that she now looked like a fly trapped in amber.

"I am going to take her to the Asklepian in Luguvalio, Do Not Inform the children."

Before she could even take a breath to reply He had disappeared taking Emily with him leaving only the pool of slowly drying blood and a few shards of glass. Sarah sighed and instinctively began to clean up the mess her friend had left behind.

CHAPTER TWENTY-FIVE

TABITHA AND ELI

Tabitha awoke slowly and became painfully aware that sleeping in a chair was certainly not good for his back. Conjured chairs may look pretty but they were always tailored to the caster.

"I need to ask how she does that so effortlessly." He mutters rubbing the sleep from his eyes.

His quiet speech had awoken Eli who was looking at him bemusedly. Without speaking Tabitha got up and headed to the bathroom leaving Eli in the same predicament. Eli slowly shuffled himself into a sitting position, wondering how he was going to get to the toilet and other things without help. After all this could lead to other, issues. He blushed at the thought. To his left propped against the bedside table was, in his opinion a stunning cane. The same cane that Coltsfoot had dug out earlier. Not that he knew this of course. On the bedside table was a small note that read: "*Thought this might help avoid certain issues. Do look after it. I'm only holding it for a forgetful Dog. I'll add this to your service charge. M.M.C.*" Eli swore he could hear the mirth in her voice but also was curious about the use of the word Dog.

By the time he had read the note Tabitha had returned looking refreshed in a new outfit. This t-shirt was black with white writing that simply said, "LET'S GET WYRD." In rainbow lettering. Eli smirked wondering where Tabitha sourced these t-shirts. Eli picked up the cane and began absently running his fingers along the intricate yet smooth shaft. He was staring off vacantly just past Tabithas head. Tabitha watched with vested interest whilst trying not to laugh as Eli expertly fingered the well-polished rod. The next moment, Tabitha failed spectacularly and burst into fits of raucous giggles. Eli's attention snapped to him wondering what had set the other boy off. Then Eli looked down, realising what his hands were doing and snorted joining his friend in his amusement.

When the laughter had simmered to mild sniggers Eli carefully began to move himself around to allow him to get off the bed. Without prompting Tabitha was at his side, with a supporting arm until Eli had found his balance with the cane. The moment the cast made contact with the floor it seemed to shift to become more of a boot. Tentatively Eli put a little weight on his damaged leg, he found that though he felt a pulling sensation where he assumed the break to be he felt no pain.

"Could you make some breakfast please, whilst I hobble my way to the bathroom?" Asked Eli quietly.

"Sure." Came Tabithas reply already wondering what delights the pantry held, and whether the Picnickers had made a dent in it. "You don't have an aversion to sausage do you?"

"I can take it or leave it." Barely holding in his mirth.

Automatically Tabitha delved into Eli's drawers, and selected a practical outfit for Eli's current predicament. Though it helped he thought it would look cute. Eli didn't comment and began hobbling towards the bathroom door, shortly followed by Tabitha. They waited for a moment while the bedroom door spun to the locked position. Tabitha entered the bathroom with Eli placed his clothes in an easily reachable place before leaving Eli to his ablutions.

Once in the kitchen Tabitha rapidly put together a hearty yet slightly crisp English breakfast, whilst every so often having to zap a Picnicker or wayward Raccoon from trying to steal Eli's meal. In the end he gave in to these not so subtle hints and made each of the three a bowl of over sweetened porridge. After what seemed like an age Eli appeared and struggled to sit upon one of the oversized barstools. As neither boy was fully awake yet, they ate in a familiar silence broken only by the snarling of a raccoon who ate a lot slower than the bears. The clock chimed four. Tabitha's eyes widened at the realisation of the time.

"S@£t I need to get going soon you have no idea how long it takes to get up to home, even using the cairns. Don't really want to leave you in this state but..." He said trailing off.

"I know, I know. I've gotten used to having you around. But, it's the only way to keep you safe while you're with me. Besides, you'll be back tomorrow?" Replied Eli smiling softly.

"Of course 'least by then you'll hopefully only need the cane. I wonder if I leave something of mine here if you'd be able to send a portal."

"Dunno worth a try though." Said Eli through a mouthful of confusingly crunchy beans.

"Let's finish eating and clean up before she sees the state I've left the kitchen in."

Eli looks over Tabithas shoulder and gapes at the disaster that was his kitchen. He privately thought that Tabitha must have used every single utensil and dish available to make breakfast. There were packets and tins strewn all over the sides, and eggshells on the floor though strangely no eggs had made it onto the plate. Perhaps it was good for their health that they hadn't had to risk the eggs, considering the crunchy beans.

Tabitha cleared his throat in an attempt to regain Eli's attention, blushing slightly at the mess he'd caused. A few minutes later they had finished eating and Eli clicked his fingers causing the Capture Lense to appear and immediately swear as it began cleaning. He chuckled as once again every other word seemed to be being censored. They both stood and Tabitha gathered his things, while Eli made his way to the terrace.

Once he was out in the cool air of the cavern he leaned over the wall and looked down into the streets below for a moment watching this insular world pass him by. A brief respite from his confused thoughts. A slow steady drip caught his attention, and in the corner near him he saw a tiny puddle of water being fed by what must be stalactites forming far above. He shoved a dying plant in an ornate pot so it sat beneath the drip. At least this way there'd be less chance of the terrace becoming slippery, he reasoned. Behind him the door opened and out walked Tabitha wearing the warmest looking jacket he had ever seen. Tabitha pulled the hood up and approached.

"Could you send me back to where I came to get you yesterday please?" He asked gently.

"Why do you think I came out here?" Grinned Eli.

"Smartass." Muttered Tabitha smiling back.

An awkward silence fell on the boys as they looked at each other for perhaps more than a polite moment. Tabitha stepped forward and pulled Eli into a tight hug, placing a gentle kiss on the shorter boy's forehead. Immediately he stepped back before the moment had a chance to become anything more than a friendly goodbye. Eli shuffled so he stood with his back touching the unyielding metal door. He waited until Tabitha had moved level with him. Focusing on the field near the church he thrust his hand forward as though he were striking someone with his palm. His power barrelled forward like a battering ram and shattered the air just before the wall as he intoned.

"Drucapaturam."

The draw of power was immense this time, probably because he was healing, and a lot of his power was being used for that task. Tabitha saw this and moved forward quickly toward the Portal. He looked back for a moment and smiled, not bothering to say anything as the Jet-like roar would have drowned it out anyway. He could see the clearing beyond, exactly where they had been the day before, so without hesitation he stepped through.

CHAPTER TWENTY-SIX

THE JOURNEY HOME

His transit through the portal wasn't as jarring this time but he didn't think on it much as he moved away from the shards to give Eli one more smile in order to reassure him that he was fine. Eli saluted him with a grin before gesturing toward the aperture. Tabitha watched as the shards pulled back in toward the breach and reality healed itself once more. Now he was alone once again and didn't know how to feel. From within his pocket he pulled out what could easily be mistaken for a letter opener. Between blinks he now held the heavy reassuring coldness of his sword *Cold Fury*. The journey home wasn't always safe.

He moved confidently along the slightly slick path that lead around the churchyard until he had reached the bench they had occupied the night before. From his finger he pulled a ring that until now had been invisible and with a thought forced it to shift like molten metal until it now looked like a silver key. He stepped forward to the kissing gate and looked onto the flat metal where disguised by rust sat a keyhole. Inserting the key with a crackling sound from the rust and the awakening of ancient power. Once he removed the key he unlatched the gate and pushed it until it touched the other side he stepped into the confines of the curved metal. Tabitha looked at the church, as he pulled the gate until it made contact with its original position and the moment it did so he was no longer in crosstown.

His breath clouded momentarily in front of him before being ripped away by the howling wind and driving snow. He looked into the white distance and could barely make out the dim squares of light he sought. Keeping his hand firmly on the frigid metal he bent down and felt in the deep snow. After several moments he found what he had been searching for, the reassuring links of a chain. With all the effort he could muster he pulled the weighty chain and hand over hand he slowly made his way to the distant lights. Over the next few minutes which seemed like hours even to Tabitha's experienced mind, he nearly lost his footing several times and he could feel that the cold iron chain was leaving its mark on his hands. Eventually he reached the end of the chain which was attached to the corner of a small inviting cottage. He felt his way, at this point almost blinded by the snow, until he felt the warm wood of the door. With three heavy strikes to the wood he waited.

Thankfully he didn't have to wait long as the door was pulled open by a matronly looking woman, who wore dungarees, thick boots and a grubby apron. Her blonde hair almost looked like a halo in the warm light of the house. As soon as she saw Tabitha her eyes widened and she reached out yanking his collar until he fell into the house. Behind him the door slammed shut, cutting off the icy gale. He sat himself up on the floor and looked around the familiar cottage but was not afforded this luxury for long, as he was dragged bodily and deposited in a comfortable chair by the hearth which crackled merrily.

"What in the blazes are you doing out there without gloves g... I mean you stupid lad." She said in a loving yet stern tone.

"It was bloody glorious sunshine when I left yesterday, and nana didn't send gloves in her Mobius bag. I mean she sent everything else, Even a portable sink but didn't pack gloves." Replied Tabitha indignantly.

"Don't take that tone with me. You should know better by now. The weather here changes its mind more than Uncle David." She chuckled slightly. "Once you've warmed your bones, you know where the spares are kept."

"I know Auntie Ruth, right by the emergency biscuits. Mind if I have a wee snifter and a warming draught before I risk the cairns?"

"No, you should just freeze your T... Bollocks off out there for forgetting your gloves." Ruth replies already pouring two glasses of amber liquid and pulling out a small vial of red yet milky liquid. She took the other chair opposite Tabitha and threw the vial gently. Tabitha leaned forward and caught it knowing he wasn't getting the whiskey until he drank the potion.

He activated the potion as everyone does with a click that drew blood. The colour of the potion only darkened slightly as he shook it vigorously with a familiar motion. Once he was satisfied that it was mixed thoroughly as he could feel the vial begin to warm in his hand, he popped the cork and threw back the potion grimacing as he swallowed. Tabitha immediately reached forward and took the offered glass. He hated the taste of the potion, it tasted like slightly off milk filled with sugar and the burn of a fresh chilli. The whiskey rapidly chased the potion to his stomach.

"Doesn't get any bloody easier." He choked causing Ruth to chuckle.

"I know, now grab your gloves and bugger off up the mountain. Your mother told me I'm tae send ye straight home." She said her accent becoming more pronounced.

"Okay wouldn't want her getting pissy."

"You know what she's like." Ruth replied producing a pair of thick hand-knitted gloves tossing them at Tabitha.

They both stood and moved to the door Ruth also handed Tabitha a pair of goggles which he put on before he pulled up his hood. She fastened the hood so the thick fabric covered his mouth and drew him into a tight hug. Tabitha opened the door and immediately reached down into the snow and quickly found the chain to the cairn. Without another word, as the thick fabric would make his speech unintelligible anyway, he proceeded to pull himself through the deep snow once more. He didn't look back but knew she had already shut the door against the storm that was gaining momentum. After a minute or so of trudging through the snow he reached the first cairn.

The tall pile of stones stood resolute against the snow, and Tabitha used his gloved hand to reach into a gap in the stones until he found a metal handle. He pulled the handle towards him twisting it before pushing it back his mind focused on the next stop. With a lurch he felt like he had been pulled by the handle through the very stones themselves. He now stood in front of another cairn and he knew there would be another house nearby should he need it. But at this point all he wanted to do was get home. So he repeated the action and focused on the next stop. Three more times he did this until he was walloped in the side of the head by an unseen force which knocked him into the snow.

He looked round for the source of the impact and internally swore, as he noticed exactly what his assailant was. The creature which looked like a shaggy faun with the head of a lizard stood snarling at him it's razor sharp teeth bared. Tabitha immediately knew that this was a Frostaur a bastard relative of the Chimera family of Minotaurs. He scrambled to get up retrieving his sword from where he had instinctively stored it on his back after crossing the gate earlier. The Frostaur charged with a hissing roar which echoed even above the storm. As soon as it was close enough Tabitha slashed at the back of its leg, and dashed for the cairn. He knew that he had little to no chance of killing this thing as they could only be taken down properly with a spelled blade, which his was not currently. Tabitha rammed his hand into the gap as the Frostaur lurched towards him again and as he twisted the handle the creatures blade-like talons tore through his coat.

Tabitha reappeared in front of yet another cairn, and feeling no pain carried on the travelling process the required six more times. Thankfully the rest of his journey was without incident and less than ten minutes later he materialised in the centre of the vast graveyard that was the sepulchre proper. He didn't need a chain to get him the scant twenty feet to the immense red, studded wooden doors of his home. As he pushed the doors open, he felt a wave of relief to finally step into the almost cavernous entry hall once again.

CHAPTER TWENTY-SEVEN

THE SEPULCHRE

As soon as he stepped into the entry hall his legs gave out with exhaustion. He was bemused and a little shocked to see a small blue and white toy telephone with a red receiver trundle over the marble floor. It had a smiling face with two large eyes which seemed to be staring right at him The small string on its front was taught as though it were pulled by some unseen child. It stopped in front of him and began to ring, the receiver rattling as it did so.

"Don't answer the bloody phone whatever you do!" Came his mothers voice from somewhere above drawing his attention away from it for a moment.

When he looked back at the phone he nearly screamed when he noticed that it's eyes were now bleeding profusely. He pushed himself away from it as it began insistently nudging his leg. The ringing noise was getting louder. The next thing he knew the thing was flying backwards as his mother appeared and whipped it away with a broom. He looked up at her and smiled. Her black hair was pulled back in a bun the stretched out any wrinkles she had. She had her favourite red lipstick on which stood out against her snow-white skin. Though ever mention snow white to her at your own peril. His mother reached down and pulled him up from the cold floor. He's used to being manhandled by his family thankfully.

"Come on to the kitchen before the bloody thing comes back, appeared on our doorstep a week ago and has took over the ground floor since then."

With that she strode away leaving Tabitha little choice but to follow her. They walked quietly to the corner of the entryway under the sweeping staircase. Down the servants stairs and into the dungeon-like kitchen below. Happiness floods through Tabitha as he spots Nana Graveminder in her usual spot by the well stoked fire. The kitchen was filled with smoke unrelated to the fire as it was billowing from Nana as she smoked a long wooden pipe. He gave his mother a perfunctory hug before making a beeline to Nana whom he gave a firm loving hug and sat on the thick hand made rug at her feet. Mina sat across from her mother in a less impressive chair.

"Back already my lad eh? Can tell you, didn't see this one coming in a month of Sundays." Nana said, her accent broad but not as pronounced as some in the family.

"Well, it seems I'll need to get you a new jacket made, what happened?" Mina asked in a clipped voice.

"Frostaur at Cairn four." Replied Tabitha tiredly.

"I'll send your Uncle Nigel with his boys when this storm settles. Can't have them too close to the cairns. I wonder if one of the repellents needs re-filled." Mina stated, though her voice was starting to soften.

"Probably best if you have a bite to eat and head up to bed, I know the woman said midnight but the last one of these I heard of the discomfort started about two hours before." Nana said kindly.

"But it's only about half six isn't it?" Tabitha asked confused.

"No dear, it's coming on half nine about now."

"I left Crosstown at like half four though?"

"It'll be the storms drastically slowing everything. Being hammered by three across the mountain range." Nana said waving her pipe dismissively, spilling hot ash on the floor.

Before Tabitha could reply a bowl of steaming beef and vegetable broth was thrust under his nose by his mother, whom he hadn't even seen move. Gratefully he began to eat it, not having realised how hungry he was as it felt like he had just eaten a little while ago with Eli. When the bowl was drained of the hearty broth, he stretched and accepted a potion bottle from his Nana who seemed to be able to pull these out of thin air. He looked at the liquid inside which was a deep blue and had what looked like flashes of white glitter, it always reminded him of the clear night sky. A sleeping draught then.

"Better you be out cold during this as early Ascensions are a lot more painful than a normal one is." His Mother said softly. "Go on off with ye."

Tabitha stood stiffly and once more hugged Nana Graveminder and then his mother, tighter this time. He left the kitchen and made his way through the familiar house narrowly avoiding an encounter with the creepy new inhabitant.

As soon as he reached his tower and prepared himself he took the potion ignoring the taste. Within moments it had pulled him into sleeps embrace.

Far below in the kitchen his mother and grandmother worried as to what was to come. Mina showing a lot more emotion than she had ever shown Tabitha. Nana sat stoically providing her usual air of strength to her daughter.

Hours later as the graveyard clocktower tolled midnight the two women who had not moved since they had sent their child to sleep, felt an awe inspiring torrent of power thunder through the halls. In the distance far above they heard a heart wrenching scream that spoke only of pain. They both wept silently knowing that they could not interfere in any way even to comfort Tabitha. So instead they spent the rest of the night comforting and consoling each other secure in the knowledge that Tabitha would be safe in the world now. But both feared for the path his life had now been set upon. As the first rays of the sun brought morning's light the storms cleared and with that an eerie stillness and silence fell across the entire mountain range. When Nana Graveminder's husband returned from a night in Crosstown he found them both fast asleep by the dying fire.

CHAPTER TWENTY-EIGHT

BREAKFAST AT TABITHA'S

As the bells rang ten, the air inside the grand ballroom of the Sepulchre exploded into shards of reality and Elijah stepped for the first but certainly not the last time into its restful halls. Nana Graveminder was sat on the long oak table as though she was a girl a quarter her age.

"Impressive my lad, but no need for the theatrics. Maybe tone it down a wee bit." She said grinning her false teeth slipping slightly.

"What do you mean tone it down?" Eli asked curiously, before bowing to the head of the family. "You probably already know who I am, as I assume you are the infamous Nana Graveminder. My name is Elijah Duskphizer."

"Aye lad I know who you are, and yes you are right I am Nana Graveminder. By tone it down I mean portals when I were a lass, watching a lad that looked very much like you, were silent and there was none of this wasting energy with shards of reality. Just an observation."

"Before I forget, Madame coltsfoot sends her apologies but asked me to give you this." From within his cloak he produced a small paper and handed it to her, after walking forward leaning heavily on his cane no cast in sight.

She unfolds the note, quickly reads it and snorts. "Fiver my arse, she still owes me fifty. Right lad come on, we'll get down to the kitchen. Mina has gone to get Tabitha."

With that she hopped off of the table linked an arm through his and she guided him out of the ballroom into a long gallery full of Graveminders past and present. Before he knew it they were entering the kitchen and he was seated to the right of the head of the table one spot down from Mina. The long table was lain with breakfast dishes of all types and around the table sat many of the current Graveminder clan. To Eli's left on one of the two chairs at the head sat a man with tawny skin who was looking at Eli intently. After several minutes of this the man spoke, his accent though broadly Scottish had an Indian lilt.

"Hello Eli, told you next time you saw me I'd look very different." He said with a smile.

Eli sat thinking about this for a moment before the light of realisation flickered on in his head and he smiled.

"Matt?"

"Aye that's me Matthias Grav'mindar or should I say Matthias Graveminder?"

"It's good to see you in person again."

"You too, we will get a chance to catch up properly one day a long time ago."

Matthias turned as Nana Graveminder sat down next to him and immediately they began to talk quietly. Eli didn't quite understand why he was here, he felt like he was intruding on a family occasion yet no one had made him feel that way. The room quieted as Tabitha entered, and everyone began to clap and cheer causing Tabitha to blush profusely. He sat down at the other side of the table opposite Eli and began to help himself to food. Eli noticed that in the centre of Tabitha's forehead was a Rune that was surrounded by decorative markings. Finally Tabitha looked up and noticed Eli and his face broke into a smile that spoke of pure joy.

"Eli what are you doing here? I thought I would be going and meeting you back at home?"

"Home?" Smiled Eli, he heard Mina and Nana Graveminder both snort as Tabitha blushed.

"You know... I meant at your place in Glight." Tabitha Stuttered.

"Yeah. Home. So going to tell me what happened last night?" He asked. The table fell silent awaiting Tabitha's reply.

"I'll tell you later, I'm still processing a lot of it." Tabitha replied quietly, causing the table to erupt into quiet groans before the previous conversations resumed.

"Tabitha, we have a small gift for you." Said Mina. She handed Tabitha a small box.

Tabitha opened it and gasped at the contents, inside lay a silver cuff which was engraved with delicate Runes and other Spellwork. In the centre of the cuff was a beautifully inlaid silver book with a mother of pearl cover. It was about the size of a matchbox. When Eli looked back at Mina and then around the table he realised that several others had similar but not identical cuffs on their non-dominant hand. Though he felt like he was intruding on a private moment he watched avidly as Tabitha put the cuff onto his left hand and it immediately became a well fitted solid bracelet. Tabitha flicked his wrist and suddenly was holding a much larger version of the book that was on the bracelet. His face now showed undisguised happiness, as he flicked through the ancient pages.

"The Grav'mindar Grimmerie." He spoke reverently. For a few more moments he examined the pages before changing it back to its previous form. "I can't believe I inherited the ability to use it."

"It's always been up in the air which pillar you'd use dearie. I did hope you'd follow this path though. Now eat up and show your friend around for a while. You need to be back in Glight by five." Said Nana Graveminder happily.

This seemed to be the queue for everyone to eat so Eli did so. Every time he looked away his plate seemed to fill until he couldn't eat any more. Once this was done several bottles of champagne were opened and a toast was had to Tabitha and then for some reason Eli, apparently the family knew the story of his meeting and saving of Matt. Finally after what seemed like hours they were shooed away by the others after a round of hugs, Nana having said that she knew after that moment they wouldn't meet again until august. Tabitha was instructed that Coltsfoot would be waiting for them to arrive at five sharp, as she was taking them to the Bluemoon Market in Crosstown.

They spent the rest of the day exploring the Sepulchre, Tabitha and his younger cousin Ellie who insisted that they allow her to come with them as she knew *all* the best places to show people. As it turned out she even knew a few interesting places that Tabitha had never found. Eli didn't really take in the details of the sights as he had a feeling that he would get more chance to explore this wonderous place in the future. He did however spend several minutes taking in the main building. It was a huge quite intimidating manor that had several towers, the tallest he had been told was Tabithas room. They took Eli to the top of Ben Nevis via the Cairn which he found did not make him feel ill as most of the other Magickal transit methods he had encountered in his lifetime.

He enjoyed taking pictures with he two on the snowy mountaintop and seeing the sights there was to see there. When they returned to the Sepulchre proper it was mid afternoon and they were fed by the family members that milled about the kitchen. All in all, it had been a really fun day for Eli. They sat on a bench closely, whispering as Tabitha filled him in how the power had torn into him and branded that Rune on his forehead, this Rune showed that the Pillar of Wytchcraft had accepted him. Most Wytches hid their mark and forgot about it especially as it made some people nervous. Tabitha however said that he would keep his on show as he was proud to be a Wytch. At the end of the day if Leanai of the Wyrd Branch and others could wear the Draiohba in public why couldn't he? Eli agreed wholeheartedly. Tabitha said that on his birthday his Leanai heritage might show, but if it didn't he was happy to be himself.

Finally the clock tower signalled that the hour was nearly five o'clock so they stood, loosely holding hands, for Eli's support mind you, as Eli summoned a portal, this time he took on board Nana Graveminders advice and pictured it how he wanted it to be. The portal was almost silent, just a hum in the late afternoon air. The shards seemed to spin around inside the portal, which suited him fine so the stepped through. To both it felt like stepping out of the house on a breezy day, much better than previous.

When they arrived back on the terrace of the apartment, Coltsfoot had a small high tea awaiting them.

"That portal was much better, didn't blow the windows out this time." She smiled.

"I'm glad. It's lovely to see you madam, I hope you ar well?" Enquired Eli.

"Perfectly well lad, don't you worry about me, I'm near indestructible." She chuckled.

They sat chatting and enjoying the fare she had provided for over an hour before she announced that they should nap and then shower before dressing up nice to go *up top* to the Market at moonrise. She assured them that the Bluemoon Market wasn't something easily forgotten. As she said this the three of them got a slight shiver. Marigold went to her flat to rest and told them she would return to wake them at nine.

Both Tabitha and Eli automatically went into the bedroom and collapsed on the bed. Each taking a side without thought. The moment they laid their heads down, they slept soundly.

CHAPTER TWENTY-NINE

THE BLUEMOON MARKET

Several hours later, as the full moon rose into the sky in all of it's blue glowing glory, Eli, Tabitha, and Coltsfoot could be found walking up the familiar pathway from the riverbank. All were dressed quite smartly at Coltsfoot's insistence although, beneath his open shirt Tabitha wore an emerald green satin t-shirt which had the phrase, "Pay no attention to the man behind this slogan." They walked casually in no real hurry through the outlying stalls, which were still setting up. As they did so they both talked animatedly to her about the visit to the Sepulchre. She had burst into laughter which brought tears to her eyes, when Eli had told her Nana's response to her note.

"I had hoped she would've forgotten that little bit." She said between chuckles.

"Waiting for Nana to forget something is like waiting for an elephant to forget." Replied Tabitha smiling fondly.

"Right, I'm going to head over towards the hotel. Hopefully Tori managed to get that shipment of tequila in."

"We'll entertain ourselves. Though these bags are annoying but thankfully not that heavy, thanks to the charms." Griped Eli. "Why'd you make us bring them again?"

"Cos I told you so, let's leave it at that." Replied Coltsfoot crisply. Before either could reply she was already almost at the hotel, showing remarkable speed for her perceived age.

Eli was about to say something to Tabitha when he heard a soft "ooh" from him as he too took off in the direction of what looked like a flower stall. At a loss and on his own he began to peruse the nearby stalls. Nothing really caught his eye, most of it was in reality tat. Some stalls held items that claimed to repel *dark forces* and others sold decks of mass produced tarot cards. A mouth-watering smell wafted through the warm summer evening air, almost like a cartoon character Eli allowed himself to be led by the smell. The smell itself was the unmistakable scent of fresh baking. As he crossed the centre of the crossroads he stood stock still, as a shudder tore its way through his body. He was about to investigate when a bony finger tapped him on the shoulder.

As soon as he had almost jumped around, expecting an attack he immediately calmed, when he came face to face with what appeared to be a harmless fortune teller. She looked exactly like these sorts of people do in every film right down to the wart on her nose and copious amounts of shawls.

"Ahh lad, got something for ye." She said her voice rattling like a bag of pennies.

"Really?" Eli asked almost bored and slightly distracted.

She reached into a small knitted bag and pulled out an envelope. Eli gasped as it was almost rammed into his hands, and within a blink she was gone. Her final words hanging in the air.

"Open this when the river fills your view and the blue moon is your only light."

Eli looked at the envelope and realised it had no seams, immediately he wrote it off as probably just some non-magickal hokum and roughly stuffed it into his pocket as his attention was drawn again to the area that had garnered his attention earlier, the road beneath his feet. At first glance nothing seemed off about this particular patch of road, it seemed no different to those around it. He bent down and touched the road which felt hot to the touch. Unlike the cool tarmac a few feet away. He decided to head in the direction the others had and observe the crowd to see if anyone else noticed. Once he was safely in the corner of the crossroads near the hotel, where he could see Coltsfoot deep in conversation with a very worried looking Tori and a hooded figure, he looked back towards the centre of the road.

In the course of the next several minutes he watched as almost every person human and Leanai alike seemed to almost trip as their attention was drawn by whatever was going on in the centre of the road. So many people had noticed this that a sense of foreboding settled over the marketgoers. Apparently he was not the only one observing this phenomenon as at the other corners of the crossroads people were standing just as he was. On a whim he switched his vision to his seight for the first time since his gilding. He was almost sick as he seemed to be able to pick up more information than he was able to before. The very centre of the crossroads was lit up like a thermal map getting hotter and wider by the moment. As he switched back to regular sight something strange caught his eye. The tarmac was beginning to bubble and peoples shoes were beginning to stick to the surface of the road. Something wasn't right, obviously. At this point though he was unsure what to do.

He couldn't seem to catch Coltsfoot's eye nor Tabitha's. His mind was made up when the road began to bubble more violently and obviously, visibly glowing with heat. Eli could feel a wash of heat emanating from that point. Without another thought and mirrored by several of the others who had, like him, been observing he threw his hand into the air and muttered "*Tripnine.*" The word held power, the pulsating Lense launched from his hand like a rocket and hung high in the air. It hung there flashing rapidly between blue and red for a moment before it exploded into multiple smaller identical orbs which blasted to the ground.

The Inquisition were not the only arrivals, as a moment later the molten road exploded outwards in a furious torrent of searing flame. Molten tar covered several people their anguished screams pierced the night air. From this almost volcanic eruption several monstrous lizard-like creatures clawed their way from the pillar of fire. By this point the marketplace was chaos, people running in all directions and screaming. Eli, strangely calm, took a moment to examine the creatures.

Four strong they numbered each one almost identical, though different in small ways. Each one was around ten feet long and looked as if they were made from magma. Though, the almost glass-like screeching their bodies emitted as they moved made Eli think they were more like obsidian. From the crystalline scales that covered their back, intermittent blasts of heat and pure fire erupted. Anything behind them was either set ablaze or incinerated instantly. One of the creatures focused it's many glowing eyes on him and let out an almost familiar roar this got the attention of the other three. Eli panicked slightly and pulled out the shrunken staff from its holster on his waist and without making it grow, he used it almost like a wand. The blast of raw power he sent towards the closest creature did nothing but serve to annoy it. It reared up on it's hind legs and spat towards him. He managed to dive out of the way in time, good thing too as the railings behind him had been reduced to slag.

Eli was pulled out of the way by his hair as another globule of probably acidic spit was sent his way. His saviour turned out to be Coltsfoot who began dragging him roughly through the crowds as the night air became filled with the sound of air-raid sirens.

"Citizens, seek shelter. We will deal with this." Came the magnified voice of an arrogant sounding male Inquisitor.

Eli heard Coltsfoot snort as she dragged him toward Tabitha and grabbed him too. As they approached Tabitha had been unceremoniously filling a herbalists satchel with everything he could get his hands on. Before either could comment he spoke hastily.

"The woman took off and told me if I could make use of anything to take it. She said that at the end of the day her stall would probably be burnt down anyway. She hoped."

The three of them moved quickly down the rapidly emptying streets, Coltsfoot seemed to be looking for something. She led them past a closed grocery store and down an alley, behind them they could hear several roars and the rapid scraping of glass. They were being pursued.

"Eli. Portal. Now." Ordered Coltsfoot.

"Where?" Asked Eli.

"Scotch side, Gretna and then I'll tell you where after that."

They looked to Tabitha to make sure he was ok, and noticed that he was rapidly tearing flowers head from stem. Almost automatically he was stuffing the heads into a wide jar. Coltsfoot was about to ask what the bloody hell he thought he was doing but was stopped short by a single finger held up. Seconds later the mouth of the alleyway was filled with the creatures. The very bricks of the buildings were beginning to melt and warp. Tabitha sealed the jar and began to shake it vigorously. Inside the flowers began to glow and change to a uniform deep blue colour. From the jar the buzzing of a kicked hornets nest sounded. He threw the jar overhead towards the slowly advancing lizards. On impact with the floor the jar shattered releasing a swarm of flying flowers. As the flowers swarmed around the lizards, still buzzing each began to release torrents of water rapidly filling the alleyway with steam. Eli decided this would be the best time for the portal to be open. He turned behind him, *"Drucapaturam"* he intoned. The world fell away quietly in font of him. Behind them one of the lizards had, unfortunately for it, swallowed a mouthful of the aggressively attacking flowers. It made a sound not to dissimilar to that of a stovetop kettle before it exploded. The three were knocked through the portal by the bow wave of the explosion thankfully before the deadly shards. For the first time Eli closed the entry aperture as they crossed the threshold.

CHAPTER THIRTY

DUDE WHERE'S MY LEGS?

The three somersaulted as they were ejected from the portal onto the cold grass of Gretna Green. For a moment they sat like dazed children ears ringing. Eventually Coltsfoot got up and brushed herself off, the others followed suit. She produced a cigarette from the folds of her dress, it was lit by the time it reached her lips.

"Well that wasn't how I imagined tonight." She said sounding every bit as old as we all imagine she probably is.

"What were those things?" Eli asked panic still edging his voice.

"Them, lad haven't been seen 'round these parts *in my lifetime.* They're called Vulacdrek, creatures from an old world. Elemental spirits called from volcanoes usually used as hunters."

"Why did they attack?"

"No idea, could be a fluke." Just remember when Eli was fighting that Portal Rune and lost the battle to hold his lunch?

"Weird." Tabitha said.

"Nice use of Floramancy there kid." Said Coltsfoot proudly causing Tabitha to blush. "Now no time to hang about I'm off home. You two I advise to go to Luguvalio. I hear the river gardens are lovely on a blue moon." Like every other time she had told them to do something she was gone before they could argue.

"I really wish she wouldn't do that, she'd slap us if we did that to her." Said Tabitha in a sulky voice.

"No use crying over spilt potion, grab on and we will go see what she's on about. Sounds like she doesn't want us going back to Glight for a while."

Tabitha moved easily into Eli's embrace and gasped as he felt the power of the Traveling Spell envelop them. Moments later they were stood in front of a fountain in the Luguvalio park gardens. A soft breeze rustles through the nearby trees and the flowers in the flower beds. In front of them the river flowed ever forward serenely. The only light was from the nearby bridge and the turquoise light of the moon from high above. He gasped at the romantic scene before him. From where he stood still tucked close to Eli, neither feeling the need to move apart, he could feel an alien buzzing from Eli's pocket.

"Eli. As *interesting* as the feeling from your pocket is. Why is it buzzing." Tabitha queried.

"No idea." Then he remembered the envelope the strange woman had forced on him. Looking at the scene before him her words now made sense. "Hold on." He said squeezing his hand between them, eventually reaching his pocket and retrieving the aforementioned envelope.

The moment the envelope was exposed to the moonlight a seam formed with softly glowing light, and the envelope sprang open. Inside, strangely was what appeared to be a tarot card.

"ELI LOOK OUT!" The shout rang out from the direction of the bridge. Eli looked around and saw a silhouette which combined with the familiar voice, could only belong to Thedas. "BEHIND YOU!"

Both boys whipped around as one and looked behind them as Thedas had instructed. On the pergola above, only a few feet away was the remaining Vulacdrek softly snarling at them. Now that they had noticed it, it began to slowly increase its body temperature, having lowered it to prevent detection.

"TRAVEL!" Roared Thedas who was now sprinting across the bridge.

Once more the card began to tremble in Eli's grasp and he felt compelled to examine it. As he did time itself seemed to slow to an almost glacial pace. The card showed a picture of an ancient looking deck of cards raining down. One of the cards which showed #0 *The Wanderer* balanced precariously on one point. The title of the card Eli held was #1 *Geam Teh*. From above the Vulacdrek roared and started to pounce. Tabitha grabbed onto Eli in fear spurring Eli to initiate the travel as he turned the card over to read the words "has just begun" scrawled in a strangely familiar hand.

In an instant they were traveling towards Crosstown. They could both feel home getting closer, when the maelstrom of reality became brighter, almost blinding and began to resemble the eye of a glittering sandstorm. The travel jerked, separating the two mid transit. Pain tore through Eli. Over the roar of the travel a scream answered the one he had not realised he had let out. It felt as though the travel and the searing pain had lasted years.

The travel unravelled whilst he was mid-air. Luckily, the Floor wasn't as hard as it looked. Almost as if it was designed for this form of ingress. Momentarily, Eli took in his new surroundings which to him looked almost identical to those of an ancient Mayan Temple, like he had seen in history books as a child. He was about to stand up when something felt strange. Before he could think of this Tabitha came screaming down from the sky. Landing in a heap next to him causing him slight pain. He looked towards Tabitha and recoiled as from the waist down he was missing some jewels and some legs.

"Dude where's my legs?" He exclaimed loudly. Tabitha swore he could hear the interrobang in Eli's question.

"Huh. Neat. I kinda like it." Tabitha said whilst looking around. Then he realised his voice and Eli's sounded different. He looked in a conveniently placed reflective surface and gasped as he now had a pair of kitten ears and slight fangs. Looking back at Eli he noticed that Eli's Draiohba now matched the beautiful multicoloured metallic scales of his tail. His wings now had a vibrant copper as their main colour much like his changed hair. As Eli chuckled slightly at Tabithas ears, which by the way had replaced his human ears though their absence was covered by much lengthier hair, Tabitha noticed that Eli had a pair of needle-like fangs. Ignoring this for a moment Tabitha examined the chamber in which they had arrived. He paled and said with all seriousness to Eli.

"I don't think we are in Crosstown anymore..."

The Fuinnestra loses connection to the goings on, on that strange planet. We the Archir hope your voyeuristic tendencies have been sated for now. Only time will tell what's happened and where they are. But unfortunately not in this volume of the Fuinnestra. Don't forget to tip your librarian if you haven't actually purchased this device. All we can say now is thank you for reading and we are sure we will see you soon.

The beginning...

ABOUT THE AUTHOR

There are many things that have inspired me to write, the important ones all root back into my childhood. I won't go long into detail, but it would do everyone some good to understand the reasons behind my writing choices and style.

You see I, like many of you, didn't have the happiest of childhoods; I had very few friends, and I always thought I was alone. Maybe I was and maybe I wasn't but that's neither here nor there. No-one is at fault for my lonely childhood, I was different, quiet. The problem for me was there were a lot of reasons I was quiet and withdrawn. As I entered my teenage years, the dominant one was the struggle with my sexuality. Other kids seemed to know this before me, whether they did or did not know is irrelevant, they acted on it and yet I did not help matters. When backed into a corner, I reacted with my mouth. I used words as weapons. Now I hope to use my words to bring a smile to someone's face when they need it. In reflection, I realise that all of this is just part of growing up; in a small close-knit town such as home. People notice things and sometimes differences unnerve them. I thought I would leave that town never to return, yet I did return. For me alot of what I perceived was bullying at the time was just childhood. For me, the best laugh is I could easily sit down with 99% of my former classmates and have a chat and a catch up. I hold no ill feeling to any of them now, because without them I wouldn't be who I am today. Not that I condone bullying of any sort, but in my own little world as in life... there are always two sides to every story. Also, in writing this book, I realised, I never left. why would I? I created a fantasy world that I love, a world that I now want to share with you.

As I grew up, I didn't go outside much, instead; I spent the lonely summer days staring longingly out of the window watching the other kids playing and one day picked up a pen. On those days, the first iteration of Crosstown was born. It was and remains to me a place filled with Magick, secrets and lots of hidden places and friends. Only I knew and would only ever know them. Or so I thought. My Mother and her glorious cast of friends, my "Aunties" whom I love and to this day and still give that honorific. They all seemed interested in what I spent my time doing and what I was doing with so many pads of paper. You know, I looked at some of those notes the other day. I realised how far I have come as a writer. I also see how little my imagination has changed, just matured.

My Aunties and my Mother are the reason I love crafting strong female driving characters as driving forces for my stories. These characters are not all light or good mind you. Just as all my male leads are not strong and competent. Just wait until you meet Elijah. Then you'll see what I mean. My summer evenings hold memories of sitting with a book in the garden as my Family laughed around me. Once I remember sneaking a drink from my Uncle thinking I hadn't gotten caught, but I had. He laughed and handed me a small glass of coke with a grin and a wink; the coke tasted strongly of vodka. One of my Mother's friends had been on holiday and brought back some particularly strong black vodka. Boy was I sick after that, my Uncle laughed hard until my 5 foot and a little bit Mother, let rip at him. I can still hear him defending himself, laughing along with everyone as I prayed for the first time but not the last, to the porcelain god. It still brings a smile to my face.

The most prominent of influences in my life were my Grandparents, John and Betty. You'll meet them later. They lived and worked bars in my early life and my Grandad lived them in his last ones. You see because my Mother working all hours to support us including, making sure I had the amazing Christmases full of presents, food and fun, just like all the other kids. I spent a lot of time living with my grandparents. They were there for me when I through the childhood hardships and scholastic rivalries, when my mother couldn't but they were *all* there beaming with pride every Christmas when I was part of the School play whether it was at the beginning as a cardboard tree or in my final production where I played Charles Dickens, one of the leading roles. I became deeper involved in my writing and more withdrawn because of the pressures of school and after they diagnosed my Grandad with cancer of the throat when I was thirteen. I needed the escape more than ever. He told me he would be there to buy me my first legal drink. When I left school, I left home then came back to care for him. As just after my 18th birthday we were told that it was back. So, he had lived up to his promise. Four months after my birthday to the day, I had become his 24-hour carer, dealing with his medication and much more near the end, he lost the battle.

In what was the hardest and strangest week of my life, I met Death and lost the closest thing to a father that had stuck around in my life. But I realised that Death, like everyone else, is just doing their job, they're not scary. Being forgotten is. And that's why I write, it's my job now to make sure that the characters and worlds that I dream up, get to the page. Hoping I can light the way for someone in a black time, or just help them pass the time until it's over.

There's more I can and will say about others in my life. But starting at the beginning seems apt as this is my first book.

Lightning Source UK Ltd.
Milton Keynes UK
UKHW012001190820
368517UK00006B/111